MICHELLE LYNN ROSS

# There's No Place Like Home

FAWN
CREEK
PRESS

First edition

ISBN: 979-8-9999310-3-0

Editing by Jones Novel Editing

This book was professionally typeset on Reedsy.
Find out more at reedsy.com

*For Justin, Rachel, Felicia & Jordyn*
*my Happily Ever Afters.*

# Acknowledgments

Even after spending the better part of a year to write this book, I still can't believe it's actually done. None of this would have been possible without the love and support from my community.

First, I want to thank Jones Novel Editing for her help with bringing this story to life.

Thank you to my husband for sacrificing his sleep while I repeatedly woke him up in the middle of the night with my obnoxious typing. Thank you for always cheering me on, encouraging me to do new scary things and being my best friend.

Thank you to my daughters for being my motivation to chase my dreams.

Thank you to my friends and family for listening to me yap about my silly love story for the last year. I'm sure there for a while, it seemed like I would never get it done.

Thank you to Mrs. McGlathery for encouraging me to keep writing when I was a teenage girl, just writing sad poetry.

And lastly, thank you to you, the readers, for picking up this book. I hope you enjoy it and you fall in love with the fictional town of Fawn Creek as much as I did.

# Author's Note

**What a whirlwind adventure this has been!**

When I first started writing this novel, it was nothing at all like what it ended up being. But I did what I'd wanted to do since I was a kid—I sat down and wrote. And I wrote. And I edited and changed things and moved things around. By the time I hit the publish button, it was more than just a story. It was about a community that I've come to love so much.

I've always been told to write about what you know, so writing about life in a small town was a total no-brainer. That is, after all, the life I know and love—the support of a community, the friendships, the journey of being an adult right alongside the same people you went to grade school with. And the things that aren't so great—the gossip, the nosy neighbors, the small-town quirks that make you roll your eyes one minute and smile the next. I wanted to capture all of that and make it feel relatable—I wanted it to feel like home.

I've been a reader my whole life. From devouring *The Baby-Sitters Club* books as a kid to speeding through every Nicholas Sparks and Sophie Kinsella novel I could get my hands on as an adult, I've always loved stories. I love visiting new places, but one thing remained the same with every book I read, movie I watched, or TV show I got obsessed with—they never happened in Kansas. Those stories sparked my imagination and even inspired a few vacations, but they never quite felt like home. And while Kansas might not be a top travel destination, it has a beauty all its own. I wanted to show that—and maybe even make a few readers feel a little less alone.

Fawn Creek, Kansas, is a fictional town. It's named after a township just down the road from me in Southeast Kansas. The town itself is heavily inspired by my hometown of Caney, Kansas, with a few familiar places and faces that pop up throughout the series. But I still wanted to rename it so I could move things around and give it more of a Hallmark feel.

**Here are a few little Easter eggs from *There's No Place Like Home*:**

*The sunflower field* that Tyler sees on her way into town was real. It used to sit on the north end of town, and whenever it came into view, I knew we were home. It's been gone for a long time, but memories of those yellow blooms will always feel like home to me.

*The rooster,* named Fernandez, was inspired by my friend's daughter's imaginary friend. The rooster itself was part of the original storyline, and even after many edits, I couldn't bring myself to cut him. (Doesn't every cute little town need a random animal running around somewhere?)

*Short Creek* was a real dance hall and saloon in Caney when I was younger. It's since closed and the building has been sold, but the memories remain. My favorite one? Eloping with my husband on New Year's Eve and then ringing in the new year there with our friends.

*Rio Escondido* was our beloved Mexican restaurant in town for many years and is arguably the most-missed business in Caney.

*The bookstore* was inspired by an empty downtown building that was for sale at the time. While I'm not in a position to open a bookstore of my own (nor am I very good at sitting still long enough to run one!), it was fun to dream about.

And as a little bonus—the city is putting in a Pocket Park next to that building! The idea was already in motion before I wrote about it, but I'm going to go ahead and pretend I manifested it.

Mayfest and the concert downtown are some of my favorite things about Caney. The committee works so hard to make that event a success, and I've loved watching it grow over the years.

Many people have asked if Tyler's story is based on my life. Nope. But she does have a few of my qualities. In fact, all of my heroines do, in one way or another. Writing them is my way of living a thousand lives.

All in all, this book—and this entire series—is a love letter. A love letter to my hometown, and to all the other tiny towns across the world. The locations may be different, but the heart of small-town life is always the same.

Thank you for reading my books and for loving Fawn Creek as much as I do.

**Michelle Lynn Ross**

# Chapter 1

*Welcome to Fawn Creek.* I murmur to myself as my car charges to the top of the hill, overlooking the valley that contains my hometown. As my car comes to a stop at the four-way intersection on the outskirts of the city, I find myself drawn to the open field under the Fawn Creek city limit sign. Today, the field is full of nothing but rows and rows of short green sprouts. Anyone that doesn't know better would probably assume they are beans or some other crop planted by a local farmer. However, I know exactly what is coming. Between now and July, those rows of sprouts will continue to grow, resulting in a field full of bright yellow sunflowers.

I haven't seen the sunflower field in years, but the memory of it is etched into my soul. Every summer, no matter where I'd been or where I was coming from, that familiar sight told me I was home. It's a shame that I'm going to miss it again this year.

The familiarity continues as I drive into town. Every driver I pass waves in my direction, without having the slightest clue of who I am. They don't wave because they know me. They wave because this is the way Fawn Creek is; friendly, welcoming and kind, just like it's always been.

As I drive towards the First Baptist Church, I marvel at the booming downtown business district. On the surface, not much has changed here since I left. Sure, some buildings have been repainted, and a few of the store names have changed, but the charm of Fawn Creek remains the same. I immediately notice that they closed the candy store and replaced it with a clothing boutique. However, right down the street, the flower shop, McDaniel's, has remained faithfully open and unchanged after all these years. Well, unchanged except the freshly hand-painted flowers that cover the large display windows. The bright, cheerful display puts an immediate smile on my face.

McDaniel's isn't the only business that's put extra effort into their decor. Almost every store front is decorated for the upcoming Memorial Day festivities. Every building boasts American flag bunting, and flowerpots full of red, white and blue arrangements. Per usual, Fawn Creek is fully dedicated to the seasonal festival. I expect nothing less, of course.

I pull to a stop in the parking lot of the First Baptist Church. Not surprisingly, the lot is almost completely full. I imagine by the time the funeral begins in forty-five minutes, there won't be a parking spot in sight. If that isn't a testament to how loved my Grandma Hazel was, I'm not sure what is. She was a noble woman and an active member of this community in every capacity that she could be. Fawn Creek won't be the same without her. Honestly, the world just won't be the same without her here.

I fire off a quick text to my boyfriend, Elliot, letting him know I arrived safely, after my three-hour drive into town. Immediately, my phone pings to alert me of a text, but it's nothing more than a thumbs up emoji. The lack of response feels like a punch to my gut. These past few days without Hazel have been really tough. I've tried so hard to stay strong. I know she wouldn't want me to lie in bed for days, crying over her death, but it's been hard to go through the motions leading up to today. All I can think about is how my life will never be the same without her here. She may have been my grandmother, but she was also one of my very best friends. She was my biggest cheerleader, my toughest (yet kindest) critic, and my safe place to land. My Sunday afternoons will never be the same now that I can't call her and talk for an hour over any and everything that crosses my mind.

I place my phone in my purse and then I sense the overwhelming feeling that someone is watching me. I glance towards the old brick church and spot the culprit immediately. My mother is peering out the window of the side door. As our eyes meet, she lets loose of the curtain, allowing her gaze to disappear behind it as though the moment never occurred. I take a deep breath and slowly exit my car. So much for taking my time to enter the lion's den now that I've been spotted. *Oh well, let's get this over with.* I enter the church through the side door and tiptoe into the family waiting area. I politely smile and exchange pleasantries with family members I haven't seen in a long time, except for holiday gatherings. Just as I'm getting ready to ask my cousin, Robin, where my parents are hiding, the sound of the swinging kitchen door causes me to start and make a 180-degree turn.

My mom exits the kitchen first, carrying a tray of grocery store cookies, arranged in neat rows. Her polyester dress swishes loudly as she moves in my direction. She places the tray down on a nearby table and then dramatically pulls me in for an embrace. My mother has never been much of a hugger. My childhood was not exactly filled with hugs and "I love you's", but when in public, my mother portrays the perfect motherly image.

"Hi, Mom." I whisper into her hair, taking in the familiar scent of her perfume.

She releases me, only pausing for a moment to look into my eyes while gripping my forearms. Her expression shows a deep mixture of exhaustion and sadness, and I try to remind myself to give her some grace today. After all, she lost her mother this week, just like I lost my grandma. This is going to be a hard time for everyone.

Next, I move toward my father, who has suddenly materialized behind her. "Hey, kiddo." He says, squeezing me tightly. He's wearing a pair of black slacks with a white button-down shirt. His beer belly hangs over the waistline, and the exhaustion on his face is clear as well. I can only imagine how hard this week has been for them both. Even with the best laid plans in place, a funeral is difficult to navigate. Hazel may have had everything arranged ahead of time, but I truly believe we all just assumed that she would live forever.

"Where's Elliott?" My dad asks, stepping backwards from our embrace while his eyes survey the room, looking for my missing other half.

"Oh," I pause, nervously tugging at the hem of my dress, "He really wanted to come, but he couldn't get away from work."

"Couldn't get off work, huh?" He laughs with a grunt. "You'd think being here to support you in your time of need would be more important than that silly computer lab he's sitting in." He says.

I ignore my father's snide comment, although I must admit it stung. "I know, Dad. He really wanted to, but he's working on a big project right now and just couldn't get away."

"It's hard to believe he couldn't just take one day of bereavement." He mutters under his breath.

"Well," I shrug. "Since we aren't married, he doesn't get company time off for the death of my relatives."

"Well, if you two would just get married already, you wouldn't have those problems," my mother chimes in. "It's been three years, Tyler. What are you waiting for?"

I bite my tongue and try to keep from saying something I shouldn't in the heat of the moment. Especially in the basement of the First Baptist Church. Luckily, the moment is interrupted just in time. A tiny bald man in a suit, presumably an employee of the funeral home, enters the room through a side door. "We are ready for the family." He announces solemnly. Per usual, Grandma Hazel intervened just when I needed her most.

* * *

After the funeral service at the church, I elect to drive myself to the cemetery rather than piling into the family limo with the others. My mother was resistant at first, but she wouldn't dare make a scene in front of the entire congregation. I'm sure I'll pay for that decision later, but that's a problem for Future Me to worry about. My mother will gladly add it to my list of shortcomings, I'm sure.

At the graveside service, I stand back quietly and watch as they lower Hazel's casket into the ground. The further she goes, the further I feel my heart sinking into my stomach. Years' worth of memories come flooding back instantly. She was always there for me when I needed her, for everything from my first broken bone to my first broken heart. She was always the one I turned to when I didn't know where else to go. And now? She's gone.

Suddenly, I feel a hand wrap around mine and squeeze it tightly, awakening me from my trance. I glance to my side and meet eyes with Avery, my best friend. She shoots me a soft smile and I attempt to return the gesture, but fall short. She always seems to know the right time to step in and help maintain my sanity. Goodness knows it's a full-time job. It wasn't necessary for her to come to the graveside service today, but I'm glad she did. I'm so grateful for our friendship, especially on days like today.

My eyes wander around the graveyard while the preacher speaks. I think every person here but me is crying. Suddenly, I notice my lack of outward emotion and feel extremely self-conscious.

I'm an emotional person by nature. I cry all the time; when I'm happy, when I'm sad, when I'm hungry, or excited. Hell, just last week I cried over a cat food commercial. For some reason, though, I haven't yet cried over Grandma Hazel. I've been waiting for it to happen ever since Mom called me three days ago to break the news, but so far, nothing. I know the dam will break eventually, and I'm sure it'll be at the most inopportune moment. Part of me just wishes it would happen so I could get it over with.

Don't get me wrong, I'm devastated about her passing. I loved Grandma Hazel more than anyone else on the planet. As her only grandchild, I know she loved me, too. My best childhood memories all revolve around my time with her. Every weekend, she insisted on "giving my parents a break" and taking me home with her. She would pick me up after school

6

on Friday and basically spoil me until Sunday evening, just before dropping me off for a shower and bedtime. I think she just liked to keep me around for the company. My grandpa had passed away from a heart attack when I was a baby, and she never remarried. "I'm too old to train a new husband." She would tell anyone who would listen.

Honestly, I think she never remarried or even dated just because she truly enjoyed being alone. She reveled in her solitude and when she was tired of the quiet, she would come and get me to fill the silence. She told me she'd much rather spend time with me than those "dusty old ladies at the beauty shop" and I liked to feel wanted. My mother and I weren't very close, and we butted heads more often than not. The relationship Hazel and I shared made up for the one I didn't have with my mother. It was exactly what I needed during my formative years, and I'm extremely grateful for those days.

Hazel was kind and caring, yet fiercely independent. She would go toe to toe with anyone that had ill intentions towards her family or the community. She would make you dinner or give you the shirt off her back in a heartbeat, but she would also tell you to go to hell if you needed to hear it. Hazel was truthful, honest, and strong. She was everything I want to be one day. I hope I don't disappoint her.

\* \* \*

After the service, I'm driving back through the downtown area on the way to my parents' house when a neon sign lit up on Main Street catches my eye. Without giving it a second thought, I pull into a parking spot and make a beeline for Drip, Fawn

Creek's quaint little coffee shop. The bell jingles happily as I pull the heavy glass door open and slip inside, following the aroma of freshly brewed coffee and baked goods.

From what I understand, this shop was recently purchased by new owners and completely renovated. This shop was once an outdated cafe, with brown wood paneling on the walls and yellowed ceiling tiles. The new owner transformed the storefront into a warm and welcoming space. It seems like every detail was intentionally chosen and meticulously organized. Everything is perfect, from the dark hardwood floors to the exposed brick walls and barn wood looking coffee bar. As soon as I step through the door, I feel like this is a place I could spend hours on end, working and visiting with other customers. I love the familiarity that comes with it.

"Tyler Burris, is that you?" I hear a vaguely familiar voice yell out from somewhere I can't quite pinpoint.

"That's me!" I respond, walking towards the counter, trying to find the source of the voice.

Finally, a petite body peeks out around the doorframe from the office on the other side of the room. Cassidy Martin, my childhood neighbor, comes barreling out of the doorway and across the hardwood floor towards me. I brace myself as she wraps me in a hug, lifting my feet off the ground as though I'm still six years old.

"I thought that was you on the security camera. How are you?" She asks, cupping my face and checking me over lovingly.

"I'm doing okay." I say with a small smile. "The best I can under these circumstances, anyway." I add with a shrug.

"I'm so sorry to hear about your Grandma Hazel. Today was her service, wasn't it?"

I nod. "Yes, I just left there, actually. I thought I'd better stop in for some caffeine before heading to Mom and Dad's."

She smiles softly. "I'm so glad you did. I haven't seen you in forever, but I think about you all the time. Are you still living in Oklahoma City?"

"Yep, still in OKC. Living the dream." I say with a smile, stepping out of the way as a mom enters the store with a little boy in tow. "How are you? How's Sierra?" I ask Cassidy.

"We are great! We just bought this place a few months ago, and I'm just trying to put some finishing touches on it." She gazes around the space proudly. "Sierra's getting married this summer! Can you believe that?"

That news stuns me for a second, but before I can answer, I feel a tug on my dress. Surprised, I look down to see a grinning toddler holding up a ball towards me. "Ball?" He asks. I glance towards his mom, who is ordering her coffee while balancing her phone on one shoulder. I take the ball and begin a game of catch while continuing my conversation with Cassidy. "Little Sierra? She's not old enough to get married. Is she even out of high school yet?"

I used to babysit Sierra when I was a teenager. Her parents hired me to watch her one summer while school was out because they couldn't find a reliable sitter. The two of us instantly clicked, and it turned into a year round Nanny job. They lived in the house between Avery and mine, so it was convenient for everyone. Sierra would just walk over to my house every morning and I would drop her off at school. After school, I'd pick her up and take her home, watching her until her parents got back. Everyone we didn't know just assumed that she was my little sister, because of all the time we spent together. While we aren't blood related, I've always loved her

9

like she was the sister I never had. Taking care of her was my only job when I was a teenager and still one of the best jobs I've ever had.

"Jacob! Please leave the nice lady alone." The disheveled mom calls out as she rushes towards us. "I am so sorry." She says to me. "He was rolling the ball back and forth on the coffee bar and then my phone rang..." She trails off.

I shake my head. "It's okay! He wasn't bothering me at all. I enjoyed playing catch with him." I add with a smile. The young mom thanks me and apologizes again before scooping up her toddler and fleeing from the store.

"What about you? Are you married? Any kids yet?" Cassidy gently pries. "You always have been so amazing with children." She adds, as she watches the mother and son duo that just left as they travel down the sidewalk.

Just as I'm about to respond, her office phone rings, saving me from acknowledging the stagnant state of my life.

"Shoot, girl, I have to go. You take care, okay?" She says, while she hurries back to her office to answer the phone, not waiting for my response.

*Saved by the bell.*

I step up to the counter and I am greeted by a man, probably around the age of nineteen, wearing a name tag that says Devin. After a quick glance at the menu, I order a large iced vanilla latte and swipe my card just as Cassidy emerges from her office once again.

"Hey, Tyler. Are you going to come home for Mayfest?" She asks.

Mayfest is an annual festival in Fawn Creek held every Memorial Day weekend. Friday night kicks everything off with a concert featuring a semi-famous band, with the opening act as a local musician. Depending on who the headliner is, the show usually draws in quite a crowd from the neighboring communities. The sales from the beer garden alone are a huge moneymaker for the festival.

"Eh, probably not." I shrug. "That's too many people in one place for me."

"Seriously?" she scoffs, placing her hands on her hips. "You mean to tell me, the girl who left here and moved to a city of 600,000 people won't come to our festival because of the number of attendees? You know that makes no sense at all, right?"

"Valid point." I shrug, taking my drink from Devin, and take a long sip. "But all those people aren't crammed into the middle of the street eating turkey legs at the same time either. They have a little more room to spread out in the city."

Cassidy just laughs and rolls her eyes. "Well, I'm just saying Jordan Johnson is our headliner. This will probably be our biggest show ever." She says with a prideful look on her face.

That news causes me to pause and reconsider for a moment. "Ugh, I love Jordan Johnson." I say, biting my lip. Jordan is a red dirt country singer that I have followed since the beginning of his career. It's no secret to those who know me that I'm a big fan. I have seen him perform half a dozen times at least, and he always puts on an incredible show. Unfortunately, in the city I don't have any friends that like Red Dirt Music, so I haven't seen him in years. Honestly, I don't have any friends at all in the city, and Elliott despises country music completely.

"That's a tempting offer. I might have to consider coming back for that." I glance down at my watch. "Okay, I really better get going. My parents are expecting me." I say, backing away from her to politely end our conversation. Cassidy's ability to chat your ear off sure hasn't changed since I left here ten years ago. Luckily, her office phone rings again, just in time for me to slip away.

Refusing to waste the chance at escaping, I spin on my heel to hustle towards the door. Just as I complete my turn, I look up to see a man, one that I've never seen before, standing face to face with me, but it's too late. My feet are already in motion and my body doesn't stop until it collides into his. On impact, I spill part of my iced latte down the front of his plaid button-down shirt. "Oh my gosh, I'm so sorry!" I exclaim, stepping back to survey the damage.

"Dammit. Watch where you're going." He growls through gritted teeth, with anger flashing in his eyes.

I swallow hard and turn towards the counter to gather napkins and help cleanup the mess I created. Just as I secure a handful, I turn and watch him storm out the front door. His face reddens as he makes his way down the sidewalk and disappears out of sight.

I watch, flabbergasted, as he makes his dramatic exit, unsure of how a little bit of spilled coffee could create such a problem.

*Ladies and gentlemen, I believe I've just met the asshole of Fawn Creek.*

# Chapter 2

I park my car at the end of the driveway in front of my childhood home, still in a strange haze from whatever just took place in the coffee shop. I wish I had the slightest clue what made that guy storm off and disappear the way he did. When I walked out the front door of the shop, I looked for any possible sign of him to make another attempt at my apology, but he was long gone. What a weird interaction over a little bit of spilled coffee.

Rather than going directly inside and putting myself into yet another uncomfortable situation, I decide to sit and savor my coffee for a few moments longer. I'm already going to be in hot water for taking so long to get here, so there's really no point in rushing now. I certainly can't take my coffee inside with me. That will just give my mother further ammunition to use against me. Through the windshield, I study my childhood home. Not much has changed since I lived here. In fact, not much has changed here since the day I was born. The humble two-bedroom house sits in the middle of a quiet neighborhood, just a few blocks from downtown Fawn Creek. Like most of the houses on the block, the craftsman style bungalow is covered in white vinyl siding that appears to have been recently pressure washed. (One of my dad's favorite hobbies.) The rest of the exterior is pretty plain, but neat. The original metal windows are still in place, flanked by gray vinyl shutters. Flowerbeds run the entire face of the home filled with lush green shrubbery. I recall, my mother bought those plants on clearance at the hardware store one summer when I was a kid. I never imagined they would have stayed alive all these years, but here they are, with the fresh red mulch that my dad replaces every spring like clockwork.

I make my way up the brick sidewalk and pull open the screen door, pausing for a second to take a deep breath. It's no secret that my mother and I have never had a great relationship. I've had a long life of walking on eggshells whenever I'm around her, and I don't see that changing after all these years. While it has gotten better since I moved out, it's nowhere near perfect. This is precisely why I moved away immediately following my high school graduation. By creating some distance between my parents and myself, I fully believe I did the best possible thing for our relationship. As soon as I cross the threshold into their living room, I confirm I was correct to feel anxious about today's reunion.

"Really, Tyler?" My mother stands from her spot on the couch, crossing her arms over her chest with a scowl as I enter the room.

Immediately, my heart picks up speed, as I rack my brain trying to figure out what I did wrong this time. Honestly, this could be something that happened today, or something that happened when I was seven. You really never know how far Lisa is searching back in her Rolodex. I have to hand it to her. No matter how old she gets, her memory is still quite astounding.

"Don't look at me like that," she huffs. "Like you don't know exactly what I'm talking about." Her face lands in a hard glare as she narrows her eyes at me.

Shit. Did someone call and tell her I was at the coffee shop when I was supposed to come straight here?

I stammer nervously, "I... I have no idea what you're talking about."

Her face reddens with anger. "I can't believe you stood at the graveside of my mother's funeral and did not shed a single tear. You just stood there the entire time with your head in the clouds like a teenage girl daydreaming about boys and shopping." She grumbles, pointing at me across the living room. "You looked like it bored you out of your mind and you wanted to be anywhere but there. As if it's not enough that I have to make excuses for your boyfriend not showing up. Now, I have to make excuses for your lack of feeling surrounding your grandmother's death? It was insulting and so embarrassing, especially considering how much Hazel loved you."

"Woah." I put my hand up as if to stop her unwarranted verbal attack. "That is not fair. Mom, you know damn well that I loved Grandma Hazel more than anything on this earth. You know that, Dad knows that, everyone that means anything to me knows that." I spit out, crossing my arms across my chest. "That's all that matters. Who cares what anyone else thinks?" Unfortunately, I'm used to this song and dance when it comes to her. My mother has a bad habit of worrying too much about how others perceive her and our family.

"You could have at least pretended." She debates as though she has a leg to stand on.

"You're kidding right?" I yell, throwing my arms in the air. "You're mad because I didn't fake cry at my grandmother's funeral so that people wouldn't think poorly of me? You are unbelievable." I huff and plop down on the couch with a scowl.

Just then, a ringing doorbell interrupts our argument. Mom's face loses all of its color once she realizes her screaming was likely overheard by a person on the other side of the door.

"I hope whoever that is didn't hear your little outburst." She threatens behind gritted teeth, as though I'm the only one to blame. Swiftly, she moves across the room towards the door. She takes a deep breath and then smooths her skirt before opening the door. "Pauline, hello!" She says, wearing her best fake smile.

I roll my eyes at the complete personality change that took place right before my eyes. Not that this is the first time I've witnessed such a thing. After a polite exchange with Pauline, Mom steps back into the room with a casserole dish in her hands, shutting the door behind her. She doesn't take her eyes off me as she makes her way across the room to deposit the casserole into the kitchen, almost like a silent warning that she isn't done with me yet. Naturally, I take this as an opportunity to seek refuge in my father's den.

I poke my head around the doorway, confirming that this is indeed where he's hiding, before slipping into the room. He's facing the wall, bent over a folding table, and tinkering with a gun, per usual, when I interrupt him. He turns to acknowledge my arrival and I giggle out loud at the headlamp that's strapped to his forehead.

"Hey sweetheart." He says, while the light blinds me. "What's so funny?" he teases, as I dramatically shield my eyes.

Boy, what a difference it is when you change rooms in this house. While my mother is more rigid and stern, my father is more lighthearted.

"I just wasn't quite expecting the headgear." I say, plopping down in a nearby recliner, feeling my body sink into the worn leather like it has done so many times over the past 28 years.

"Well, you know. Ever since my only flashlight holder moved away, I have had to come up with some new methods." He chuckles, his belly jiggles, and adds to the joke more than he intended it to, I'm sure.

"I can't believe Mom let you keep this chair." I change the subject, fingering a piece of duct tape on one armrest. My favorite photo of the two of us was taken in this chair. I was seven years old, and I had just finished filling my dad's hair with pink and purple butterfly clips. Next, I climbed into his lap and demanded that he read "Where the Wild Things Are" to me over and over until I fell asleep. Mom snapped the perfect photo of me with my legs crossed, reclining on dad's chest while he sported his new fancy hairdo. That photo currently resides on my mantle at home and is one of my most prized possessions.

He scoffs. "Let me? I'm going to be buried in that chair."

I raise a brow, knowing better.

"And I can keep it until I die as long as it stays in my den where no one but me will ever see it."

I shake my head. "What've you got there?" I motion towards his project on the table.

"Oh, just getting this shotgun cleaned up. I picked it up for cheap at an auction last week." He sticks a giant Q-Tip into the disassembled barrel and makes a disgusted face when it comes out black. "I don't think anyone has ever cleaned this thing before. Disgusting."

"Looks like it." I say, trying to feign interest. My poor dad. All he ever wanted was a son to hunt and toss a football with. Instead, he got stuck with me; a girl that hates the outdoors and never had an interest in sports. He took me hunting one time, but I had snuck a book with me into the tree stand, just in case we had downtime. I still remember him shaking his head in frustration when he found it. We did not get a deer that day, thankfully. Knowing me, I would have puked, or cried, or both if I would have had to take home a dead animal. He never invited me to hunt with him again and that was fine by me.

"So" Dad breaks the silence, "Hiding from your mother, I suppose?" he asks, not removing his eyes from the piece of metal he is polishing.

"Yes, actually." I huff. "Did you hear her screaming at me?"

"No, but in all fairness, I have gotten very good at tuning her out over the past thirty years." He jokes. "I didn't need to, though. I heard all about it on the way home."

"Oh, I'm sure you did." I sigh. "Honestly, I'm amazed at how you handle it. I would have gone out to get a gallon of milk a long time ago and never returned."

He snorts. "Maybe that's why I never go to the grocery store. The temptation is too great." He answers with a wink.

I roll my eyes at his stupid dad joke. I won't ever admit that I'm thankful for his ability to lighten any mood. "Seriously, though. This is why I don't come home more often. I swear every thing I do makes her mad." I sigh.

Dad climbs onto the stool next to his worktable and turns around to face me. "Honey. I know your mom is a lot to handle sometimes. Today, her emotions are running higher than usual and it's affecting everyone around her. Give her a chance to calm down and I'm sure she will see that she overreacted. She loves you so much, she just doesn't always do a great job of showing it."

"I'm sure you're right. I just hate the fact that every time we are together, it's a complete shit show."

He nods. "Me too. We don't have nearly enough time

together to waste it arguing over petty things. I'll talk to her."

"Thanks, Dad."

Per usual, Dad fixes everything.

# Chapter 3

My car rolls to a stop in front of Avery's house, and I exhale a deep breath in an attempt to shake the tension in my body after my visit with my parents. Avery's daughter is with her dad tonight, so we are taking that as an opportunity to grab dinner and have an old-fashioned sleepover. I might as well get some quality time in with my bestie while I have the chance, because goodness knows I don't make it to town often enough to hang out with her regularly. It's been a while since we had time to do this. Our sleepovers aren't much different now than when we were kids. We typically stay up too late watching old rom-coms, and eat way too much junk food. The only difference now is that we are old enough to legally add alcohol to the mix.

The ignition isn't even shut off before Avery steps onto her screened-in porch to wave me inside. I busy myself with gathering my purse and overnight bag, leaving the shoes I took off as soon as I left my parents. I climb out of the car, locking the door behind me before carefully walking barefoot up her brick sidewalk.

"I just need to change real quick and then I'm ready to go." I say, making my way into her living room. In a matter of minutes I emerge from the bathroom in a pair of leggings, a loose t-shirt, and a messy bun on top of my head, my usual look. I shove my dress and uncomfortable bra into my bag and retrieve my sneakers. "Much better." I sigh after slipping them on and tying my laces. "Now I feel like me again."

"You look like you." Avery agrees. "Let's go. I'm starving. Is it okay if we walk? I want to have a margarita."

"And I need at least 2 margaritas after the day I've had." I tell her and pause as she stops to lock the front door.

"I take it your visit didn't go well?"

"Does it ever?" I let out a small laugh. "Get this. My mom bitched me out for not crying at the funeral. And if I couldn't naturally cry, I could have at least thrown her a bone and pretended for the sake of the audience." I pause. "Of course, that was after I walked right into some jerk at the coffee shop and sloshed my drink on his chest. He stormed out of the place like I ruined his life and made me feel like crap."

"Oof." Avery says. "What did your dad say about your mom?"

"He stood up for her, per usual. Of course, he was already hiding from her in the den when I got there, cleaning a gun."

"Classic Lisa and Jerry." Avery shakes her head, laughing.

"I suppose." I say with a sigh. "I should have known I was in for it. As soon as I got to the funeral, they cornered me, wanting to know why Elliott didn't come."

"Eh.." Avery says, shrugging her shoulders, as she steps onto the sidewalk on Main Street. "I mean, it is a little weird that he didn't come with you. It was Grandma Hazel, after all. She was so important to you. You were closer to her than you are to your parents."

"I'm sure he would have, had I asked him to." I say, kicking at a rock that lays in the middle of the sidewalk. "But why burn a vacation day to come to Fawn Creek and eat casserole at my parents' house, while my mom makes snide comments to us both? I wouldn't want to do that either. Hell, I avoid his parents at every chance I get, too."

"I don't know, Ty." She says. "I just feel like, with as close as you and Hazel were, he shouldn't have waited for you to ask him. He should have just came to support you."

"You've met my parents. Should he really volunteer to be subjected to them?"

Avery stops in the middle of the sidewalk and grabs my elbow to stop me. "If he loves you, he should be willing to put up with their shit in order to be there for you when you need him. That's what relationships are all about. The good and the bad. You would do it for him."

We continue down the sidewalk in silence for several paces. I know Avery isn't an Elliott fan. She has voiced her opinion of him several times, and I hate it. She's my best friend and the one person I really want to approve of him. However, it has always felt like a lost cause.

"Besides, if he had come, I wouldn't be able to hang out with you tonight. We would have headed right back home after eating dry tuna casserole made by some random lady at the church. I have been dreaming all week about eating dinner at Rio." I sigh. "OKC has plenty of excellent restaurants, but I can not find anything that rivals their flan. Believe me, I've tried every Mexican place within 60 miles of my house." I say, approaching the bright turquoise painted building. "And there's a lot of them." I add in a whisper.

"Sounds like a good reason to move home, if you ask me." Avery teases, opening the door and waiting for me to walk inside Rio Escondido.

"Ha!" I shake my head. "Can you imagine Elliott living here?

He wouldn't last a day in Fawn Creek."

She shrugs and mutters, "You don't have to bring him."

I roll my eyes as we follow the waiter to our booth. We each order a margarita on the rocks and graze over the basket of chips and salsa.

"I mean it, you know," Avery says, breaking the silence. "I just wish you would move back already. Seriously, how dare you leave me here alone to raise a baby?" she says, poking out her bottom lip.

"Avery, I love you, but I would rather eat a jean jacket than move back to Fawn Creek. All I ever wanted was to get out of this place, and I won't give up my dream that easily. Sometimes it's nice to be where you haven't known your neighbors all your life."

Avery glances around the room. "What? You mean you don't enjoy rubbing elbows with washed up high school football players at the Mexican Restaurant on Thursday nights?"

We both steal a glance towards the bar. All four stools are filled with guys that graduated with us, concentrating hard on the television screen in front of them.

"No, I could have lived without seeing Thomas McGregors' butt-crack on a Thursday night while he chugs a red beer." I whisper. As if on cue, Thomas turns around and waves at us with a sideways grin. Avery attempts to stifle her giggle, but fails miserably.

I shake my head. "You can't even pee in this town without someone knowing about it. I enjoy the anonymity that comes with living in the city. Besides, we won't even discuss how fun it would be to live near my parents again." I say, laying down my menu. "There's no use. The only option is for you to join me in Oklahoma City."

She winces. "You could never force me to live in a town with stoplights."

"I suppose we are destined to be apart, then." I retort, biting into a tortilla chip and offering a shrug.

"And so goes the classic tale..." she adds just as the waiter walks back with our drinks.

\* \* \*

After dinner, we decide to take a stroll through downtown before heading back to Avery's house. This is one thing that I can appreciate about Fawn Creek. I have never been afraid to walk anywhere, day or night. Back home, I live in a decent neighborhood, but I can't just go downtown to take a walk unless I want to pay $10 for parking and watch over my shoulder the entire time. I certainly wouldn't be walking around at night time, either.

Sure, all small towns have problems, but in Fawn Creek I have only felt unsafe once while out in public. A group of Girl Scouts tried to sell me cookies, and I declined because I was trying to cut back on sweets. You would have thought that I stole their lunch money with the way they glared at me when I said no. I seriously feared for my life. Honestly, I never knew seven-year-old girls could be so intimidating.

"There is just something so charming about this little place." I say, gazing through a window at the flower shop. It's hard to believe there are still no chain stores or restaurants, only locally owned businesses. "There isn't an empty building down here anymore, is there?" I ask.

"Just one," Avery winks as we approach the building in question.

I pause in front of an empty storefront with a For Sale sign propped against the interior window and smile wistfully. "Ugh, the love of my life." I swoon.

This sweet little brick building was always a favorite of mine, for no particular reason at all. It just always seemed to have so much potential. The exterior is still the original red brick, and two huge display windows flank either side of the original glass entry door. It's a two story building with the potential for upstairs apartments or office space. On the surface, there's nothing special about it. In fact, it's quite simple. There's no reason for me to love this place like I do, but sometimes the things, people or places we fall for the hardest don't have to make sense to anyone but us.

Years ago, not long after I moved away, the building next door caught fire in the middle of the night. Faulty electrical wiring was the culprit, and it resulted in a total loss of that historic storefront. This building unfortunately suffered quite a bit of fire and water damage as a result. The city tried to make the best of it. They tore down the burnt building and installed a pocket park in its place. The park is now a key player in the downtown area. All spring and summer, this is where the Farmer's Market is hosted. In the winter, a giant Christmas tree is erected and the tree lighting festival takes place to kick off the holiday season. Otherwise, the space can be rented for events, food trucks come to town and park there, or citizens can just enjoy the little quiet spot in the middle of town. It's not unusual to see someone sitting on one of the nearby benches, reading a book they borrowed from the little free library nearby. That park is a true testament to this community and their ability to turn a devastating loss into a hidden gem for the city.

Unfortunately, the same can't be said for the building that's for sale. Turns out, the owner had allowed their insurance policy to lapse. Therefore, they were unable to make any repairs to bring the brick beauty back to life. So, it's just sat empty for all these years, wasting away. Until now. Now, it is finally on the market. Apparently, the owner has finally come to terms with letting it go.

Avery interrupts my daydreaming. "This poor place. I'm sure it would have been snatched up a long time ago if it didn't need so much work. It's a mess. The electrical needs completely redone, and not to mention the smoke and water damage from the fire. It's going to take someone with deep pockets and incredible carpentry skills to revive that beast." She says, as she makes her way down the sidewalk again.

I sigh and glance back at it once more. When I was a kid, I used to talk to anyone that would listen about how I was going to grow up and own a bookstore right in downtown Fawn Creek. I already had the building chosen, this building to be exact. The plan was to live on the second story and run my business down below. I would spend my days reading and sharing my love of books with like-minded people. I would help children learn to love literature by offering weekly story times. All day, I would help the citizens of Fawn Creek travel to new places just by opening the pages of a novel. I shake my head, thinking about it now. Those dreams were simple to come by when I was ten and I thought anything was possible. Now, the world has taught me that some dreams are only wishes, never meant to come true.

Avery walks along beside me quietly and appears to read my mind like she often does, something only your lifelong best friend can do so easily. "Hey. Maybe you can win the lottery and hire some hot contractor to fix it up for you. Then you can finally open that bookstore you've always wanted." She says, elbowing my side.

"Only if I can move it to the city, I'm afraid." I tell her with a shrug. "Target and Starbucks have become essential to my life, and I don't know that I can survive without them."

"Hey. We have a grocery store and a great coffee shop." She says, pointing to Drip.

I just shake my head and keep walking. Fawn Creek is great for a visit, but moving back here will never happen.

# Chapter 4

At 6:00 am, my eyes shoot open to the sound of my screaming alarm clock.

"Shit," I whisper, as I spring from the couch and dive for my phone in an attempt to silence it before it wakes Avery. I pause to listen for movement upstairs, and I am met with silence. Thankfully, I was successful.

"I can't believe I forgot to turn that off." I mutter to no one in particular as I crawl back on to the couch and rub the sleep from my eyes. Usually, I never have to set an alarm for before eight in the morning, but I did yesterday, so I could leave early for Hazel's service. I must have put it on a repeating schedule instead of a one time use, resulting in this rude awakening. In an attempt to not lose any more of my sleepiness, I lay back down on the couch and pull the blanket over my head, but it's a lost cause. Thanks to that dose of adrenaline, I'm up for the day, like it or not.

Since Avery will be in bed for at least another hour, I decide to seize the opportunity and get in an early morning walk before I head home. Maybe I'll even pop in for another latte at Drip for the drive home.

Before I can talk myself out of it, I get dressed and slip out the front door and into the fresh morning air. Immediately, the nostalgia of this neighborhood takes me back in time. My entire childhood happened on this very street. Avery and I grew up just a few blocks from here. We were neighbors, with just one house between ours, Cassidy's. Avery moved to Fawn Creek just before kindergarten started. We met for the first time on the playground at school and became fast friends. Once we found out we were neighbors, though, we were inseparable. Memories suddenly rush back to those days, causing my heart to swell. Memories filled with roller skating, back yard sprinklers, mud pies and playing in the rain in the middle of the street. Those were the very best days. We had a great life on Elm Street.

For a second, I feel a small wave of sadness wash over me. I admit, I hate the fact that my future children will never know about small town life. Don't get me wrong, I love the city, but there is just something comforting about raising kids in a small town. Mainly, I wish they could experience the safety and security that comes with small town living. I hate that they won't grow up knowing that everyone in town will look out for them, whether or not they like it. Sure, they will have a life of their own with friends in our neighborhood, but the city will just never be the same.

Fawn Creek is your typical small town in Kansas. It's the kind of place that you merely drive through on your way to somewhere new and exciting. People say that you can easily miss this place if you blink while driving through, and they aren't wrong. With a town this size, it's not a surprise that most have never heard of Fawn Creek. However, for those of us who are from here, this place is so much more than just a map dot. What I told Avery is true. I have no intention of ever moving back here, but there are definitely parts of Fawn Creek that will always hold my heart.

As a teenager in Fawn Creek, I couldn't wait to get out of this town. I think that's the general consensus among small town kids. We grow up within these tight city limits and we want nothing more than to just get out and see what else is out there. Like the rest of them, I dreamt of city lights, restaurants, shopping and the ability to leave my house without running into people I knew. More than anything, I yearned to put distance between myself and my parents. I love my mother and father deeply, but putting space between myself and them was a pivotal moment in my life. So, that's exactly what I have maintained for all these years. Thankfully, only a few hours' distance has been enough to put a barrier around my life.

Honestly, living in Oklahoma City might be the best of both worlds. I live close enough that I can drive down for a day and see my family, but I live far enough away that my family doesn't just pop in on me unexpectedly, nor do they know every detail about what I'm doing. Perhaps whenever I do have babies, I can bring them here to visit to get a taste of the small town life before we flee back to the city.

The one person I do miss is Avery. Even after all these years, it's hard to do life without her. I tried to get her to go to college with me, and dozens of times since then I've tried to get her to join me, but every attempt has been a failure. She just loves it here. On more than one occasion, she has told me she can't imagine living anywhere else, and it's always been hard for me to understand what keeps her here. We've made it work, though. Thanks to technology, we stay connected with regular phone calls and face times. It's just not quite the same.

Nearly nine months ago, Avery FaceTime'd me to say that she was headed to the hospital to give birth to Juliet, her baby girl. I squealed with excitement and immediately jumped into my car before racing to the hospital. To this day, I am so grateful that I could be there for her that day. Living so far away definitely complicates things, and I could have easily missed it. Being in that delivery room with her was one of the most important days of my life. I never understood the deep, unending love that you can feel towards another human being until I met Juliet. There was just something about her squishy little face and the scent that newborns give off, that made it clear to me I'd always love her as if she was one of my own. It was nothing short of miraculous. Watching Avery raise Juliet from a distance has been difficult, to say the least. Since I'm an only child, she's the closest I'll ever have to a niece and I love her like she's my blood relation. It sucks watching her grow from so far away.

I continue my walk down Main Street, checking out window displays as I pass through the business district. Most of the businesses are still closed, except for Drip, of course. As soon as the building comes into my field of vision, the scent of brewing coffee reaches my nose. I promise myself that I'll stop in there on the way back to Avery's house.

After passing the coffee shop, I find myself in front of the little brick building with a For Sale sign once again. My stomach flutters and sadness washes over me. Is it possible to feel an emotional connection to a piece of property? One that I have never even come close to owning? I'm not sure, but I kind of feel like that's exactly what is happening here. I've watched this building house many things over the years. But, despite the best efforts of the citizens of Fawn Creek, nothing has stuck. It's been a thrift store more than once, a gun store, a boutique and a children's consignment store. I always loved going inside to look around and dream of what I would do with it if it were mine. It's the perfect size for a used bookstore and with Drip next door, the location is perfect.

No one in my life took me seriously when I told them my dream. Well, no one but Hazel, of course. She loved to read as much as I do. When I told her my dream, she beamed and squealed excitedly, as if I told her I'd won the lottery. She said she couldn't wait to be my first customer and from there always encouraged me to make the book store happen. A part of me has always struggled with the fact that I never saw the plan through. Not only did it feel as though I let myself down, but I felt like I let Hazel down as well. It's not like she could still be my first customer now that she's gone. Still, here I am, feeling sappy over an empty shell of a store and the path I didn't explore. Pathetic.

Elliott knows this is something I've always wanted, but like others, he has always dismissed it pretty quickly. Even with us living in a bigger city, it's just seemed impossible. It would just be so hard to compete with major book retailers. They have the upper hand and they always will. They can sell things for so much cheaper than I ever could. Why would the average person spend money at my store when they could travel up the street and save twenty percent by shopping with a major retailer? Plus, Elliott has no interest in taking on debt for a business that may not make it. I understand his reasoning. Money is and always has been a top priority to him. I know he's right, but it's still a hard dream to just let go of. I shake my head, as if attempting to clear the ideas from my brain, but it's no use.

Obviously, that's just not the life that was meant for me. In a few hours, I'll be back in Oklahoma City with Elliott, where I belong. I'll be back in our cutesy little house with our tiny yard. I'll be back to living the life I wished for all those years ago. Perhaps it's time to give up and focus on other dreams.

I stop in the middle of the sidewalk and glance down to check the time. It's 7:00 on the dot, and I imagine Avery is probably up and getting ready for work. Time for one last coffee stop before I head back to reality.

# Chapter 5

Just as I enter through the automatic doors of Whole Foods, I'm interrupted by my ringing phone. I retrieve my cell from my purse and roll my eyes at the caller screen. My mother. After lunch with my parents, the rest of our visit was about as pleasant as a root canal. We made small talk over a pan of tuna casserole to the best of our ability, and I snuck out of there as early as I could.

"Hi, Mom. Everything okay?" I ask into the phone, balancing it between my ear and shoulder while I retrieve a shopping cart.

"Well, yes." She answers, already sounding annoyed. "I just wanted to check on you, to make sure you made it home. You never called me last night."

"Oh crap, I'm sorry." I say, raising the palm of my hand to my forehead. She told me to call her when I got home and it completely slipped my mind. I was so ready to escape, I completely forgot to say anything about staying with Avery. "Last night I spent the night at Avery's and just got back this morning. I actually just stopped at the store on the way home."

"I was just worried that you were dead in a ditch somewhere." She says with a hint of sarcasm in her tone.

"I know. I really am sorry, and I didn't mean to make you worry." I won't question why she didn't call me yesterday when she didn't hear from me, instead of waiting until today. I would have been very dead in a ditch by now.

"You could have stayed here last night. We have more than enough casserole in the fridge. I could have sent some home to feed you, Elliott, and Avery for a week."

I laugh. "Sorry mom. Throw it in the freezer. You and dad will be set until Thanksgiving."

"Oh, you mean the next time I'll see you?" She asks dryly. My mother rarely misses an opportunity to point out the fact that she doesn't see me nearly as often as she would like to.

*Unless someone else dies between now and then*, I think. I would not dare say that, of course. I would be the next one to die and my mother would drive up here to do the job herself. Well, she would make my dad drive her. She's not a fan of driving in the city.

She changes the subject. "Did you say you are out at the grocery store? Is Elliott with you?"

"Nope, he's working...I think. I just pulled into town and haven't even been home yet. I'm just stopping at the store to grab a few things for dinner, so I don't have to get back out later."

"I hope you have your pepper spray with you."

I pat my crossbody purse I'm wearing slung over one shoulder as I wander through the aisles. "Yep, my hot pink pepper spray is in my purse, ready to protect me from all the villains that run around the Whole Foods parking lot."

She ignores my sass. "I just hate the thought of you wandering around the city all by yourself."

"I know, but I am being safe, I promise."

She sighs in disbelief and then changes the subject. "It was great to see you yesterday. I wish Elliott could have come too."

*Here we go again.*

"Me too. He's been working on a big project and there was just no chance he could get away yesterday. Maybe we can all get together for dinner soon." I say, making an empty promise.

"You know, speaking of Elliott." Mom interrupts the silence. "Joyce told me yesterday that her son Roger is getting married next month. She asked me when you and Elliott are finally going to get married." She stammers. "I wasn't sure what to tell her."

*Real smooth, Mom.* "Well, I'm not really sure what to tell her, either." I say, balancing my phone between my ear and my shoulder.

"I just don't understand why he hasn't asked you. Why hasn't he? I would really love to have some grandchildren before I die."

It's a great question. I'll admit, I've been wondering the same myself for a while now. Still, I have no answers for her.

"Beats me, mom. Probably my sparkling personality is too much for him." I answer dryly. "Mom, I thought you didn't like Elliott, why are you so concerned about me marrying him?"

She pauses thoughtfully, just long enough that I'm not sure she's still on the line. "Oh Tyler, it's not that I don't like him. Honestly, I don't know him well enough to dislike him."

I want to argue with this statement, but she's not wrong. I don't visit often at all, but he rarely comes with me when I do. He is usually busy with work or the gym, and truthfully he's not a fan of Fawn Creek or any small towns in general. If he does come visit he's usually bored out of his mind, or making fun of the townsfolk before we've been here for an hour. I don't even bother eating a meal in town when he's with me because there is always something for him to nitpick.

"Tyler, I just want nothing else than for you to be happy. If Elliott is who makes you happy, then I want that for you. He must be something special if you two have been together for all these years."

For some reason, her words slice through me like a knife. Am I happy? Is there a reason we've been together for all this time? Why did going back home stir up all these questions in my heart? I can't get into this right now.

"Mom, I better get going. It looks like there is a gang initiation happening in the granola aisle and if I want a good seat, I need to get there early. Love you." I wait just long enough to hear her say a quick, "I love you, too." Before I press the end call button and shove the phone in my back pocket.

I know my mom means well. I really do, and believe me, she isn't the only one that wonders why I'm not engaged yet. In fact, this is the second time in two days that I've been asked about the status of my relationship. I wish I had answers to give other people, but more than anything, I wish I had some answers for myself.

Elliott and I have been together for three years. When we moved in together, I thought cohabitating would be nothing more than a stepping stone. Instead, it appears that it was more of a life sentence. We live in his parents' rental house, and they charge us a minimal amount for rent, just enough to cover property taxes and insurance. This enables us to use our money elsewhere. Because of this, we were able to pay off our cars and student loans rather quickly. With no debts to speak of, that has allowed us to each build up substantial individual savings accounts, keeping them completely separate of course. We split our bills and household purchases directly in half and try to keep things as equal as possible. It's a system that's worked well for us so far, even if the arrangement raises eyebrows among our friends and families.

I thought maybe once we paid all the debts off, he would finally pop the question. I thought so again regarding our savings accounts. Once we each had $10,000 in the bank, I was sure a proposal was coming. However, I've gotten nothing but crickets. Every time I think it's coming, I'm let down. I don't want to push him, and I don't want him to feel pressured. However, we are kind of at a point in our relationship where it feels necessary to have a discussion about our future.

Avery and I have hashed this out before, many times in fact. I tell her I don't want him to propose because he thinks he has to. She says that if I don't have this talk with him, I'm going to waste my chance to have a family. She's right, of course. It's no secret that I'm getting older, and I thought I'd be further than this by now. I was sure by 22 I'd be married and by 25 I'd have my first baby. That was the plan, anyway. Now, at 28, it may be time to realize that my plan, just like my bookstore, was nothing more than a wish. I hate to admit it, but my mom and Avery make a valid point. I'm going to have to approach this subject with him, whether or not I like it. The only question is, how?

\* \* \*

The front door opens with a click and the sound of Elliott's shoes landing on the hardwood floor echo throughout the house. I'm in the kitchen, finishing up the homemade gua-camole when I hear him.

"Hey, you!" I yell across the house before moving to the

fridge to pull out the pitcher of margaritas I have chilling in there.

He peeks his head into the kitchen. "Hey." He answers with a tired smile before moving across the room to lightly kiss my lips.

"Hungry?" I ask, nuzzling my face to his chest, breathing in his scent. I've missed him. We aren't the type of couple that needs to talk often when we are apart, but I always cherish the moments when we are finally back together.

Elliott surveys the kitchen, and I admit I'm sure it looks as though I went a bit overboard with dinner. Cooking is one of my favorite distractions and today I really need to be distracted. I just finished making steak street tacos. Between those and the rice, beans, chips, queso, guacamole, and salsa, I have just enough food to feed a small army. Every surface of our kitchen is covered with various serving bowls. I'm going to have to have the conversation with Elliott that's on the tip of my tongue or I'm going to gain twenty pounds.

Elliott places his backpack in an empty seat at the dining room table and pulls out his laptop. "How much are you going to hate me if I say I'm not hungry?" He asks, setting up a workspace on the table. "I had a big lunch today."

My smile drops immediately. I don't even have the energy to hide my disappointment after the week I've had. This was a lot of work to just feed myself, but I guess it's probably my fault for not saying anything to him first. I had shot him a text that I was home and asked if he needed anything while I was out running errands, but I had not mentioned that I was making a feast for dinner.

Reluctantly, I make my plate. After placing my food on the table, I salt a margarita glass and offer him one.

He shakes his head and waves me off without removing his eyes from the laptop. "No, thanks. I've got to get some more work done."

I frown. This is already not going the way I need it to. How am I going to have a heart to heart with him if he's too busy working to even look at me?

I carry my drink to the table and take a seat across from him. Quietly, I pick at my food while I watch him. He's typing away at the keyboard and concentrating on the task in front of him, completely oblivious to the worries that are consuming my every thought.

He stops typing, and his eyes move to mine. I smile at him, but it's obviously forced. This time he reads my expression.

"What's up?" He asks, still not moving his hands from the keyboard.

"Oh, nothing. I just don't want to interrupt you while you're working." I say, moving some food around on my plate. "Want to do something together tomorrow? Maybe we can go to the Farmer's Market?"

"Sorry, I'm going to have to work tomorrow." He says, eyes back on his screen. "But you should definitely go to the market if you want to."

I shrug in response. My attempt to have some one-on-one time this weekend is failing miserably.

"How was Fawn Creek?" He asks while he stands from his chair and moves to retrieve a bottle of water from the fridge.

"It was good." I say, leaning back in my chair. "I found out Sierra is getting married."

"I don't think I know who that is, do I?" Elliott asks, sitting back at the table, finally giving me his attention. To Elliott, Fawn Creek is like some mythical land that I tell him stories

40

about. He doesn't have any connections to the town, and why would he? He's only been there twice in the three years we've been together.

"That's the little girl I used to babysit when I was a teenager. I can't believe she's old enough to get married." I pause, waiting for him to say something, but I'm met with silence. It's now or never, I suppose. "Elliott, speaking of people getting married..." I start, moving my plate towards the center of the table and then downing the rest of my margarita. "Can I ask you something?"

"Uh, sure." He responds, finally moving his computer out from between the two of us, giving me his full attention. Unfortunately, the moment is interrupted by his phone ringing loudly on the table between us. He looks at the caller screen and frowns. "Sorry, I have to take this," He mumbles quickly before putting the phone to his ear, cutting off my febrile attempt at a confrontation.

Almost immediately, he carries his laptop to the spare bedroom to solve whatever IT Emergency has popped up at work. And of course, I'm left in the kitchen surrounded by enough tacos to feed a small army. Mindlessly, I clean up the mess and carefully pack away the leftovers while waiting for him to return. By the time I wipe the counters down, I have not only lost hope of seeing him again before bedtime, but I've also lost the courage to push the issue any further. With that, I down the rest of my second glass of margarita and send myself to bed alone.

# Chapter 6

My eyes flutter open on Saturday morning and I slide my hand across the bed to reach for Elliott in the dark. Instead, all I find is an unmade side of the bed. It's obvious that he never came to bed last night. Unfortunately, I am almost relieved by the revelation. The last thing I want is to wake up and have to continue our attempted conversation. I've lost any sense of courage I was feeling yesterday.

I roll to my other side to retrieve my phone and check the time. It's 8 am. There's a dull headache behind my eyes, the aftermath of the tequila I had before bed, I suppose. That's what I get for having nothing but coffee and one taco before drinking, I guess. I put the phone back down and pull my blanket tight around my body, trying to will myself back to slumber. Just as I close my eyes once again, my phone vibrates on the table next to me, jolting me back awake.

**Caroline: Hi girls. Still up for hot yoga and brunch today?**

*SHIT. This day keeps getting better. I totally forgot that was today.*

The phone buzzes again.

**Mandy: Yes, please! I feel like an absolute cow. I can not wait to get my sweat on.**

I pick up the pillow next to me and press it into my face before letting out a scream. Hot yoga is the last thing I want to do today. Hanging out with Caroline and Mandy is the next-to-last. These women are both just so, for lack of a better term, plastic-y. They both walk around in expensive clothes with their fake boobs and designer purses while driving $80,000 cars and turning down their noses at everyone else around them. They are just so different from anyone else I have ever been friends with, and I clearly don't fit in with them. In fact, they are the exact type of women I generally try to avoid. They are the girlfriend and wife of Elliott's two best work friends, Logan and Greg, so I don't really have a choice but to play nice. Considering the fact that I still have no friends here in the city, I have to at least try to befriend them. Working from home is nice, but it makes meeting new people nearly impossible. Especially when you are an introvert.

Elliott has been begging me to get to know them for a while now, so that we can all do things together. Therefore, when they invited me to tag along with them on a Saturday, I knew I had to accept the invitation.

**Me: I'll be there! Can't wait!**

**Caroline: Yay!**

**Mandy: See you girls at Namaste at 9!**

With a huff, I roll out of bed and stumble towards my closet. I'm not really a fan of name brands, but my mom is. Well, scratch that, she is a fan of people *thinking* she can afford name brands. With that being said, this year she bought me some knockoff Lululemon leggings for Christmas. I've never been inclined to wear them, mainly because I rarely do any type of exercise, or have a reason to put on athletic wear. I tend to live in lounge wear. However, today they are just what I need. I already feel self-conscious when I'm around these ladies. They are both so perfect and I'm just, well... me. I know I don't fit in with them at all, but at least I can dress the part.

\* \* \*

Fast forward to 8:45. I pay for parking and carry my gym bag and the yoga mat I bought for this outing towards Namaste, the yoga studio. Immediately, I spot Mandy waiting outside the door on a bench, staring straight down at her phone, oblivious to the world around her. Even from a distance, she looks flawless and intimidating as hell. She's wearing a black crop top with matching leggings and white sneakers. Her bleach blonde hair is in a perfect high ponytail, and her French manicured fingers loudly tap on her phone screen.

"Hi" I say nervously, as I approach her.

"Hey." she says back, not bothering to look in my direction. After probably a full minute of awkward silence, she pulls a water bottle out of her bag. "Ugh, where is Caroline? We will not get a good spot inside if she's late."

As if on cue, we look up to see Caroline rushing across the street towards us. She looks just as flawless as Mandy does. She's wearing an olive green crop top and legging combo, with a high teased ponytail. If I'm not mistaken, they are wearing the same outfit, just in different colors. I glance down at my own clothes. I paired my fake leggings with a bright pink fitted tank top. I thought I looked cute when I left the house, but now, in the presence of these two, I feel so much less polished. Honestly, I didn't know my self confidence could get any lower than it was already, but here we are.

"Ugh, sorry, guys!" She says, stopping in front of us. "I had a hard time finding a place to park. The parking lot is almost full already. I had to park next to some old crappy Honda." She whispers that last sentence, with one hand covering her mouth like she's saying a bad word. "Hopefully they don't scratch my Wagoneer when they leave."

Caroline turns to look at me. My mouth is slightly hanging open and I can't hide the look of confusion on my face.

"I try to only park next to cars that are newer and nicer, so hopefully the owner will respect the surrounding cars when they are getting in. I never get door dinged by other nice vehicles." She explains.

"Oh, yeah, that makes sense." I say, trying to remember what direction she came from. Not far from here, I parked my Honda in a busy lot. Surely there is no way she was talking about my car, right? My car isn't brand new, but it's far from old and shitty. I shake the thought from my head. No, she has to be talking about an older Honda with missing hubcaps and duct tape holding the mirrors on and dents all over the body. I can not let myself get worked up for no reason.

"You guys ready?" Mandy asks, already sounding bored. She picks up her things and heads towards the door without waiting for an answer.

I obediently grab my bag and follow along in her path. Mandy has kind of always struck me as a bitch, while Caroline is at least a little warm and welcoming. I have mentioned this to Elliott before, and he agreed Mandy is kind of gruff, but that's just her personality. She's a nurse and from the stories Elliott tells me, she deals with a lot of stupidity daily, making her a bit cynical. Basically, he told me she has a very low tolerance limit for people, but he swears she's a great person, at least as far as Greg says.

45

I suppose I haven't spent enough time with the two of these ladies to really pass too much judgment on them. Caroline works in Pharmaceutical Sales, so she spends a lot of time in and out of doctors' offices. I think she is just naturally good at being nice and bubbly towards people, whether or not she means to, because it's a key component of her job.

We pay our fees and quickly sign our waivers. Normally, I would at least pretend to read the paper I am signing, but today I feel like I have to rush so I don't get left behind. I feel like a third wheel already, or like someone's annoying little sister that has to tag along, even though no one wants her there. Carefully, I lay my mat down on the floor in the large yoga room just as the instructor enters the room.

"Hi ladies! I see a few unfamiliar faces in here today. I'm Gail and I'll be your instructor." Her eyes land on me and she sends me a gentle smile. "We are going to get started in about five minutes. This is a great time to get some water and take a potty break." She announces in a very calm but kind voice before leaving the room once again.

"I better run to the restroom." I whisper to Caroline before slipping out of the room. She nods in response while busying herself with some light stretching.

On my way back, I pause just long enough to notice Mandy and Caroline through the window. They are huddled together and giggling, engrossed in some sort of joke between the two of them. I smile to myself, thankful that Mandy's mood seems to be lifted. Maybe she's defrosted a bit and will at least be tolerable for the rest of the day. That feeling of relief doesn't last long, though. As soon as I walk back into the room, they both look at me and abruptly stop talking. It's obvious that they were talking about me or talking about something they didn't want me to hear. Suddenly, I feel like I'm thrown back into high school and stuck working with a couple of mean girls on a science project. It takes every bit of strength in my body to not gather my things and leave. I am way too old to be subjected to people that make me feel like I don't belong, but somehow here I am. Instead, I try to hide the fact that my feelings are hurt and I take a seat on my mat just as Gail walks back in to start the class.

"Welcome everyone." She announces. "Once again, I am Gail and I'll be leading today's hot yoga session. We are going to get started with a brief warm up while this room works to reach a balmy 99 degrees, since the door is now shut."

I look around the room with wide eyes. 99 degrees? The rest of the attendees look on as though they've heard this opening information too many times already.

She continues, "Please remember, if you get lightheaded or dizzy, take a break. Get out of the pose and get a drink of water. Don't die. It'll make me look really bad."

The class erupts in light laughter after that last line, and I wonder again if I should have left when I had the chance. *What have I gotten myself into?*

* * *

I make my way into the lobby of the yoga studio and lean against the concrete wall. Slowly, I allow my body to melt until I am sitting on the floor. The cold concrete immediately works to bring my body back down to its normal temperature. I sip my water and try to steady my breathing while begging myself not to pass out.

The door to the studio swings open and out walk my yoga companions. Caroline has my yoga mat and gym bag under her arm, while Mandy follows along behind her, looking annoyed as usual. Immediately, Caroline moves to sit next to me. "Tyler, are you okay?" She asks, her eyes searching mine.

My breathing has finally returned to normal, and the feeling of embarrassment has taken over instead. "I think so." I respond with a nod, while wiping sweat from my forehead.

"Did you get lightheaded?" Mandy asks accusingly.

I nod and down the rest of my water bottle. "I don't know what happened. I was doing okay, but suddenly I felt like I was going to fall on my face during downward dog. Child's pose didn't make me feel any better either, and I just had to get out of there." I cover my eyes. "That was so embarrassing."

"Did you eat today?" Mandy asks, sounding annoyed, as she shifts her bag from one shoulder to another. It's clear that I have ruined her Saturday morning and she doesn't bother to hide it.

I shake my head. "No, I didn't want it to upset my stomach before class."

"What about water? Did you drink water this morning?"

I wince. "I had coffee on the way to the studio."

Mandy rolls her eyes. "I know you probably don't workout a lot," Mandy says, looking me up and down with an obvious judgmental eye, "but you have got to eat before working out and you have to hydrate before hot yoga." She finishes with her arms crossed over her chest. "Or you might, oh I don't know, get lightheaded and pass out."

"Noted for next time." I mumble, as I stand up from my spot on the floor, steadying myself against the wall.

Caroline places a hand on my shoulder. "Let's go next door

for brunch. You need to eat something," she says kindly. "We can beat the crowd since class isn't over yet."

"Food sounds great." I agree and obediently follow her out the door, avoiding eye contact with Mandy.

When we step through the door of Yolk, the ultra hip brunch restaurant next to Namaste, I am immediately taken aback. Everything from the marble tiles to the crushed green velvet chairs and booth seats scream luxury. I've never even been to such a beautiful restaurant, and certainly not for breakfast. I'm more of an Ihop kind of girl, to be honest.

The hostess leads us out the door onto the back patio. It's May in Oklahoma, and it's still cool enough in the earlier part of the day to sit outside and enjoy the weather. I'm thankful for the outdoor seating. I'm too sweaty and gross to feel comfortable tainting their plush velvet chairs with my sweaty backside, and the fresh air will hopefully help me feel better while I wait for my food.

Our waitress comes to take our drink order, and we all settle on infused water with cucumber and lemon. As she walks away, we study our menus. It doesn't take me long to decide on Eggs Benedict, my favorite. Satisfied with my choice, I close my menu and the other two follow. As soon as the menus hit the table, the incredibly attentive waitress is back. "Have we decided?" She asks, holding her pen over her notepad.

"Yes, I'll have a green smoothie." Mandy says, not making eye contact with the server at all. She places her menu on top of Caroline's and goes back to her social media scrolling.

I mentally add this to the reasons why I can't stand Mandy. You can tell a lot about people based on how they treat their server at a restaurant, and she is basically acting like ours doesn't exist.

"I'll have the same." Caroline pipes up, handing the stack of menus to me.

Suddenly, I feel like I can't order food. They're already in better shape than me, and I don't want to stand out more after my embarrassing stunt today.

"Make that three." I tell the server, with a soft smile. I already know I'm going to regret this decision.

"So, I have something to tell you, ladies," Mandy says in a singsong voice. She digs in the change portion of her wallet and slips something onto her left hand. She holds up her perfectly manicured fingers and braces for our response.

Caroline gasps loudly, causing the rest of the restaurant to turn and look our way. She pulls Mandy's hand closer to investigate the giant rock that is now dominating her left hand. "Mandy, it's beautiful. When did this happen? How did he do it?" Caroline pries.

She grimaces a little. "It's almost embarrassing to talk about." She starts. "Last night was our one year dating anniversary, so he tried to recreate our first date. He took me out for dinner and then for a walk in Bricktown. Just as we reached the bridge, he got down on one knee and proposed."

"Aw, that sounds sweet." I say, taking a drink of my water, trying to avoid the sting. If only she knew that I would kill for a "boring" proposal like that.

"I guess, but he could have at least taken me out to a nice restaurant. Not Bricktown Brewery." She says with a shrug, not bothering to hide the disappointed look on her face.

"No, Tyler's right. It's cute." Caroline adds, trying to console her friend. "Do you have any ideas about setting a date yet?"

"Not yet. It's going to be huge, like the event of the century, so it'll probably take another year and a half, if not two years, to plan it." She takes a drink. "It has to be perfect."

The two of them lose themselves in conversation about venues and colors while I quietly sip my water. It's not long before the waitress is back with our smoothies. As she places mine in front of my face, I try to hide my disgust. What in the hell did I order? I lean over and look at the thick green concoction in my glass. To add to my disgust, the drink gurgles and a large piece of spinach surfaces to the top.

My tablemates immediately each take a sip with satisfied looks on their faces as if they are eating a four course meal. I follow, not knowing what to expect. It doesn't taste like much at all, to be honest. It's like a flavorless, ugly milkshake. Why would anyone order this on purpose? I look at the ladies with me again and their perfectly toned bodies. This is exactly why I'll never look like them. I like the taste of food too much.

"So Tyler," Mandy says while absentmindedly stirring her smoothie, "How long have you and Elliott been together?"

Sigh. *Here we go.* "Just about three years," I say, mimicking the stirring motion she is making.

"Oh. I didn't realize it had been that long," Mandy says nonchalantly. "Any plans on getting married yourselves?"

"Um...well" I start, trying to decide how to answer, just as we are interrupted.

"Hey ladies!" A high-pitched voice breaks through the nervous conversation and a gorgeous brunette pops up in between Mandy and Caroline. She obviously shops at the same place as these other two. She is also wearing the same crop top and legging set, with a high ponytail, only in pink. They look like they could model for a Lulu store poster, the same outfit all in different colors.

"Jess!" Mandy says, standing from her seat to move to hug

her. "Guess what?" she says, but then holds her left hand up to show off her ring before Jessica can guess.

"Holy crap! Congratulations!" she squeals and hugs her friend. "I'm so excited for you!" Mandy and Jessica hug tightly. When they release, Jessica leans across the table towards me with her hand out. "Hey, I'm Jessica."

I shake her hand. "I'm Tyler."

"This is Elliott's girlfriend," adds Caroline.

"Oh, I work with Elliott. He's a great guy," Jessica says with a smile. "It's so nice to meet you. Well, girls, I have to get over to my table. We just took a spin class and I am starving." She waves to us and turns, walking back to her table. Her perfect ponytail swaying behind her, against her tanned and toned back.

"Bye!" the ladies at my table call to her as she walks away.

I take another sip of my chunky green smoothie, trying to drown my sorrow and counting down the minutes until I can get out of here.

# Chapter 7

I hug my yoga mat close to my chest as we walk down the sidewalk towards the paid parking lot.

"Oopsie." I hear Caroline say behind me. "Tyler," she says in a loud whisper. When I turn, she motions for me to come towards her. "You have a tear in your leggings. I can see your panties." She says softly.

I sigh. Of course, I do. Damn, these fake ass leggings couldn't even last for one wear. Just one more thing to ruin my day. I stop in the middle of the sidewalk and pull a long sleeve shirt from my gym bag, before tying it around my waist.

"You know, there's a Lululemon just around the corner," Mandy says. "You should go see if they will replace them. They look like you've never even worn them."

"Oh" I pause, trying to figure out how to get myself out of this. "It's not a big deal." I say, in an attempt to brush it off.

"Mandy's right." Caroline says, "Those are way too expensive to fall apart like that. Let's just go right now."

SHIT. "Oh no, it's okay. I'll go another time." I wave them off.

Mandy side eyes Caroline and I see it. "Isn't that kind of out of the way for you? You should really just go now." She says, pulling my arm, trying to lead me around the corner of the sidewalk. "If you are afraid to ask them, I will. They know me there."

I put my hands down at my sides and take a deep breath. "I really appreciate it, but I need to get home."

"It'll only take a second." Mandy says with her arms crossed.

Caroline smiles softly, "Come on, you are being kind of silly."

I let out a deep sigh. So much for the one thing that I thought would make me fit in with them. "They're not real, okay?" I look back and forth at the two horrified women as I make my confession. It's almost as though I told them I'm an alien. "My mom bought them for me from some wholesale group for a Christmas gift. I have never been in a Lululemon in my life and don't really plan to. The fanciest store I shop at is Target, and I'm okay with that."

"Oh, okay," says Caroline, obviously at a loss for words.

"I knew it." Mandy mutters.

Okay, that's all I can take for one day.

"Thank you both for your invite today." I say, clapping my hands together a little too loudly and causing even myself to startle. "But I really need to get going." Without another word, I turn and bolt towards the crosswalk, taking advantage of the blinking WALK signal. Don't cry. I beg myself. All I have to do is make it to the safety of my car and then I will be free to have the breakdown I fully deserve after this terrible day.

I enter the parking lot and stop short when I spy Caroline's dark gray Wagoneer, parked right next to my "shitty" Honda.

"And the hits keep on coming." I mumble under my breath.

I grab the door handle and climb inside, immediately starting the engine. My tears burn as they brim in my eyes.

Don't cry, at least not until they're gone. I beg myself. I scroll through my phone, trying to look busy while I wait for them to get in their cars and drive away. In reality, I am just looking for the nearest Sonic. Screw hot yoga and screw nasty ass chunky green smoothies. That's not me and it's not who I'll ever be. I'd rather live the rest of my life alone in this town than try to force myself to be someone I'm not.

What I need right now is a greasy breakfast burrito and a Diet Dr. Pepper with a lime wedge. I may live in the city now, but I'm not ashamed to admit that I find a familiar comfort in a Route 44 soda that nothing else in this world can provide. I can't explain it. It just tastes like home.

Just as my yoga companions drive away in their overpriced vehicles, my car makes a dinging sound, indicating that something is wrong and my day is about to get even worse than it already was.

*Perfect. My shitty Honda is going to live up to its name today.*

I check the display and find that I have a flat tire. Since the coast is clear, I climb back out of the car and quickly discover the culprit. My passenger side back tire looks like it's melting into a puddle on the pavement. Fantastic.

The tears I have been willing to stay inside my body have no other choice than to race down my face. Clutching my phone, I scroll to Elliott's name and press the call icon. He answers on the second ring.

"Hey. What's up?" He asks. I can hear typing in the background. He's still at work.

I sniffle. "Elliott, I'm having the worst day of my life." I take a breath. "I went out with Caroline and Mandy today. First, I nearly passed out at yoga. Then, I was peer pressured into drinking some nasty green smoothie. After that, my fake leggings ripped and my ass was showing to the entire world, for who knows how long. Now my shitty Honda, which I didn't even know was shitty until today, has a flat tire in a parking lot downtown." My words fly from my mouth without taking a breath.

I'm met with dead silence on the other end, no typing, no voices in the background.

"Elliott, are you there?" I ask, sniffling again.

I hear the typing commence. "Yeah, I'm here."

"Did you have me on mute?" I ask, my face glowing red with anger.

"Yeah, sorry. Greg stopped by to ask me something." He pauses, "Sounds like a terrible day, babe. I'm sorry."

I let out a loud sigh. "I know you are working, but is there any chance you can come help me change my tire?"

Silence again.

"Hello?"

"You pay for Roadside Assistance through your insurance, right? Why don't you just use that?" He answers, still clearly sounding distracted.

"Please tell me you are kidding right now."

"I mean, I'm just in the middle of work and..."

I interrupt before he can continue. "So instead of taking a break to drive ten minutes to come help me, you want me to call Triple A and then possibly wait for hours for someone to come help me?"

"Well..." He trails off.

"Whatever." I huff. "Nevermind. I'll figure it out." I end the call and let out a loud groan. How can he be so smart and such a freaking idiot?

I shake my head in disgust and call the one person I can always rely on to save the day.

"Hello?" He answers the phone on the second ring.

"Dad. I have a flat tire. Can you walk me through changing it over the phone?"

His soft chuckle rattles through the phone. "Is this one of those internet pranks?"

"No." I sigh. "I'm stranded in downtown Oklahoma City with a flat."

"Where's Elliott?"

"Working." I mumble in response.

"Oh. Too busy again. That sounds about right." He sneers. "Tyler, what are you doing?"

"I'm sitting in my car in a parking lot having a mental breakdown?" I supply, trying to understand what he is getting at.

"No, with him. What are you doing?" He repeats. "Tyler, I love you and I have tried to be supportive, but can't you tell that this is wrong?"

"Because he can't come change a tire for me?" I sigh. I know exactly what he is getting at. I am just too emotionally exhausted to hash this out right now.

"No, because if he wanted to make you a priority, he would. He would have been there for the funeral. He wouldn't leave you stranded to fend for yourself downtown with a flat tire. You deserve better than this, and it kills me to see you settle for less than you deserve."

Another tear escapes through my eyelashes. He's right, but I can't think about it right now. I just need to handle what's in front of me. There is no way I'm going to discuss the current state of my relationship with my dad right now. Especially when I'm not even sure what the current state is.

"Dad, can you please help me?" I ask, putting an earbud in

my ear. I need to focus on the task at hand before I deal with the rest of the shit show my life has become.

"Of course, open your trunk."

# Chapter 8

Defeated and exhausted, I unlock the front door and walk into the house, thankful to find it empty. After the day I've had, the last thing I want to do is stand face to face with Elliott. I'm still pissed at him for not coming to save me today.

After leaving downtown, I got some actual food for a late breakfast. Then, I drove to the nearest tire shop and had my tire repaired. It was the last place I wanted to spend my Saturday, and of course I was stuck sitting in the waiting room for an hour and a half, but at least it's done. If only the rest of my life was so easy to fix.

I round the hallway and make a beeline for a much needed shower when I hear the front door click open and Elliott slipping off his shoes onto the hardwood floor. Immediately, all the tension from the day returns to my body. I bite my lip and try to decide my next move. No part of me is ready for a confrontation and I'm too mad to pretend like everything is okay. I could quickly rush into the shower and put off seeing him for that much longer, or I could tackle this... whatever it is... head on. Just as I turn on my heel to make my way towards the bathroom, the sound of his voice stops me.

"Tyler! You in there?" He calls out as his footsteps pad across the living room towards the hall. I take a deep breath and plaster on my best attempt at a smile before turning to meet him. "There you are." He smiles. "How was your day?"

Those words are enough to make me lose my pleasant facade. "Terrible, remember?" His blank expression tells me he's already forgotten about my call this morning. I sigh in frustration. "I went to hot yoga with Caroline and Mandy and I almost passed out during class. My pants ripped wide open, and I got a flat tire." I listed back to him.

"Oh yeah. I forgot I talked to you earlier." He runs a hand through his hair and leans against the wall in the hallway. "I guess you got the tire straightened out then."

I grimace. "Yep, I changed it myself and then went to the tire shop to get my old one repaired." I let that sink in for a moment and place my hands on my hips. "Good as new now."

"I didn't know you knew how to change a tire."

I shrugged. "I didn't. I called my dad, and he walked me through it. He didn't want me to be stranded in downtown Oklahoma City for hours waiting on Triple A to show up." I snarl.

He rolls his eyes. "Okay, Tyler. Sorry, I can't just run out of work to save the day after you've been out with your friends at workout class and drinking mimosas." He mutters.

I scoff. "Nope. I was out with YOUR friends, trying to make them like me so that I can make you happy, just like you asked me to." I shake my head, remembering my morning. "And for the record, it was terrible. Every single second of it."

He smirks and starts to respond, but then closes his mouth and just shakes his head. "I'm sorry you had a bad day." He offers and opens his arms towards me.

I close the space between us and let him envelop me in a hug. "I'm sorry for being snippy. It's been a really long day and I have a lot on my mind." I say into his chest.

He squeezes me tighter and kisses the top of my head. "Why don't you get cleaned up and we will go get something to eat for dinner? Tacos fix pretty much everything, right?"

I hug him tighter and feel relief wash over my body, thankful for a chance to reconnect with him. "It's a date." I say, into his chest, before wiping the stray tear rolling down my face. Maybe I am letting my emotions control me a little too much. Maybe my life isn't so bad after all.

\* \* \*

"Another margarita?" the server asks as he approaches our table. Naturally, I had just taken a huge bite of my street taco.

I shake my head quickly while trying to chew and swallow my mouthful of food. My last margarita was a little too strong and I'm sure if I have a second one, I'll have to be carried to the car after our meal.

Elliott smiles and reaches across the table to squeeze my hand. I squeeze his hand back. This is exactly what we needed; an uninterrupted date night for the two of us. Everything I've been worried about just seems silly now. Just as I lean down to take another bite of my dinner, I notice a commotion out of the corner of my eye.

It all happens rather quickly. A server approaches our booth with a plate of sopapillas, complete with a lit candle sticking out of the top of the stack, and gently sets it down in front of me. Confused, I look down and read the words "Will you marry me?" written across the bottom of the plate in chocolate syrup.

My eyes move to Elliott's and my heart hitches. I'm waiting

for him to make a move, but his face has turned pale, and he is frozen in place. He shakes his head quickly at the server and says, "Wrong table."

"Oh! I'm so sorry! My mistake!" the server exclaims, before quickly snatching the plate from in front of me and placing it down on the booth behind Elliott.

I watch painfully as a man that can't be over the age of twenty years old moves from his seat to kneel in front of an already crying young blonde woman. She says 'yes'. They kiss and I fly from my seat towards the bathroom. I barely make it inside the stall and close the door before I begin to cry. I sit down in the stall and bury my head in my hands as I let the tears puddle into my lap. In a course of mere seconds, I went from excited and eager to completely heartbroken and let down. And all he can say is, "Wrong table." I can't do this anymore. I move from the stall and stand in front of the sink to blot my face with a wet paper towel. After fanning myself for a few seconds, I look at my reflection and determine that's as good as I'm going to get. Time to face Elliott and the rest of the restaurant that I just ran from while fighting back tears.

As soon as I round the corner to our table, his eyes meet mine. I try to read his expression, but there's nothing there. He throws some cash down on the table and stands as I approach him.

"Ready to go?" He asks, just above a whisper, obviously embarrassed by my reaction.

I nod and turn towards the door, leading him through the building, past the rows of yellow and turquoise booths and out the front door into the quiet evening air. I settle into the car and put on my seat belt, not removing my eyes from the passenger side window. We drive in silence for several blocks before he speaks.

"Tyler." He says just above a whisper, not moving his glance from the windshield.

"Elliott." I respond quietly, willing myself to not start crying again.

"What the hell happened back there? Why are you upset?"

I bite my lip and close my eyes, begging my brain for the right words to say to him. Willing myself to not turn into a sobbing mess.

"You really don't get it, do you?" I ask, turning my entire body towards his. I pause for him to respond, but I'm met with silence. "Elliott, for half a second I was so excited. I thought that proposal was for me, and then to find out that it was intended for another table?" I shake my head. "That was so embarrassing."

"So, let me get this straight." He turns to look at me. "You're mad at me for a mistake that the waiter made?"

I huff, louder than I probably should have. "No, Elliott. I'm not mad at you over what he accidentally did. It's that I'm disappointed. I've been waiting for three years for you to propose to me and for a second, I thought it was happening tonight. For a second, I was so excited and then completely heartbroken."

He doesn't respond, and that hurts even more.

"Elliott. I hate even having this conversation, but I can't just skate around it anymore." I swallow hard and with every bit of courage I have left, I ask him. "Are you ever going to propose to me?"

He quickly hits his blinker and turns into our driveway. After a smooth stop, he puts his Tesla in park and turns to face me. Sadness is all over his face. "Tyler..." he whispers. "I don't see myself ever getting married."

Instantly, I feel sick to my stomach and I regret starting this conversation at all. I feel tears building in my eyes once again. "Did I do something wrong?" I ask between sniffles.

He grabs my hand and pulls it towards him. "It's nothing to do with you, Tyler." He relaxes into his seat, almost as though this has been weighing on his shoulders for ages. "I just don't think I'm the kind of guy that gets married and has kids."

I take another deep breath. "What about me?" I ask quietly, staring down at my hands.

"Tyler…" He lets out a small chuckle. "Nothing has changed for me. I still love you and I'm not going anywhere. I just don't think we need a piece of paper to tell people we are in a relationship."

My brow furrows. "So, you want to be with me, but you don't want to marry me?"

"Exactly." He responds with a shrug, as though I've been acting like an idiot for no reason.

I wring my hands together. "So, that's that, huh? You don't want to get married and you don't want a family, so suddenly that means that I can't have those either?"

He sits in silence.

"Do I really not get a say in any of this?"

More silence fills the car. I shake my head, trying to decide where to go from here. I think I already know the answer, but I'm too tired to fight anymore.

# Chapter 9

I wake up in the late afternoon and pour myself a cup of coffee before settling into the couch with a throw blanket. Elliott left me a note on the fridge that he went to the gym and for that, I am so thankful. The last thing I need right now is to restart last night's conversation. After we came inside, I crawled straight into bed and by the time he was out of the shower; I was busy pretending to be asleep. It wasn't long before his breathing steadied and I was safe from having to continue our conversation. I laid in bed awake, replaying our conversation in my head repeatedly until I finally fell asleep sometime around three this morning. Per usual, all the late night thinking and worrying did nothing for me. I'm still just as sad and angry as I was last night when I got out of his car and I highly doubt I'll be over it soon.

What I need is an honest sounding board that will tell me the truth, even if I don't want to hear it. I grab my phone and fire off a text to Avery.

**Tyler: Hey. Is this a good time to call?**
**Avery: Sure! I just got Juliet down for a morning nap.**

I immediately hit the call command and Avery answers on the first ring.

"Hey. What's going on over there?" She asks. "It must be

some type of emergency if you want to talk on the phone."

I nod, as if she can see me. She's right. She knows me all too well. I hate talking on the phone. Mostly, I blame it on the fact that I've been traumatized by working in customer service for years. You can only get screamed at over the phone so many times, for things that you have no control over, before you just start avoiding phone calls all together. This is part of the reason I do customer service via chat and email now.

"I need life coaching." I sigh.

"Well, I'm covered in spit up. My hair is in a rat's nest and I slept for a grand total of 27 minutes last night, so I think you have come to the right place." She replies, in an attempt to sound as reassuring as possible.

"Perfect." I laugh, trying to lighten my mood. I spend the next several minutes recounting my experience from yesterday morning. Afterwards, I finish with a deep breath and stare at the wall above the television while I brace myself for Avery to respond.

"That sounds horrific." She finally agrees.

"That's just the tip." I admit, working up the nerve to fill her in on Elliott's startling confession from last night.

"That's what she said." She mutters in a low voice.

As much as I want to giggle at her stupid joke, I can't. I don't have even a bit of humor left inside of me anymore.

"Nothing?" She asks, sounding playfully annoyed. "I get nothing for that? That was a classic."

I moan, still unsure that I want to hash this out right now. "I don't know how to lead into this, so I'm just going to say it. Last night Elliott told me he has no desire for children or marriage. Not now, not ever." As the word ever leaves my lips, I feel a tear gently rolling down my cheek. I quickly wipe it away as though I am attempting to hide it from someone.

"Wait, what?" She pauses for a second. "I thought you guys were on the same page about this stuff?"

I sigh. "I don't know. I guess he changed his mind, or maybe I just assumed that I knew what he wanted. Regardless, he doesn't now."

"What about you? Has your mind changed?"

"No." I answer quickly. "I still want nothing more than to have a baby of my own and a husband. Not a live-in boyfriend until I die. What does he expect? For us to be sixty years old, introducing each other at the golf club as each other's girlfriend and boyfriend?" I sigh, sinking deeper into the couch.

"And he decided now was the time to spring this on you because...." She drags on. "Because you weren't already hurt enough after losing your grandma, so he decided to make it worse?"

Ouch. She's not wrong, though. His timing was less than stellar, but I admit I brought it on myself.

"Well." I wince at the looming confession. "I started it. My mom got inside my head this weekend. She called and was asking me when we were going to finally get married. I decided she was right and that I needed to talk to him. But, I was afraid to ask, until last night. There was a proposal at the restaurant we were eating at."

"Oof." Avery breathes out.

"Girl, you have no idea." I moan, remembering the night before. "The server accidentally gave me the dessert plate with the proposal written on it. I thought it was for me. Elliott went white as a ghost and almost died in front of me before telling the server he was at the wrong table. I was so hurt I ran to the bathroom stall crying."

67

Avery's breath hitches. "Oh, Ty..."

"Yep." I continue. "And as you can probably imagine, it just kind of imploded from there. I asked why he hasn't proposed to me and he told me exactly why." I sigh. "Now I kind of wish I could go back to being ignorant about the whole thing, to be honest."

"That's understandable." Avery agrees. "And it was also fair for you to ask him. It sucks that this whole situation had to happen in order for you to do it, but you deserve to know where you stand."

"I guess so." I sigh. "But now I just feel like I've been punched in the gut."

"Well, what are you going to do now?" She asks, gently.

I reposition myself on the sofa. "Well, I was actually hoping you would make that decision for me." I mutter.

Avery laughs. "Not a chance, sister. But I will give you my unfiltered opinion if that's what you would like."

"Please."

"All your life, you have dreamed of being a mom. You're amazing with kids. You have the patience of a saint. You know what it's like to have a crappy relationship with your own mom, so you know exactly the type of parent you want to be. If you stay with Elliott, then you have to accept the fact that you will never have that. Is that another dream you are willing to just throw away? You've already given up on your bookstore. Are you willing to give up on having a family, too?"

I sigh, quietly, but don't respond.

She continues. "In my opinion, Elliott is fine, but he is not the love of your life. If you stay with him, then you are doing nothing more than settling. I think if you settle, you are going to look back on your life in 5 years and regret it."

I frown and wipe the tears from my eyes. She's right. I hate it, but she's right.

"I'm just saying," Avery continues. "I think there is a guy out there that will move mountains for you and that will love you the way you deserve to be loved. A man that would die to wife you up and have babies with you. Please don't settle for good enough."

I wipe my eyes again. The tears are flowing quickly now. "What if you're wrong? What if this is as good as it gets?" I sigh.

"Tyler, you need to be honest with yourself. What you have now isn't even good. That man will never give you the life you want." Avery pauses for a beat. "There is better out there, but you will never see that if you don't make a move. There's only one way to find it."

"Avery, I don't even know where to go from here.... literally. I don't have anywhere else to live. It's going to take months to find a decent apartment to move into." I reason. "I can't stomach the idea of living with him as a roommate for months while I try to find somewhere else to go."

"Come home." She pleads, sounding hopeful. "You work remotely so you can work from anywhere. You could stay with your parents until you find a place to rent. Hell, you could even sleep on my couch."

I groan. "Avery, I don't want to move back home. I've worked so hard to distance myself from that town and from my parents. I can't move back now."

"Then think of it as a long visit." She pleads. "Come stay during the summer while you find a new place to live in OKC or wherever it is you want to live."

"I don't know...." I say, trying to weigh my options.

"Come on. We've never had a summer together as adults. We can take Juliet to the lake and go out on weekends when she's with her dad. Please?"

The sound of slamming doors in our driveway interrupts my thought process. I rush to the window and peer through the blinds to find Elliott making his way towards the front door. "Avery, I gotta go. Let me think about all of this, and I'll let you know what I figure out."

"Good luck." She says, still sounding hopeful as I disconnect the call and put the phone in the pocket of my sweats.

I don't think even luck can save me now.

Elliott breezes past me into the kitchen to retrieve a bottle of water. When he returns, I'm sitting on the sofa with my arms wrapped around my knees, holding them close to my body. No matter how hard I try, I can't stop the tears from flowing. I know what must be done. I'm terrified to speak.

Elliott takes notice of my stance and sits next to me on the sofa before reaching out and stroking my knee. "Tyler, are you okay?" He prods, softly.

I shake my head. The words are on the tip of my tongue, but for some reason, sitting here with him, I can't will them to come out of my mouth.

Elliott reaches out to take my hand, and briefly I allow it. He uses his thumb to trace circles on the top of my hand. "Are you still mad about last night?" He asks.

I pull my hand back and place it in my lap. "Elliott, I'm not mad. But I am upset and hurt, and it's not just about last night, it's about a lot of things." When he doesn't respond, I continue. "Elliott, I love you and honestly, until last night, I thought that you and I agreed about a lot of things."

He scoffs, "So, we're back to this again?"

I bite my tongue and attempt to remain composed. "Yes, we're back at this again. THIS isn't some slight disagreement, Elliott. THIS is the state of our relationship, and the state of my life. It's the fact that last night you basically told me you had made the decision that we are never getting married or having children, and I have no say in the matter."

Elliott's posture goes rigid. He straightens his back and a look of annoyance comes over his face. "Tyler, I can't help how I feel. There's nothing wrong with living together and not having kids. Think of all the traveling we could do. Think of all the spare time and sleep we could get. I wish you could see how great life is going to be."

I sigh. "Elliott. That may be the life that you want, but that isn't the life for me. And it's not fair for you to make that decision without even as much as hearing my side in the matter."

He shakes his head. "Ty, I don't know what there is to say that hasn't already been said."

I press my palms against my forehead and take in a deep breath. "That's okay, because I do." I turn to face him. "Elliott, this isn't going to work. We have got to end this before we waste any more of each other's time." My eyes search his for any sign of what he is thinking.

"Tyler. We've been together for three years." He says, shaking his head. "We have built a good life together and you just want to throw that all away?"

I take a deep breath and stand from the sofa. "Elliott, the only one of us that is enjoying this life is you. I have waited patiently for years for my life to begin and for the things that I've always dreamed of, but you have only been focused on making yourself happy."

"That's not fair." He says sternly.

"No." I interrupt him. "What's not fair is for you to completely disregard what I want and how I feel."

"You are what I want." He says, standing from the sofa and reaching out to grab my hands.

I pull my hands back. "No, what you want is a roommate that will pay half of the bills and have sex with you." I shake my head. "That's not me. I'm a whole person with feelings and dreams and I deserve someone that will love me as much as I love them. And that someone isn't you."

He rolls his eyes. "Tyler, where are you even going to go? It's not like you can just move into a new place this weekend."

I shrug. "I don't know, but I'm going to go back home until I figure it out."

He laughs. "To Fawn Creek? You can't be serious. There's nothing there. Do they even have Wi-Fi yet?" He jokes. "Why don't you just stay here and sleep in the guest bedroom until you can find a new place?"

I shake my head. "No, Elliott. My mind is made up and the sooner I leave, the better off we both are going to be. I will not stay here and risk changing my mind. It'll only delay the inevitable." I pause and look over at him once more. "Either you can help me pack, or you can get out of my way."

And with that, Elliott storms out the front door, once again leaving me to handle everything on my own.

In just under two hours, I have all of my belongings packed, mostly in trash bags, and loaded into the back of my crappy Honda. Slowly, I move through the house that I've called home for the past two and a half years. All this time, I was sure that if I ever moved again, it would be because Elliott and I were purchasing a bigger house to raise our growing family. I never imagined that the only one growing here would be me.

As I leave the key on the counter, I pull my phone from my pocket and call Avery once again.

"Hey, you okay?" She answers quickly.

"Does your offer still stand for me to sleep on your couch tonight?" I ask, as I walk through the front door of my Oklahoma City home for the last time.

# Chapter 10

"Auntie Tylerrrrr.... Time to wake up." Avery sings from across the room, stirring me awake.

I open one eye and find Juliet hanging onto the couch, inches from my face, drool dripping from her face and hands.

"Hi sister." I say to the sweet smiling baby in front of me.

She smiles in return and then grabs a handful of my hair with an adorable chuckle.

"Okay, I'm up." I say, wincing. I gently untangle my now drool covered hair from her hand before sitting up on the couch. No wonder Avery gets no sleep. Avery moves to scoop her up just as I shuffle to the bathroom. Moments later, I'm settled back on the couch with a coffee, holding it close to my chest when Avery and Juliet reappear. It's just after 7:00 am.

"Morning," Avery says as she rounds the corner and buckles Juliet into her car seat carrier that's sitting on the floor.

"Good morning." I reply with a yawn. "Don't worry, I'll be out of your hair and off your couch soon. I just didn't have the energy to go to my parents' last night. I needed at least a night before telling them that my life is a complete shit show."

"You're welcome to stay as long as you want and you know

that."

"I know and I love you, but your couch is terrible." I smile.

"That's for a good reason." She says, "It keeps the amount of company down. At least until I can get the moat built around my property."

I stop and picture Avery's house surrounded by a moat full of alligators with a drawbridge, right in the middle of Fawn Creek. Honestly, it sounds like an introverts dream. Really, it's more something I would enjoy than she would. She loves to pretend to hate people, but she can't stand to be home in the quiet for more than a day. "You're a genius. I'll remember that for my next place."

She taps the side of her head and winks.

"Really." I say, "Thank you for letting me crash here last night."

"It's no problem at all." She shrugs as she throws Juliet's bag over her shoulder. "Let me know how it goes with your parents, though."

"Will do." I nod and take a long sip of my coffee. I need to get that done sooner rather than later. If I hurry, I can catch my dad before he leaves for work.

* * *

I lean forward and press my parents' doorbell, anxiety coursing through my veins. I feel like a child knocking on a stranger's door, anxiously waiting for them to answer so I can retrieve my baseball from their backyard. If they knew I was coming, I would just walk in, but the last thing I want to do is walk in and scare them. Or find my dad walking around naked. I shake my head, frantically trying to clear that thought from my brain. Living here with them again is going to be terrifying to say the least, but hopefully Avery is right and it'll just be through the summer. My breath hitches just as Mom swings open the screen door.

"Tyler! What are you doing here? Are you okay?" She looks worried and I'm sure my tear-streaked face doesn't help. My mom's expression seems to give my body permission to let go and I do.

Immediately, my face is covered in a steady stream of tears. Mom holds the door open wider and motions for me to come inside. "Come here. What happened?"

I follow her inside and plop down on the couch, pulling a throw pillow into my lap and clutching it to my chest. "Is Dad still home?" I ask between sniffles.

Within minutes, the three of us are settled in the living room with a box of Kleenex in my lap while I tell them all about my weekend from hell.

"I don't know what to do. My entire life has turned upside down in the last 24 hours and I feel like a failure." I breathe out heavily. "Everything was under control and just the way I wanted it, but now it's just... gone." I bury my face in my hands. The tears are flowing faster now and my breathing is more labored. "I'm almost thirty, single, and homeless." Slowly, I turn towards my parents. "I know you guys enjoy being empty nesters, but can I stay here until I figure out what to do next? It won't be long, I promise."

"Actually." My dad begins. "I think I have a better solution." He says, before getting up from the couch and moving towards the kitchen.

I turn to face my mom. "What is this about?" I ask, almost

afraid to find out.

Before my mom can respond with anything more than a wink, my dad reenters the room. "Now Tyler, of course, you are more than welcome to stay here with us if you want to. We love you and would never turn you away. However, last week we picked up some paperwork from Hazel's safe deposit box. Last night, we finally had time to sort through it when we found she named you as the person to inherit her house, as well as half of the money from her estate. The money will take some time to travel through legal hoops, but really there is no reason you couldn't move into the house now." He says with a smile. "The house isn't much, and it could use some updates, but with a fully paid off mortgage, I bet you could make it work." He ends with a wink.

I shake my head. "I don't understand. Why would Hazel have left the house to me?" My eyes brim with tears once again. I haven't lived in Fawn Creek since I graduated from high school. Hazel was very familiar with the fact that I had no intentions to come back to my hometown. It made no sense for her to leave it to me to deal with, instead of leaving it to my parents who live right down the street.

"Maybe she was hoping you'd come back to Fawn Creek one day." Mom offers. "Hazel always wanted nothing else than to see you live out your dreams and be happy."

"This is so much to wrap my head around." I say. "It's unbelievable that she would do that for me." I snatch a tissue from a nearby box and blot my eyes. My mind is running in a million different directions. How did I walk into this house with my world crumbling around me, only to be leaving with this incredible lifeline offered to me by Hazel?

* * *

After a quick call to my boss, to use a personal day while I get settled into my new home, my dad and I venture over to Hazel's house to see what it will take to get me settled in.

While dad goes to inspect the exterior of the house, I experience a quick struggle with a janky doorknob and I push my way inside. Running my hand along the wall in the dark, solely working by memory, I locate the light switch and illuminate the room. Thankfully, my parents hadn't yet disconnected the utilities. One less thing for me to deal with right now.

I move through the little house slowly and take everything in. There are two bedrooms, one bathroom, a dated kitchen, a small dining/living room combo, and a small utility room. After my grandfather's death, Grandma Hazel sold her home in the country and moved in here. She specifically chose this place because of the small stature. Her country home had sat on twenty acres and the chores were never ending. The amount of work was manageable when my grandpa was alive. He enjoyed mowing and working in the yard. Hazel, on the other hand, did not. She just wanted a small space she could pay a local kid twenty dollars to mow twice a month, and to be close enough to walk around town if she wanted to.

This was the first place Hazel had ever lived on her own. She moved out of her parents' house and directly into that farmhouse with Grandpa Karl after their wedding. Over the years, she had made that farmhouse homey, but she did everything with him in mind. It was his house too, after all. So, she decorated with lodge like touches to work around his deer and elk mounts hanging on the walls. When she moved into her new place in her fifties, she started from scratch and she made this place just as unique as she is. Hazel, who despised being called Grandma, was so young at heart. No matter her age, she was always far from old. Every inch of this house reminds me of her funky, eclectic self.

Every decorative piece in the house was carefully chosen, and always unique. It's been this way for as long as I can remember. Most people decorate their houses following trends, but not her. What was trendy was never a concern to her. She was more concerned about surrounding herself with the things she loved. Every week, she would venture to a surrounding town in search of treasures at local thrift stores and garage sales. We never knew what she might find. She might bring home a random ceramic rabbit one day and a collection of old whiskey bottles to use as vases the next. Somehow, while most of us never quite understood her vision, she always did. She made it fit right in with her decor, almost as if that piece was made for her. This resulted in a light and airy space filled with funky feminine touches everywhere. And now, it's all here for me to sort through. *Thanks Hazel.*

Just then, Dad steps into the entryway and interrupts my walk through Hazel's antique store. He smiles softly. I'm sure after dealing with me throughout my teen years, he is terrified of being alone with me post breakup. Who can blame him? I cry far too easily, and I don't blame him for treading lightly. "I walked all around the yard. Everything looks good out there. I think you'll be fine to move in today if you want to. It really shouldn't take too much to turn this into a place that you can call home."

I nod. "I think this'll be perfect while I try to decide where to go next." My eyes move to meet his. "Just please remember, I don't plan to stay in Fawn Creek forever. This is just a pit stop while I try to figure out what to do next."

"Well, then what I would do is clean this place up, empty it out and do some updates. Then, when you are ready to get back out of here, put it on the market. The money you make, plus your inheritance, will be plenty to help you buy a new place somewhere else." He pauses. "Maybe by the time you're done here, you will know what you want to do. And if not, it doesn't matter because no one is making you go anywhere."

I ponder on what he says. "You're right. I think a good reset is exactly what I need, and this is probably the best place for it to happen." I say, agreeing with him. "But don't be surprised if I am gone by the end of summer."

Dad hugs me. "Don't be surprised if you fall in love with Fawn Creek and decide to stay forever." He whispers.

*Doubtful.*

\* \* \*

Avery pushes through the front door and steps around the mountain of bags in the center of my living room. She plops onto the couch in a huff and shakes her head. "I can't believe you fit your entire life into the back of a Honda Accord."

"Well, if it makes you feel better, I was selective." I frown, looking down at my heap of personal effects. "Basically, I only took my clothes, books and what I can't replace. I sold all of my furniture and household stuff when I moved in with Elliott years ago. That house was pretty small, so I tried to be very selective about what I brought in. Honestly, I was a borderline minimalist."

80

"Well, don't worry." Avery says with a chuckle as she stands and moves around the room. "For every item on the planet that you resisted buying in the last few years, Hazel bought seven." She picks up a clown cactus pot from a shelf and holds it up dramatically, giving it a side eye. "What are you going to do with all this.... stuff?"

I raise a brow and swipe the vase from her hand. The clown is holding his pants open and a very dead cactus is poking out from the top of his waistband.

"First off, I'm being buried with this, so be careful with it." I say with a smirk before swooping it out of her hand and putting it back on the shelf. "It just needs a new plant. I don't know about the rest." Even for such a small house, there is a lot to sort through. That's going to be a huge job by itself.

"Was your mom upset Hazel left the house to you and not her?"

I shake my head. "I don't think so. Mom actually did a good job today. Normally she adds to my anxiety, but today she was everything I needed in a mom. Maybe she's just excited to have me home for a while."

"So," Avery takes one more look around the room, "What's the plan here?"

I shrug. "Clean this place up, paint and get it on the market. I think I should be able to knock it all out by the end of summer."

"Or... you could clean it up, paint and stay in Fawn Creek forever." She winks. I knew it wouldn't be long before she tried to talk me into settling down here.

I roll my eyes and rip open the first trash bag of clothes, emptying it onto the floor. "Fawn Creek is charming. I will give you that." I say, beginning to sort my clothes into piles. "But city life has spoiled me. In the city, I can get my food and groceries delivered. Things are open past 8:00 at night and I can go outdoors without running into people I went to preschool with. Plus, my parents don't know my every move."

"The gas station is open til nine." She adds with a smirk. "Besides, there are plenty of opportunities to stay out after 8 pm. Take this weekend, for example."

I try to recall what she's talking about, but I come up empty. "What's going on this weekend?"

"Duh... It's Mayfest." she says, eyeing me suspiciously.

I frown. "Damn. I really should have hung out with Elliott for one more week." I say dryly. The last thing I want to do is spend a weekend surrounded by the entire community. By this afternoon, word will already be around town that I'm back and I can only imagine the stories people are going to come up with.

She rolls her eyes. "I already got you a ticket for the Friday Night concert so you aren't getting out of it. On Saturday morning, we can go check out the food and craft vendors."

"Or," I begin. "We could skip it and I could stay home all weekend reading a book." I say, pulling a book from my pile and waving it in the air.

Avery plucks the book from my hand. "First off, no. I haven't had my best friend at a Fawn Creek Festival in years. You aren't getting out of this, and I know you would be so mad at yourself if you missed getting to see your favorite singer performing downtown." The fact that she knows me well enough to know I need to see this concert warms my heart. I have to admit, I need a little bit of fun in the middle of all this chaos.

"Besides, you'll have that read before Friday, anyway." She shrugs.

"It's like you know me."

"Just a little." She says, plopping the book on the end table, on top of an ivory doily.

"If nothing else, I'm predictable."

# Chapter 11

*Cock-a-doodle-doo!!!!*

The sound jolts me awake from my deep sleep. In a panic, I sit straight up in the darkness and try to catch my breath. My eyes frantically search the bedroom for the source of the sound that woke me up. Surely it wasn't an actual rooster. Since when do people have chickens in the middle of town? Maybe I was just dreaming about farm animals. That's logical, right? It's not like I've been getting much rest lately.

The scream of the bird pierces through the silence again. It's so loud, I'm half expecting to find it perched on my footboard.

I climb from the bed and walk to the nearby window, pushing the heavy lace curtain aside. Startled by the rooster's face looking back at me through the dirty windowpane, I jump back. He's perched on something outside and it's giving him the perfect boost to stand there and scream at me.

"Get down." I yell, tapping my finger against the pane, being careful not to hit the glass too hard. "Go!"

Luckily, it's just enough to scare him. The rooster flaps his wings and floats down from his perch, disappearing into the dim morning light.

I shuffle back to bed and climb under the blankets, burying myself as far into the pillows as I can, hoping I can go back to sleep. The old digital alarm clock on the nightstand brightly proclaims that it's only 5:47 in the morning, and I don't need to clock in for work until nine. Last night, I got just enough unpacking done to set up my new workspace amid all the chaos that is this house.

All I want right now is another two hours of sleep before I have to force myself to rebuild my life. Just as my eyes close and I feel myself drift off, the evil yard bird lets out another squawk as if he is trying to get in one last word. "Fine! I'm up!" I scream back at him, kicking off my blankets in what I will admit is borderline tantrum material. My first official day in my new house is already shaping up to be a nightmare.

Angrily, I climb out of bed, and move to the kitchen, stopping short at the coffeepot. It never crossed my mind yesterday to run to the grocery store and get coffee. Mom and Dad had come over and removed all the food from the house after Hazel passed, to keep pests away, so the cabinets are completely bare. I ordered pizza for dinner last night but what I would do this morning never crossed my mind.

According to Google, Drip opens at six. I waste no time getting dressed and moving towards the door to head downtown.

I pull the door closed behind me and head towards my car in the driveway before I stop dead in my tracks. This is the first time in years that I can walk to where I need to go instead of driving across town. Drip and the rest of the downtown business district are only a few blocks away and the weather this morning is perfect. I might as well take advantage of a morning walk while the opportunity is there.

Without a second thought, I shove my key into my pocket and make my way downtown. As I walk, I take the opportunity to really examine the neighborhood for the first time. It's quiet, and no one is out moving yet. Of course, it's before six in the morning, so who knows what it'll be like by this afternoon? Based on the lack of bikes, sidewalk chalk art and children's outdoor toys, I assume that most of the neighbors are older, like Hazel. The street is filled with quaint houses connected by brick sidewalks. The yards are maintained and clean, every flower bed is full of fresh flowers and mulch. It's neat and pristine.

I make a promise to myself that I'll get out in the evening and try to make myself known to my neighbors. I know how people in small towns can be, and I sure don't want them to be alarmed by seeing me coming in and out of the house.

Or, on second thought, I could hide inside my house until I leave again. That actually doesn't seem like a terrible idea, now that I think of it. I mean, that would ensure that I can do exactly what I came here to do; rest, reset and get my shit together so that I can sell this house and move back to the city as soon as possible. Or some city... or really just any place that isn't Fawn Creek. The more connections I make, the harder it'll be to leave.

As I approach Drip, I frown at the open sign that still isn't illuminated. I glance at my watch and confirm, it's just after six o'clock. They should be open by now. As I get closer, I notice the vinyl lettering on the door states 6:30 as the opening time. Although I'm a bit frustrated about Google lying to me, I decide this is just a part of learning about my hometown all over again. I'll just get in a bit of a longer walk and then grab coffee on the way back to the house. I have a lot of work ahead of me today, so this is an excellent opportunity to get plenty of exercise and fresh air.

Besides, this is the perfect time to listen to an audio book.

I pull my earbuds from my pocket and get ready to immerse myself in a romance novel for the duration of my walk. As usual, it's just another predictable story about two people who realize they are in love after a decade of friendship, my favorite. Sweet and light, with a happily ever after at the end. I wish real life could be as predictable.

Elliott always made fun of these books. He enjoyed telling me how unrealistic the stories are, and how they create unrealistic expectations for women to hold towards men. I'd roll my eyes and brush off his comments, telling him to let me live my life. Sure, sometimes they are pretty unbelievable, but let's be honest, the real world is terrible. At the very least, when I pick up a romance novel, I know that there will be a happily ever after at the end. If nothing else, it's reliable, it's safe. If only the same thing could be said for reality. Besides, it gives me hope that maybe one day, I'll get a happily ever after of my own. Or maybe Elliott was right. Perhaps I'm just a hopeless romantic.

Fawn Creek is great in its own little ways. This is the town that raised me and it will always have a spot in my heart. It's like a warm hug from your favorite person, but even hugs get annoying and claustrophobic after a while. Fawn Creek will always be home, even if I don't want to actually live here.

I leave the business district and make my way towards the city park. The park is right at the edge of downtown and serves as a city gathering place just as much as a place for kids to play. It houses a pavilion, a gazebo, picnic tables and plenty of play equipment. There's a wide sidewalk all the way around the square, each lap measuring a quarter mile. This is a fact I remember well from when I was a kid and thought I was going to be a runner. It wasn't long because I realized I hated running and I hated waking up early to get a run in before the heat of summer.

As I walk, more memories made in this park quickly come flooding into my mind. My sixth birthday party was in the park pavilion. I still have pictures of Avery and me with blue cupcake frosting on our faces and party hats on our heads. We played so hard that day and got so covered in sand that we had to ride home in the back of my dad's pickup truck. Our moms wouldn't let us into their cars.

Next, my eyes move across the park to the gazebo. It seems like just yesterday I took my prom photos over there. I had a date, some Steve guy I don't think I ever spoke to again after that night. I took one photo with him, to be polite, but quickly moved on to taking photos with Avery instead. We took our own series of awkward prom poses, while Grandma Hazel played photographer. I don't think I'd ever seen that woman laugh so hard as Avery and I quickly changed poses and made silly faces at the camera. My mother, on the other hand, was mortified. She told us we were causing a scene, and she went to sit in the car until we were done. I shake my head and sigh, thinking back to how mad she was at us. A scene? We were the only ones in the entire park and who cares what anyone else thought? We were just a couple of kids, and we were having fun while we could. I'd give anything to go back to those days now. Life was so easy and carefree. Now, everything is stressful and exhausting.

I finish my loop around the park and make my way back towards downtown. In that small amount of time, Fawn Creek has woken up and people are moving around. It's Tuesday morning and the citizens with long commutes are already getting in their cars to head to work in the surrounding cities. I've always wondered why people lived here, but drove thirty to forty-five minutes to work. Why wouldn't they just move closer to their jobs? I suppose some of them love the community that much, but it's hard for me to wrap my head around. Avery is one of those people. She's tried to explain it to me a million times, but it's a lost cause. I guess the people that get it, just get it... and the rest of us just pretend to understand.

Before long, I'm back in the heart of downtown and I find myself in front of the little vacant storefront once again. I look down the street and make sure no one is coming before I step closer and peer through the window. Lightly, I touch the doorknob and I feel butterflies flutter in my stomach.

"What are you doing up already?" I hear a voice from behind. I jump and quickly turn towards the sound. It's Avery, pulled into a parking spot at the curb, with her window rolled down. Busted.

I walk towards her car. "I got woken up at 5:47 this morning by a rooster. He was perched outside my bedroom window, screaming at me. And then, I realized I didn't go get coffee last night, so I took a walk while waiting for Drip to open."

Avery frowns. "A rooster? Who in that neighborhood has a rooster? You aren't allowed to have chickens in town." She says, as she opens the car door and grabs Juliet's carrier. "Weird. How was your night?"

I lead her towards the coffee shop and hold the door open for her. "It was nice and quiet. Just what I needed so I could wallow in self pity. I got started on some decluttering, but I have a long road ahead of me."

Avery places Juliet's carrier on the floor of the shop and I immediately bend down to the smiling baby to say hello. I've decided my first goal during my stay will be to teach Juliet to say my name. "Can you say Aunt Tyler?" I coo to her. "What about Ty-Ty?" I add.

"Hi girls!" Cassidy yells out to us from behind the counter, interrupting my talking lesson. "Tyler, I thought you already left town." She raises a brow at my appearance.

I stand from my kneeling position and face Cassidy while I search for the right words. "Well... I did and now I'm back. It looks like I'm going to be home for a few months." I say, hoping this will be enough information.

"I see..." Cassidy responds, wiping her hands with a towel. Her curly blonde hair is held back in a claw clip and she's wearing a black apron over her t-shirt and jean combination. She looks relaxed, more so than she ever did when I was a kid and she was busy working the corporate life. "Are you staying with your parents?"

"Actually, no. I am staying at Hazel's. I'm going to get it cleaned up and updated so it can go on the market."

"Hmm.. I saw your mom on Sunday at church. She mentioned nothing about this." Cassidy looks concerned.

I shrug. "Yeah, it all happened pretty quickly."

She raises a brow. "I see. Did your boyfriend come with you?" She presses.

"It's a long story, but no." I smile weakly before giving her my order and sliding my card across the counter.

"I have time." She says with a soft smile.

*I'm going to be here for a while.*

* * *

I'm just stepping onto the porch with a large iced latte in my hand, as well as a bag from the grocery store, when my phone rings. I set my cup down on the concrete porch and pull my phone from my pocket. Avery's name is on the caller screen.

"Hey!" I say, answering the call. "Missing me already?"

"Hi, my best friend in the entire world." Avery says, her voice dripping with the fakest sweetness I've ever heard.

"Oh my gosh, what do you want?" I ask jokingly.

"I need you to do me a giant favor today." She says. "Are you back home?"

"Just got here. I stopped at the store to grab some coffee and some groceries. What's up? Did you forget to unplug your straightener again?" I ask, finally winning the war against the doorknob and stepping inside. I make a mental note to run to the hardware store and pick up a new one as soon as possible.

"Listen, that was only one time." Avery says, defensibly.

"But you left it plugged in for an entire weekend." I recall. "I still don't know how your house didn't burn down."

"ANY-WAAAAY." Avery says loudly, trying to change the subject. "The babysitter just called. Juliet is running a fever, and she needs to be picked up. My mom has a doctor's appointment today, and I have a meeting this morning that I can't afford to miss. Is there any way you can watch her for me until lunchtime? I promise she is fairly easy to deal with. I'm sure it's just from teething, but the daycare lady has some pretty strict rules about fevers, regardless of the cause."

"Sure! We will make it work." I say, wondering if I can pull of working with a baby on my hip. "Do you want me to just stay at your place?"

"Oh, my gosh. Thank you so much." She immediately says, with her voice full of gratitude. "Normally, yes, I would have you stay at my place, but the bug guy is supposed to stop and set off a bomb under the house today. We have a spider problem. So I'd rather you girls not be there. Can you keep her at your place? You can stop and grab the playpen from my house. Everything else she needs is in her diaper bag."

"Sure. Send me the daycare lady's address and I'll head over there."

"I owe you big time." Avery says. "She's already had breakfast at daycare. She will be ready for a nap around 10. I'll try to be there before she wakes up."

"Sounds good. We will be just fine."

"Thank you again. I'll text you her info. Bye." Avery says, hanging up the phone.

As I pull into Avery's driveway, my phone pings with a text from Avery.

**Avery: Okay, I don't know the address, but the babysitter is Madison King. I'm sure you remember her from school. She lives in the white house next door to our old Junior High Science teacher, Mrs. McBride. She has a cute little blue welcome sign and a 15 passenger van out front.**

I slowly blink twice. Is she for real right now?

**Me: Wouldn't it have been faster to just ask her for her address instead of all of that? Small-town people are so damn weird.**

**Avery: Not like you've ever known what half of the street names were, anyway.**

**Me: Valid point. But I have this fancy thing called GPS. It even works in Nowheresville.**

**Avery: The playpen is in the closet. Thank you again.**

I enter the code on Avery's door and run inside. Quickly, I locate the playpen and lug it to my car. Of course, even after rearranging everything in my trunk, I still can't get the thing to fit back there. I sigh and carry it around to the backseat until I remember that I have to put a baby back there. Dammit, this must be why all moms drive giant cars. It isn't because they have that many kids, it's because their kids just have that much shit.

Within a few minutes, I'm on the other side of town, pulling up in front of a cute little white house with a blue welcome sign just like Avery told me I would. As soon as I get out of the car, I glance over at Mrs. McBride's house. Nothing on her porch has changed since I was probably seven years old, including her concrete goose that she dresses up for every season. It's currently wearing a yellow rain jacket with a matching hat. That damn goose is more stylish than I am, and I bet it has more clothes than I do. I pause to wonder if it has its own closet, but then quickly remember I have a task at hand.

I walk up to the door of the home daycare and it swings open as soon as I step foot onto the wooden porch.

"Tyler Burris! How are you?" A skinny blonde girl bounds out of the house and attacks me. Okay, maybe she doesn't actually attack me, but she definitely pulls me into a hug that kicks my fight-or-flight response into overdrive. Why does everyone in this town think I want to hug them? Does no one have personal boundaries here? Has it always been like this and I just blocked it out?

"Hey! How are you?" I say, trying to search my memory for whatever Avery told me this girl's name was, but I come up blank.

"I'm good!" She beams and stands staring at me for a beat too long. "Thank you so much for being able to come pick up Juliet. Avery's lucky to have a friend like you."

"It's not a problem at all." I smile softly. "I am in a bit of a hurry though...."

"Oh yeah, of course," the woman says, opening the door wider and handing me a diaper bag. "She's already had breakfast and she should be about ready for a nap around 10. Just give her the bottle in the side pocket around 9:45."

"Perfect." I say, taking the bag and baby carrier from her. I glance down at Juliet, to get an idea of how she is actually feeling. Juliet looks up at me and shows me a wide gummy grin.

"Hi, sister. Want to go to Aunt Tyler's?" I ask her.

She coos in response.

I smile down at her before turning towards my car. The weight of the carrier almost takes me down. *Sheesh, this thing is heavy.* I wonder how Avery totes the carrier all over the place. She made it look effortless at the coffee shop this morning. I would probably never leave my house if I had to carry this contraption everywhere.

"Nice seeing you!" I yell over my shoulder, not stalling to see if the sitter says anything back. I'm too busy fighting for my life to carry Juliet down the stairs.

I get back to my car and heave the carrier into the backseat, making sure Juliet is facing backwards. It's only then that I realize I have no clue how I'm supposed to belt the car seat in. I try to remember how Avery does it, but I feel like she has a plastic base in her car that this thing snaps into. I've spent plenty of time babysitting over the course of my life, but it's never been with any actual babies. Every kid I've ever watched has been at least in a booster seat. I sigh and grab Juliet again, lugging her back up to the daycare provider's house.

After one quick knock, the provider sticks her head back outside.

"Hi." I say. "Do you know how to buckle this into my car?"

She stares at me, bewildered for a second. "Oh, like with the lap belt?"

"Sure? I have actually never put a kid in my car before." I laugh.

"Umm... you just pull it across and..." She stops talking when she notices the look of confusion on my face. "You know what? I'll go do it. Can you just stand in here so I'm not leaving these kids unsupervised?"

"Sure!" I say, stepping into the living room.

She grabs the car seat from me and slides through the front door.

I smile down at the kids sitting on the carpet staring at the television. A cartoon about a blue dog mesmerizes most of them.

"What's your name?" A little girl with pigtails turns to ask me.

"I'm Tyler. What's yours?" I ask in response, bending down towards her.

The little girl ignores me and looks back at the television as though we never spoke.

Another little girl comes toddling out of the kitchen with a sippy cup in hand. She's wearing hot pink bell bottoms with an AC/DC shirt and a big pink bow in her hair. She frowns as soon as she sees me. "Why does your hair look like that?" She asks me, staring at the messy bun on top of my head.

"Uh... Well." I think. "I just haven't had time to fix my hair yet today."

"My mom says you aren't supposed to go places if your hair is messy." She tells me sternly. "People will think you don't have a house to live in."

"Piper, that's enough." Interrupts the daycare lady as she walks back into the house. "Okay, Juliet is all ready to go." She says, holding the door open to me with a smirk. "Sorry that kid it a little spicy sometimes."

I laugh. "I'm sure it keeps your day interesting." I saw with a wink.

She sighs and chuckles. "You have no idea."

"Thank you so much." I say, as I move out the door. "Bye." I say to the room full of kids, with Piper being the only one to wave back. I don't know why, but I like that feisty kid.

# Chapter 12

I lean over the playpen, lowering Juliet to the mattress before I cover her up with her favorite thin pink blanket. Relieved as I watch her as she peacefully snores. I've been rocking this baby for the last thirty minutes, while simultaneously working, and Juliet just finally drifted off to sleep. Luckily, my job is all about customer service through chat and email. I may not type as quickly with a baby balanced in my lap, but I could still get quite a bit accomplished. Just as my arm fell asleep, so did she. I back away from the sleeping child, feeling victorious, but not for long. Suddenly the room fills with the sounds of loud steel guitars, shaking the windows. It's almost as though there is a concert happening right outside the guest bedroom where Juliet lays.

My eyes widen in fear as I look down at the sweet sleeping face. "Please don't wake up," I beg her in a whisper. For whatever reason, the babysitting gods are smiling down on me today and she continues snoozing away quietly, as though nothing else in the world is going on. She looks so sweet with her arms outstretched over her head, and a tiny bit of drool escaping from her lips. Thank goodness.

I tiptoe through the doorway and let out an exasperated sigh when I reach the living room. Flinging open the front door, I step into my yard, my eyes surveying the surroundings. There's no one to be found, only the familiar sound of Rob Zombie's *Dragula*. I rush to the side of the house, in search of the music source. The only thing I find, though, is a Bluetooth speaker next to an abandoned pile of tools. The speaker is up on top of a tree stump between my house and the one next door as though someone had just put it there and ran away. I speed walk to the device and smash the power button. Instantly, the music dies, and silence is restored to the neighborhood once again.

I glare at the brick house next door, and immediately march towards it to find the owner of the speaker. I step onto the porch and loudly knock. The door must not be latched all the way, because it flies open as soon as my fist makes contact. I cautiously lean into the doorway. "Hello?!" I call down the hallway into the dimly lit space. A figure emerges in the darkness at the end of the hall, causing me to jolt.

"Can I help you?" A deep voice booms out as the figure moves closer to me. As he walks into the light, I can't help but think that the man looks familiar, but I'm not sure from where. He's wearing blue jeans with a baseball cap on backwards. His t-shirt is hanging from the back pocket of his jeans and his tanned, chiseled abs are on display. He's nothing short of gorgeous, and I can't help but stare at his exposed muscles for a little longer than necessary.

"Can I help you?" He asks again. His face is hard to read. I can't decide if he's annoyed by my presence or concerned that I pushed myself into his house. That's when it hits me and I remember where I've seen him before. Drip. It's the Asshole of Fawn Creek, once again. Suddenly, the anger I was feeling when I left my house is back with a vengeance and I'm reminded of why I'm here.

"Um, yeah, you can help me. You could start by being mindful of your neighbors." I say, pointing to my house. "There's a sick baby in there trying to take a nap. I spent half an hour rocking her and had just got her to sleep when suddenly you thought it was a good time to have a heavy metal concert right outside my window. I really need her to rest so that I can work. You know, you aren't the only person on the planet, right?" I glare at him with my hands resting on my hips.

"Okay." He holds his hands up. "First off, I didn't know anyone was there. That house was empty the last I knew. Second, Rob Zombie is rock, not metal."

I huff. "Honestly, I don't care what genre he is. No one should be subjected to it without their consent. Especially a nine-month-old baby." My lips form a line and I stare at him with crossed arms.

"Calm down, Karen. It was an honest mistake." He shrugs. "I was just getting ready to work on the privacy fence when I came back in to grab my phone. I was opening Spotify when the washing machine had just finished. So, I stopped to put clothes in the dryer. I guess my Bluetooth automatically connected, and it played through the speaker."

"Did you seriously just call me a Karen?" I fume. *What a jerk.*

"It fits, doesn't it?" He asks with a shrug. "You're the one coming up to my door to scream at me over a mistake."

Now, I'm fuming. "Like you should talk! I accidentally bumped into you at the coffee shop and you acted like I ruined your life. You don't have to walk around being a jerk."

"Well, if you weren't walking around with your nose in the air, you might be able to see people that are walking around behind you. You aren't the only person on the planet, you know." He snarls, turning my words back on me.

I shake my head. "I don't have time for this." I turn on my heel to stomp back to my house and then spin my body back towards him once more. "Keep your shitty music down. I'll just call the police next time."

*The Asshole of Fawn Creek strikes again.*

I walk back into my house, absolutely fuming. How dare that asshole call me a Karen? And where the hell does he get off saying that I think I'm better than anyone? I am the last person that would look down on other people, especially when it's for no good reason. If that jerk is my neighbor, there is no way I'm going to make it through the summer here. I'd almost rather live with my parents than deal with that jackass on a daily basis.

\* \* \*

I spend the rest of Juliet's nap replaying the scene in my head repeatedly. I carry the laptop to my bedroom to work on de-cluttering my closet while I wait for customer correspondence to come through, and luckily it's a slow day. If nothing else, my goal is to get my clothes off the living room floor and on hangers before I go to bed tonight. No matter how far I get into the task at hand, I just can't get over what just happened. Sure, yes. I came out of the gate swinging so his attitude wasn't completely unwarranted, but what he said kind of hurt my feelings.

I've never thought of myself as a person who looks down on anyone else. My mother, on the other hand? That is her exact M.O., which is why I strive constantly to not be that person. I rack my brain, trying to remember our initial meeting at Drip. What could I have possibly done to come off as a snob? Nothing immediately sticks out to me, but again I was distracted because of Hazel's funeral.

The anger in my body is the exact fuel I need to get to work on cleaning. Hazel was a collector of many things, including her extensive wardrobe. She had an outfit or costume for every occasion. Her closet and dressers are crammed full of those pieces. I begin by making piles on the bed of different clothes. Before long, I have the floral quilt covered in piles of dresses, tops, pants and skirts.

I stand back and shake my head at the sheer amount of polyester before my eyes. I have no clue what I'm going to do with all this stuff, and just the thought of hauling it all to the thrift store downtown feels overwhelming. How do you just discard all the pieces of your favorite person?

"Knock, knock."

I jump as Avery interrupts my thought process and enters the bedroom.

I narrow my brows at my friend. "Hey, how'd you get in here?"

"The door was unlocked. I figured you did that so I wouldn't wake Juliet when I came in." Avery answers with a shrug before plopping amongst the piles of clothes on the bed.

I shake my head. "No, I definitely locked it after I got into it with the asshole next door this morning." I make a mental note to run to the hardware store for a doorknob after work.

Avery scrunches her nose. "The asshole next door? Are you talking about Andrew?"

I frown. "I was too busy listening to him tell me what a terrible person I am to ask for his name."

"Beard, dark hair, chiseled abs?" She asks.

"That's the one." I roll my eyes. Although I won't admit it to her, I definitely noticed his abs and the v at his waist running down the front of his jeans. He may be hot as hell, but the fact that he's an asshole doesn't do much to help him. I quickly run through the recap with Avery over what happened today.

She shakes her head, taking in every detail. "So weird. I've never known Andrew to be anything but kind to everyone. I wonder what you did to get his boxers in a wad."

I shrug. "Beats me. All I know is, now I have a reason to get this house done as fast as possible so I can get the hell out of here. A jerk neighbor is the last thing I need to savor in Fawn Creek."

"He'll be gone soon enough." She winks. "That was his grandpa's house. He's been coming up from Texas from time to time to get it cleaned up and updated to go on the market. Surely he's about done by now."

I feel a wave of relief come over me. It's not like I have anywhere else to run to anytime soon. Honestly, I have no clue where I'm going next. I have no reason to go back to Oklahoma City. I had no friends, family or really anything else that I'm missing. Elliott was it. For years, my only identity was working remotely and waiting for him to get home each day. My friends were really just the partners of his friends. The house belongs to his parents and never really felt like mine. Hell, that's even more obvious now that I was able to pack everything I owned into the back of my four-door sedan and drive it back to Kansas in one trip. As much as I hate to admit it, the longer I spend away from him, the more I realize that I have no actual idea who I am anymore. My entire persona was "Elliott's girlfriend." and I was just standing by waiting to be upgraded to "Elliott's

Wife." Now, I'm none of those things and I'm honestly not sure who I'm supposed to be next.

"What do we have going on here?" Avery asks, eyeing the clothes piled around her, breaking my concentration on my existential crisis and bringing me back to reality. "New wardrobe for your new house?"

I roll my eyes. "Calm down, these are Hazel's old clothes. I just need to figure out what to do with them. Do you think I'll completely overwhelm the thrift store if I show up with 18 trash bags full of old lady clothes in tow?"

The horrified look on Avery's face tells me my plan isn't going to work. "Please don't."

I frown. "Avery, I know you are sentimental, but I am not. There is no way I'm going to hang on to all of this stuff."

"You don't have to keep it all, but definitely look through it first before you just toss it out. Hazel had some cute stuff for an old lady and I bet there are at least some things you can hang on to and add to your wardrobe." She pauses. "And when you're done, I'll go through what's left. I love vintage clothes."

"Don't lie, you love all clothes." I interrupt.

"True." She shrugs. "Then we can have a big yard sale."

I frown. The idea of setting up tables full of Hazel's belongings so that people can haggle over the price just doesn't sit right with me. Avery reads my mind, as usual.

"You can either do that and make a little bit of cash, or you can give it all to the thrift store and who knows what will be done with it." When I don't agree quickly enough, Avery sticks out her lower lip into a pout. "Please? I need a reason to go through my house too, and this will be the best motivation to get it done."

I huff. "Fine, but only for one weekend. Whatever is left over is being donated, and I'm moving on with my life."

"Don't be bitter." Avery side eyes me. "Some of this stuff around here will bring in some money. Money you'll need to buy the building downtown and open your bookstore." She winks. "I saw you peering in the windows this morning."

I frown. I was hoping she would have forgotten all about that after the chaos of today. "Avery, I told you I'm not staying in Fawn Creek. And I can't afford to open a bookstore. It'll never make it in a town this size."

Down the hall, Juliet coos.

"Great, now you woke my baby." I add with an eye roll.

Avery sighs. "That was a nice little break while it lasted. Duty calls." She says before climbing off the bed and moving to the next room to retrieve the now screaming infant.

"Just so you know, she didn't do that when you were gone." I call after her.

"They're always worse for their mothers." She jokes back. "I'm going to take her home so you can get back to work. Just try to play nice with the neighbor, okay? You never know when you might need some allies around here."

I raise a brow at Avery as we move towards the house. "Allies? You make it sound like Fawn Creek is a war zone, not a tiny town in the middle of nowhere."

She turns back to look at me before heading out the door. "All I'm saying is, Fawn Creek is a much different place when you look at it as an adult, instead of somewhere you couldn't wait to escape from as a kid. I bet it won't be long before you see how strong this community is, but you have to embrace it by playing nice."

# Chapter 13

After Avery leaves, I grab my laptop and move on to the guest bedroom to attack another closet and pack away the playpen. Avery told me to keep it, just in case I need it again, which I'm sure I probably will. Not that I mind. I've seen Juliet more in the last two days than I have since the day she was born. I want to soak up every second that I can with her while I'm in Fawn Creek for the summer.

After a bit of a struggle, and a short YouTube tutorial, I fold the playpen back up the way I found it and lean it against the wall next to the closet. I fling the closet door open and let out a sigh of exasperation. Of course, this closet is just as full as the other one was. Immediately, I pull hangers from the metal rod, piling everything on the full size bed. After the clothes are removed, I grab the bright blue plastic totes from the floor and pull them towards the center of the room. Just as I yank on one final tote, I hear something that resembles a hissing sound. Instinctively, I jump backwards, just in time to see something long and dark slither against the back of the closet. IT'S A SNAKE!

"Shit!" I scream out, and without wasting another second, I race towards the front door. As soon as I reach the edge of the yard, next to the street, I let out another squeal. My body is trembling and I feel woozy. I hate snakes.

My mind races. How did a snake even get into the house? How long has it been there? Have I been living with a snake for the past two days? What am I supposed to do with it?

Still shaking, I pull my phone from my back pocket and call my dad. After three rings, my call goes to voicemail. Frustrated, I call Avery on FaceTime.

"Hey! What's up?" She answers quickly. I can tell from the background that she's standing in her kitchen.

"Ahhhhh!" I let out a shriek and hop from one foot to another, recalling my slimy roommate before I can answer her. "There's a snake in the bedroom closet."

"Is this some sort of metaphor that I'm not understanding?" She asks, setting the phone on the kitchen counter and moving backwards to allow herself and Juliet, in a highchair, to fill the camera frame.

"No, there is a literal snake in the bedroom closet. I found it when I was putting the playpen away. What do I do?" I can't help but squirm again, thinking about that snake being inside the house with me for the last twenty-four hours, and with Juliet while she was napping.

"You could use a shovel? Maybe there's one in the garage?" Avery suggests.

I violently shake my head. "Absolutely not. There is no way in hell that I am going near that thing." I say, not taking my eyes off the door. "Is there someone I can call for something like this? Like animal control?"

"Hmmm." Avery pauses thoughtfully. "We have a dog-catcher, but he only does it in the evening after he gets home from his day job. Maybe you could go next door and ask Andrew for help?" Avery mutters with a smirk.

I let out a loud sigh. "Hard pass." I answer immediately. If I never see that jerk again, it'll be too soon. "Maybe I can handle it myself, after all. What's the likelihood this snake is poisonous?" I reply, dryly.

"Venomous," Avery corrects me. "Well, there's one way to find out. If it bites you and you die, then it's venomous."

I roll my eyes, trying to think of any way I can get around this that doesn't involve Andrew. Maybe I should try my dad again? But, it's too late. I turn to the sound of crunching gravel as I spot Andrew crossing his driveway towards me.

"Everything okay?" He says. "I heard screaming. I was under my house or I would have been over sooner."

Great. Just one more thing for him to judge me over.

"There's a snake in the house." I say, trying to appear calm, although internally I can't stop shaking. "And I don't know what to do about it."

He smirks and shakes his head, almost as though he is trying to keep from laughing. "I'll be right back." He says, and without waiting for a response, he disappears towards his garage. Within moments, he returns with a garden rake in his hand. "Where is it?" He asks without breaking his stride.

"In the guest bedroom closet." I say, slowly moving towards the house, but he steps ahead of me and hurries towards the door. "Last door on the left down the hallway!" I call to the back of his head.

I turn my face back towards the screen and look back at Avery. "What if he can't find it?" The mere thought of a snake on the loose in my house makes me ill. There's no way I could stay here with that thing running loose.

"He will." She snickers. "It's not a big house."

"If he doesn't, I'm sleeping on your couch tonight. And

possibly every day until I find a new place to live." I warn her.

For half a second, I wonder if I should text Elliott and beg him to take me back. A rooster has already harassed me. I've had an altercation with my jackass neighbor and discovered a snake. I've only been living here for just over twenty-four hours. Things aren't looking great for me. Maybe this is a sign that I really don't belong here. Perhaps instead of staying for the summer, I need to just list this place and get back out of town.

Just then, Andrew walks out of the house, with a long black snake hanging from the end of the rake.

"Is it poisonous?" I shout to him, taking a step back, my heart picking up speed once again.

"Venomous," Avery corrects me once again. I roll my eyes at the phone screen.

"Nope, just a rat snake. He's a good guy," He says, carrying him across his backyard towards the alley and disappearing along the fence line.

I turn my face back towards the phone to shoot Avery a disgusted look, only to be interrupted by Andrew's return.

"Did you kill him?" I ask, although I'm not sure I want to know the answer.

"No ma'am. Those snakes eat mice, and they kill the bad snakes. We want that kind around here. I threw him in the treeline behind the alley."

I scrunch my nose. I don't like the sound of this. "You don't think he will come back to my house, will he?"

"I wouldn't if I were him." He replies with no emotion, obviously a dig at me.

If he hadn't just saved my life, I'd say something shitty in return, but just this once I'll keep my mouth shut.

"Thank you for your help." I say, trying my best to smile. "I appreciate it."

He doesn't respond, just waves over his shoulder as he makes his way back to his house, wasting no time for conversation.

I hate myself for it, but I can't help but let my eyes linger as he walks away. Why does he have to be such a jerk and so freaking hot at the same time? Dammit. His horrible attitude ought to be enough for him to completely turn me off. However, his eagerness to help me just hours after our confrontation causes me to wonder if he isn't such a jerk after all. I bite into my lower lip as I watch him disappear.

"I saw that." Avery interrupts me. I forgot I still have her on FaceTime.

My face reddens. "You saw nothing." I mutter.

"Nothing except you checking him out. Pretty sure you were picturing him naked. You know, makeup sex can be a lot of fun after an argument." She wiggles her eyebrows. "And for the record, blue collar guys can do some great things. Much better than the nerds that you're used to."

"Goodbye." I sigh and disconnect the call before stuffing my phone back in my pocket. There is no chance I'll be getting involved with a guy like that.

* * *

The bell above the door at Drip rings cheerily as I push my way through on Wednesday morning. I have to admit, while I'm fully capable of making coffee at home, I'm loving the routine of a morning walk and a fresh coffee before starting work for the day.

"Hey there, beautiful," Cassidy shouts across the room. "I just love seeing your pretty face here every morning." She says, moving towards me to envelop me into a hug. "It's so good to have you home." She whispers into my hair while squeezing me tight.

When she finally releases me, I offer her a half smile. I admit it, I'm enjoying the quiet and simplicity of small town life. Everything is just so much slower than what I've been used to after all these years. "It's good to be back." I reply, worried that I might mean that a little too much.

"How's the house going?" She asks, moving to the counter to take my order.

"Sugar free vanilla cold brew latte please, a big one." I wink and hand her my debit card. "Slow. Sorting through all of her things is a lot of work, but I'm getting there." I yawn and stretch, waiting for my coffee. "Avery talked me into having a yard sale." I grumble. "Once all the extra stuff is gone, I think I'll be able to make some actual progress."

Cassidy shakes her head softly, obviously reminiscent of my late grandmother. "That Hazel. She was quite a collector."

"Of EVERYTHING." I add with a laugh as she wipes my cup off with a rag and slides it across the counter to me.

"Have you met that neighbor of yours yet?" She asks, wiggling her eyebrows. "He's a cutie."

I sigh. "Yeah, we've met." I respond, not allowing myself to elaborate any further. "He's okay, I guess." I say with a shrug, trying to sound aloof to the entire thing. "I hadn't really noticed."

"Oh, come on," she says as she leans across the counter towards me. "A young, single girl like you hasn't noticed that?" She raises her brows at me. "I don't believe that for a second. Have you seen him without a shirt on?" She fans herself dramatically with her hand and I stifle a giggle.

"Okay, yes. He is nice to look at." I admit, "But I'm in no position to be ogling him. Don't forget, I just got out of a long-term relationship, and the last thing I need to do is get tangled up with another man." I pause. "Besides, I'm only staying here for a few months. Getting involved with someone, anyone, would just further complicate things."

"Whatever you say, sister." She says, handing my card back to me. "But if I was your age, I would be all over that. There's nothing wrong with having a little fun." She adds with a wink.

"I bet you would." I tease back with a laugh.

"I'm old and married, not dead." She replies with a chuckle.

Just then, the door jingles again, and in walks Andrew, toolbox in hand.

"Speak of the devil." Cassidy mutters with a wink.

I feel my face turn red when he turns to nod in my direction. I've successfully avoided him ever since the snake and music fiasco yesterday and now I'm not really sure how to act towards him. In all honesty, I feel like a jerk for needing his help after yelling at him. Of course, I haven't forgiven him for calling me a Karen, either. Why is everything so damn confusing?

He puts his toolbox on the ground and goes back out the door.

"What's that about?" I ask.

"Oh, he's doing some work around here for me today. He's a contractor, so I'm taking advantage of his time in town."

"Oh." I say, nodding. Maybe I need to make nice with the contractor next door while I deal with my fixer upper. It's probably too late after our last few interactions, though.

While I'm lost in thought, an older woman walks through

the door and approaches the counter. I don't know her, but I recognize her face as a Fawn Creek regular. She has to be close to Hazel's age, or maybe older. Hazel always seemed so young for her age.

"Oh, honey." The woman says to me, reaching her hand out to squeeze my shoulder. "I heard all about what happened."

"Uh.." I drag out my confused expression, unsure how to respond to her.

"I can't believe your husband was cheating on you with the maid." She whispers. "His loss though."

I blink slowly as she turns her attention towards Cassidy and places her order for a small black coffee, leaving me dumbfounded. Husband? The maid? Is this what the people of Fawn Creek are saying about me? I shake my head and try to make sense of what just happened. With a raise of my hand, I wave goodbye to Cassidy and make my way towards the door. I need to get home and get ready for work, and out of this weird situation.

I reach the door just as Andrew appears on the opposite side. His hands are full of tools. Quickly, I pull the door open and hold it for him to make his way inside.

"Thanks." He offers with a soft expression. It's not quite a smile, but it's nicer than anything else I've gotten from him in the past. I decide to count that as a win and make my way back to Hazel's. Maybe I can at least get along with my neighbor. But that's the only goal. I don't need my heart broken again.

# Chapter 14

"You about done?" Avery asks, as her can of hairspray meets the counter with a clink.

"Just about." I assure her as I lean over the bathroom counter to apply a layer of mascara.

I have to admit, spending the evening getting ready at Avery's bathroom counter has been a bit nostalgic. It's almost as though we're back in high school, huddled together at her vanity mirror, getting ready for the winter formal. We always got ready at her house, because my mom would have never let us leave the house with makeup on.

If only she could see us now. Actually, come to think of it, I wonder if my parents will be there tonight. If they sold 1200 tickets, and the population of Fawn Creek is 1200... Math isn't my best subject, but something tells me I'll be having to hide beer from my parents tonight, just like the good ole days. I grimace at the thought of running into them tonight.

Avery appears to read my mind, as usual. "You are not going to get out of going tonight. Don't even try."

I sigh. "I'm not trying to get out of it. It's just... I'm just a little nervous about going out in public for the first time since I've been back in town." I admit. "I've never done things in this town as an adult. Some of these people make me feel like I really am still just a teenage girl, you know?"

Avery nods. "I don't think that feeling ever goes away." She sighs. "I still have a hard enough time remembering I'm a grownup. But, I promise you, no one in this town will care that you, an adult woman, are having a couple of beers downtown at the concert. As long as you don't make an ass out of yourself, they won't notice. And don't worry, your parents never come to the concerts."

I let out a sigh of relief. "Good. Keeping some distance from them isn't as easy now that we live a few blocks apart." I pause. "I don't know that you're right about people not caring about what I'm doing, though. Wednesday some old lady told me she was sorry that my husband cheated on me with the maid."

Avery laughs and motions for me to follow her down the hall. "The maid, huh?" She shakes her head. "Damn, I haven't heard that one yet."

"I didn't even know I had a maid." I roll my eyes. "She must have only been sleeping with Elliott because I was the only one keeping that house clean."

Avery laughs. "People are wild. I can't wait to hear what else is happening in your life."

"I'm sure we will hear it all tonight."

Avery shrugs. "Meh, who cares what people say? Besides, we have other things to worry about, like finding you a husband."

I scoff. "No thanks. I am not in the market for a husband, especially not in Fawn Creek. That's the fastest way to get stuck here."

Avery smiles just on one side of her mouth. "I know. That's why I'm going to find you one, so you can't leave me again."

When my expression doesn't change, Avery frowns. "Fawn Creek isn't so bad, you know. And I really love having you here."

I turn and face her, putting my hands on her shoulders. "Avery, I love that you love it here so much." I pause. "But the small town life just isn't for me." I smile and change the subject. "Maybe we should find you a husband instead."

"Fat chance," Avery says, while she sets up her ring light in the living room. "Cory will make sure that I never have a normal dating life ever again." She snickers. "He's going to continue to run my life either until Juliet is grown or until he falls into the dam and drowns while his drunk ass is fishing."

I frown and watch her get just the right angle with her phone camera. I wish I could say that Avery is joking, but sadly, she's not. Cory is terrible. He's controlling, abusive, manipulative... the list goes on. When Avery and Cory began dating, he seemed like a great guy. She was happy, and he was head over heels in love with her, at least as far as anyone could tell. They got engaged pretty quickly, but no one gave it a second thought. Avery was so happy. We just thought that she had finally found the right person. It all changed after she found out she was pregnant with Juliet. Suddenly, Cory didn't have to put on a show anymore, because he had her under his thumb and he knew it. Quickly, he became controlling. He told her how to dress and what she was and wasn't allowed to do. He dictated who she was and wasn't allowed to be friends with. It was disheartening to watch my bubbly social butterfly of a best friend suddenly become a pile of mush that couldn't make a decision for herself. I thought she would never come to her senses again, to be honest. It didn't matter what I or anyone else said. She was just not herself anymore. She seemed to think she had no way out. That is until he hurt her. When she was six months pregnant, he lost control of his anger and she ended up in the hospital. He only spent one weekend in jail, but that was just enough time for her to pack her things and get out of his house.

She may not be with him anymore, but he still has her under his thumb. He still questions what she does, spies on her, and picks fights. Then suddenly he is begging for her to go back to him. I'm constantly living in fear that one day she will, but I think Juliet helps to keep her strong. Although she has made a lot of progress, I am looking forward to the day when she is finally free from him. When she's ready. Hopefully that'll be sooner rather than later.

"Come on." She commands, breaking my concentration. "Let's get a couple of pictures before we leave. We will post them on your Facebook and Elliott can eat his stupid heart out over what he's missing."

I frown. After all the time we spent together, you'd think that I wanted him to see that I'm happy and thriving. But, I don't. I don't care how he feels about my new life and honestly; I don't care what he's doing either. For so long, I thought he was my soulmate, but if that was the case, it wouldn't be so easy to be away from him, would it?

\* \* \*

I pause at the entrance while Cassidy attaches Avery's wristband. Turns out, Cassidy's a member of the Mayfest Committee that helps run the entire festival. I'm not sure when that woman ever takes a break. How could she possibly have time to run a business and help keep the tourism of Fawn Creek alive? I can hardly remember to move my clothes from the washer to the dryer before they mildew.

"Avery!" calls a voice out of nowhere. We both look over to see her daycare provider with a beer in each hand, flagging my friend down.

"I'll go get us a couple of drinks," I say, nodding towards the beer garden, happy to avoid standing around talking to people that I don't know.

While in line, I take part in one of my favorite hobbies, people watching. It's only 7:15 pm and the main act doesn't take the stage until 8:30, but the concert is already in full swing. The city blocked the street off with caution tape and plastic fencing, creating a makeshift concert arena. The stage is at the end of Main Street, overlooking the entire downtown area. Most of the shops have stayed open for the show, and people are popping in and out of the stores, shopping bags in hand. The other end of the street is full of food trucks and a couple of beer gardens. Dozens of lawn chairs filled with people are lined up, waiting for the show to start. A handful of concert goers are already two stepping in the streets. From college aged couples to daddies and daughters, everyone appears to be having the time of their lives. While I'm watching the dancers, a couple of small kids come barreling towards the line and I step back quickly, just in time to avoid being run over. When I step back, my heel lands on top of something that I wasn't expecting. Panicked, I turn my body in a complete circle and begin my apology to the unsuspecting victim.

"Oh, gosh I am so...." But I stop short when I find myself face to face with none other than my neighbor, Andrew. "Sorry...." My smile falls and I feel my face grow warm with embarrassment.

"Seriously." He sighs. "I'm beginning to think that you have

117

no spacial awareness."

I scoff. "Maybe you shouldn't have been standing so close to me and you wouldn't have been stepped on." I say, crossing my arms over my chest, but with a small smirk on my face to show that I'm not angry. What I don't quite expect is this new flirtatious tone in my voice.

He leans in towards me and whispers. "Believe me, I would have stood back, but this dude behind me has been breathing down the back of my shirt since we got in this line. I don't know why he thinks he needs to be so close to me, but his breath is hot and sticky. I'd way rather be close to you than be close to him."

I snicker and look over the back of his head to see who he is talking about. The heavy breather behind him has to be over six and a half feet tall, has long greasy hair and is definitely standing six inches too close. His beer belly, which is not completely covered by his Metallica shirt, is nearly smashing into Andrew's back.

"Okay." I say in a low voice, "I'll forgive you for being in my bubble if you forgive me for smashing your toe."

"Deal." He says, slightly leaning into me. It's not lost on me that I really don't mind the proximity of his mouth to mine. "Does this mean we're friends now?" He raises a brow at me and shifts his eyes from side to side.

I offer him a shrug. "I mean, I don't know if I would go that far." I say with a smirk. "But you saved me from a snake, so maybe we are just no longer mortal enemies?"

"Okay, I'll take what I can get." He laughs. "I'm Andrew. I don't think we've officially met yet." He sticks his hand out to shake mine.

I smirk and shake his hand. "I'm Tyler. It's nice to meet

you." I move forward in the line to order my drinks, thankful for the chance to start again. "Well, I guess I'll see you around." I say with a wave once I have my drinks in hand.

"I'm sure you will." He winks.

* * *

The night draws on while I sit on the curb next to Avery, sipping on my seltzer and enjoying dinner from the taco truck while we take in the festivities. I'll admit one thing: Fawn Creek knows how to throw a festival. Everywhere you look, people are laughing, singing, dancing and just spending time together. The entire scene warms my heart and makes me realize a bit of what I have been missing all this time. I can't believe these concerts have been occurring for the last few years and I have never come back for one.

"Are y'all ready for Jordan Johnson?" The announcer calls out to the crowd. All of Main Street is suddenly filled with the sounds of excitement. We all yell and clap as loud as we can while Jordan walks onto the stage. We inch closer, but by the time he strums the chords for the second song, Avery finds herself a distraction.

"Hey, I'll be back." She says into my ear while she grips my forearm. A tall, handsome cowboy is standing a few feet from her, waiting. I watch as they move to the middle of the street and begin to two step. The smile plastered on her face gives me a little bit of hope that maybe she will be okay after all. She deserves happiness more than anyone else in the world.

While she's dancing, I turn back towards the stage and lose myself in the music once again. I sing along to every word, never taking my eyes off of Jordan. This is exactly what my soul needed. I've needed to feel connected to something, anything. For months, hell, maybe even years, I feel like I have just been floating through life. Not actually enjoying anything, but merely participating, just being. I can't remember the last time I actually did something that I enjoyed doing, rather than just going through the motions. It hasn't been a priority for a long time, but now I can feel what I was missing. I was missing out on life. I was missing out on joy and merely settling for good enough. The reality of it is, I had settled. All this time, I thought I was living the life I wanted. Now, I think I'm starting to see that I was forcing myself to want the life I had.

The realization hits me hard, and I have to admit, it hurts. You truly never realize how low you've been until you've left the valley and you are looking back. Suddenly, a tear rolls down my face, followed by another and another. Normally, I would be so embarrassed to be standing downtown crying, but not tonight. Tonight, the tears feel like the exact cleansing my soul has needed for so long and I'm going to let them fall. Besides, there's no better place for them to fall than at home.

"You alright?" a voice breaks through my thoughts and brings me back to reality.

I turn and see Andrew standing next to me, with concern in his eyes.

I smile and wipe my face with the back of my hand. "Just having a moment. I'm fine, thanks."

He nods and turns his head to the stage, but doesn't move from where he's standing. His presence soothes me more than I'm expecting, and I like it. He's not forcing me to talk, he's not touching me. He's just being nearby, and it's enough.

The next song starts and I steal a quick glance at him. He's singing along, just like I am. Our eyes meet and we both smile.

"Are you a Jordan Johnson fan too?" I lean forward and shout into his shoulder.

"Super fan, actually." He answers with a wink. "This is my tenth show, I think. I've lost count."

"We'll have to compare notes sometime. I bet we've been to some of the same shows." How crazy is it to think that we've probably crossed paths at concerts and had no clue?

"Looking forward to it." He says with a smirk before turning his head back to the stage.

I smile to myself. This guy may not be too bad after all. I blush, realizing that I might actually like him a little. It's been so long since I had a crush on someone, I almost forgot what it feels like.

When the concert ends, and the crowd clears, I scan the crowd, looking for Avery.

I turn to Andrew. "Have you seen Avery Thompson?" I look around nervously. "Last I saw, she was two-stepping with some cowboy, but it's been a while. She and I are supposed to walk home together."

He shakes his head. "No, but I'll help you look for her." He offers.

I gladly accept his help. There are still so many people on the street, slowly making their way out of the concert gates.

Andrew and I take off through the crowd while I hold my phone to my ear. I try to call Avery twice, but both calls go unanswered. Suddenly, the crowd on the sidewalk clears and I spot her, leaning against the wall near Drip. There's a man in front of her, leaning towards her with his hand braced against the building next to her head. At first, I think maybe she's in a make-out session with the hot cowboy, and I almost turn the other way to give her a few minutes. Unfortunately, I'm wrong and it doesn't take my eyes long to adjust and see that she is talking to Cory.

I grab Andrew's bicep to stop him and I feel a tiny pulse of electricity run through my body when our skin connects. He turns to face me.

I nod my head in Avery's direction. "There she is. She's talking to her ex."

He frowns. "It doesn't look like it's going well." He says with a mutter.

"I promise you it is not. He's a complete tool bag, and I wish he would stay away from her." I shake my head. "He's incredibly controlling and has hit her before."

"Well, let's go interrupt them, then." He says, grabbing my hand, pulling me toward Drip. For a second, I freeze. Our hands fit together perfectly. It feels natural and safe, and I don't want to let go. But also, I'm scared to death at how much I'm enjoying this.

As we approach Avery and Cory, I can hear that they are arguing.

"You're a terrible mother." Cory says, pointing a finger in her face. "You should be at home with my daughter instead of running around town dressed like a whore. It's not like you ever let me see her. You should let me have her if you aren't going to bother to take care of her."

"Cory, you don't even try to see her. Your mom keeps her during your visitation time. Please, just leave me alone. I am allowed to have a life," Avery says, trying to move out from under him, but he grabs her arm and holds her in place.

"Take me to see her right now." He demands. The vein on his forehead looks like it's about to explode.

"Dude, let her go," Andrew yells, pushing his way towards them and putting a firm hand on his shoulder.

Cory turns to look at us. "Fuck off," he says to Andrew before turning his attention back to Avery.

Andrew takes a deep breath and I'm afraid that he might hit Cory, just as a Fawn Creek police officer rushes between them and grabs Cory by the back of his shirt.

"Are you going to leave her alone, or am I going to take your ass to jail, Cory?" The officer growls at him.

Cory throws his hands up and steps back. "Shit, I'm going, okay?" He yells while he backs away. "I was just trying to talk to her."

"That's not how we talk to women. Keep walking." The officer stands firmly, pointing down the sidewalk. When he disappears around the corner, I close the space between myself and Avery.

"Are you okay?" I ask, as I notice a red mark on her arm from Cory's grip on her. "He left a mark on you."

"If you want to press charges, I'll go get him." The officer says to Avery, eyeballing her arm. He sounds almost excited to cuff Cory.

Avery uses her hand to rub the red mark on her arm. "I'm fine." She rolls her eyes. "Nothing will happen anyway besides him getting more pissed off at me. It's not worth it."

The officer and Andrew exchange a look.

"I'll walk them home. Thanks, Derek." Andrew leans in to shake his hand.

"Call if you need me." Derek tells Andrew. "And Avery? If you change your mind, call up to the station and we will do a report."

She nods. "Thanks, Derek. I'll be fine."

# Chapter 15

"Are you sure you don't want to just stay with me tonight?" I ask Avery as we cross the street and step into her yard. "I don't like the idea of you being home alone after that scene downtown. What if Cory shows up?"

"I'll be fine." Avery answers in the darkness. "As soon as I get inside, I'll lock my door and go to bed. I don't think Cory will mess with me after running into the cops, anyway. Derek probably scared him off."

I exchange a look with Andrew. "Okay," I tell Avery, "but you seriously better call me if you have any problems."

"Promise," she says, holding up her pinkie.

I interlock my finger with hers. "Do not break a pinkie promise." I say in a grumble, attempting to sound as intimidating as possible, but falling short, as usual.

Avery laughs. "Goodnight. And Andrew, thanks for walking us home."

"No problem." Andrew says, shoving his hands in his pockets and kicking at a piece of gravel on the ground.

We stand quietly in the yard and wait for Avery to disappear inside before we finish the two-block walk to our houses.

"So." Andrew interrupts the silence. "What brought you back to Fawn Creek?"

"How did you know I ever left?" I laugh nervously.

"Well, I've heard things around town." He trails off.

"Of course you have." I mutter with a roll of my eyes. I can only imagine the things that he's heard about the shit show that has become my life.

"That's the beauty of a small town."

"Something like that." I let out a sigh. "Well, long story short, at the beginning of this week, my boyfriend of three years and I split up, resulting in me being without a place to live. Of course, this was the week after my grandma passed away."

"Oof." He breathes out. "That's a hell of a couple of weeks."

"The worst." I agree. "Hazel left me her house, so at least it gave me somewhere to live in the meantime. I'm going to clean it up and get it ready to sell. Hopefully, by the end of summer."

"Where are you going next?" Andrew asks as he quietly strolls along next to me, shoving his hands into his jean pockets.

I pause for a second to think about my answer. "That's the fun part. I have no idea. Honestly, I haven't had time to think about much this last week."

"Why not stay in Fawn Creek?"

We step into my yard and I lead Andrew to my porch by motioning my head in that direction. "I don't know. I just... I never pictured myself back here." I say, plopping down on the porch swing as he moves to sit beside me. "When I left this town as soon as I graduated high school, it's because I had always planned to live in the city and that's what I've been doing. Until this week, anyway." I shake my head. "I thought this place was a part of my past."

He nods quietly. "That's understandable. It's almost like a

rite of passage, you know? Like it's ingrained in all small town kids to want nothing else but to get out of their hometown. To see the world." He looks at the sky wistfully for a second. "But few actually get the chance to do so. And most of those that manage to get out end up coming right back."

That last statement of his hits me a little harder than I expected it to. Am I just another statistic? Just another person who couldn't break away from her small town roots? No. That will not be my story. This is just a blip. A pause, if you will. I look to my side and see Andrew studying me while I battle my internal crisis on the wooden porch swing next to him.

"So, what's your story?" I ask, although I already know part of it. The last thing I'm going to do is admit I've talked to anyone else about him. Unlike him, I don't want to look like a stalker.

"I live in Texas and I own a construction business there." He motions his head towards the house next door. "My grandpa used to live next door to Hazel. He raised me and my little brother." Andrew smiles softly, but it doesn't quite reach his eyes. "He passed away earlier this year, and he left the house to me. This is the first opportunity I've had to come back here and get the place ready to list."

"Wait." I turn to him. "You grew up next door? I practically lived with my grandma growing up. How do I not remember you?"

He chuckles. "Oh no, we grew up on a farm outside of town. Grandpa didn't move here until my brother and I grew up and moved away." He pauses to look up at the sky. "Grandma passed and then the farm became too much for him to handle, so he sold it off and moved to town. He and Hazel were close friends. She was always checking in on him and baking him pies." He says with a smile.

I grin. "Hazel was such a good person. I miss her." I say with a sigh.

He nods. "She really was."

"Well, how much longer until your house is ready to list?" I ask, changing the subject before I start crying for the second time tonight.

"Realistically, if I really worked at it, I could have it ready next week." He stands and yawns, stretching his arms above his body. His shirt rides up and gives me a glimpse of the abs I saw during our last encounter. I quickly look away, hoping he didn't catch me staring. He doesn't, as far as I can tell. "I don't know, though. I've been kind of taking my time and enjoying being back home. It's been nice to slow down and get back to my roots of handyman service, like by helping Cassidy at the coffee shop."

I nod. "Who's running your business while you're here?"

"I scheduled a break between jobs so I could come do this. Took three weeks off, the longest vacation I've ever had." He laughs. "I have some great guys back home to help me out, and I found them plenty of work for the time I'm gone, so they aren't going without pay."

I laugh. "You know, most people vacation at the beach or the mountains, not in Southeast Kansas."

He just offers me a shrug. "Well, I better be getting home. It's late."

"Wait, I have to ask you something." I say, with a raised brow. "Why did you call me a Karen? And why did you say I think I'm better than everyone else?" I frown. "That's really not me at all."

He scrunches his nose at me. "I was kind of hoping you had

forgotten about all of that."

I scoff, "No way. It actually kind of hurt my feelings, to be honest."

He frowns. "It really was a dick move. I'm sorry." I nod in agreement and he continues on. "Honestly, I didn't know who you were when I saw you at the coffee shop. I just saw that you were all dressed up and wearing heels and carrying an expensive purse, so..."

"So you just assumed that I was a snob?"

He pauses. "I might have assumed that you weren't from around here. I was so nervous that day." He shakes his head. "I had spent all day trying to psych myself up to go from business to business, introducing myself as a licensed and bonded contractor, hoping to make some business connections and do some side work while I'm in town. And when we collided, you covered my only nice button up I brought with me in milky coffee."

I raise a brow. "So you freaked out, ran out the door and.."

"And ran home to wash my shirt." He laughs.

I shake my head. "Why were you nervous? If you have your own successful contracting business, that should speak for itself, shouldn't it?"

He nods. "You'd sure think so. But, I was a bit of a wild child when I was a teen and I've found that people in small towns don't tend to forget that stuff easily." He shrugs. "So basically, I'm starting from scratch, trying to make a name for myself all over again." He smirks. "I asked Cassidy who you were when I went back, and she told me you were Hazel's granddaughter, who was visiting from the city. Grandpa Charlie had told me a lot of stuff about your mom. Mostly, he said she likes to pretend to be a little more uppity than she is. I assumed the apple didn't fall too far from the tree, and I let my assumptions take over when you confronted me."

My face reddens and I stare down the street, avoiding eye contact with him.

"But." He says, breaking the silence. "I was wrong. You are nothing at all like I thought you were. You're the exact opposite, actually."

I raise an eyebrow at him. "You should probably know I didn't buy that expensive purse. It was a gift from my ex-boyfriend's mom. It wasn't my style, but I carried it to make her happy. I left it there when I left him." I say with a shrug. "Also, I might have judged you a little, too. I was secretly calling you the Asshole of Fawn Creek."

He chuckles. "I deserved it." He pauses for a second, but then turns to make his way towards the stairs. "I better get home. It's late."

I nod and watch him walk across my yard before I call out. "Hey, Andrew?"

"Yeah?" He says, turning back towards me.

"I was wrong about you, too."

"I know. Night, Tyler."

"Night."

* * *

My eyes flutter open just after nine o'clock on Saturday morning. As soon as my eyes open, my brain is overrun with the events of the previous night. Mostly, I rerun my late night chat with Andrew. I'm still not sure what to think of it, but maybe, just maybe, he and I can be friends. And only friends.

I shoot Avery a quick text to make sure she made it through the night and then shuffle to the kitchen to make coffee. As I make my way to the couch, cup in hand, my phone vibrates with a text.

**Avery: I am alive and well. What time do you want to meet downtown?**

*Ugh. More peopley activities.*

**Me: I just rolled out of bed. What if I meet you at Drip at 10:00?**

**Avery: Works for me. Are you bringing your boyfriend?**

**Me: I don't have a boyfriend.**

**Avery: I don't know. Andrew was hanging out awfully close to you last night.**

**Me: We are just friends.**

**Avery: We'll see how long that lasts. That's a lot more than you guys were a few days ago.**

I roll my eyes and toss the phone down on the couch next to me. Andrew and I will not be a thing.

* * *

Devin, the barista, slides two iced lattes across the counter to me just as my phone pings. It's Avery letting me know she's here, waiting outside. I thank Devin and quickly grab our drinks to meet her. As I step through the door, she looks at me like I just saved her life by bringing her a coffee.

"Oh, bless you." She says with a sigh, taking the drink from me and inhaling a long sip. "Are we getting too old to stay out as late as we did last night?" She asks, leaning on the handlebar of the stroller. "I like to think I'm still young and fun, but damn, then I stay out after 9 pm and have to question my entire existence."

We stroll down the sidewalk towards the car show. "Yes, we absolutely are. I don't remember the last time I stayed out until 10:30, but I'm going to need at least a week to recover from it." I say with a yawn.

She sighs loudly. "When did this happen? We aren't even thirty yet."

I raise a brow. "We're getting close, though."

"Shut your mouth." Avery glares at me. "We still have a couple of years."

"Morning ladies." A voice interrupts our conversation and we both turn toward the sound. Derek, the officer from last night, is standing on the sidewalk holding a coffee in one hand and a dog leash in the other. His German Shepard is sitting quietly at his feet, overlooking the crowd downtown. He's off duty now, but still has that stance, like he is ready to spring into action at a moment's notice.

"Morning!" we say in unison back to him.

When we get a little further away, I lean towards Avery. "The hot cop was checking you out."

She steals a glance at him and then rolls her eyes at me. "Whatever. He just feels sorry for me after that scene last night."

"I think he wants to protect and serve you." I mutter, bouncing my eyebrows at her.

Avery shakes her head and takes another sip of her coffee. "We're just friends."

"I've heard you say that about him before. He's the one from the hospital, isn't he?" I raise a brow in her direction, recollecting that Derek had shown up at the hospital when Cory got arrested for hurting her.

She nods. "Yes, and we were just friends then, too." She steals another glance at him before looking back at me. "I told you. You saw that mess last night. I am at Cory's mercy for the rest of my life. I couldn't date if I wanted to."

I frown at my best friend. I hate this for her. "But that isn't fair. You guys are over. You deserve to have your own life."

She shrugs. "I know. I guess life is just like that sometimes." She continues walking in silence, and I follow next to her wordlessly. I hate this for her and I wish I could say the right words to make her feel better. I just have no idea what those words are.

We move through the car show, taking in the beautiful classic cars lining the street. The city blocked the entire downtown business district off, just like last night. Now, instead of being filled with concert goers and beer gardens, Main Street is full of classic cars, street vendors and the sounds of classic rock music.

Neither of us are really car fanatics, but the prideful faces of the old men sitting in lawn chairs behind their cars light up as we pretend to be. A lot of work and money goes into projects like these. I know because my dad has been working away on his grandpa's old Chevy pickup for most of my life. We stop in front of a silver Corvette and I notice a disgusted look as it crosses Avery's face.

"What's wrong with you?" I whisper out of the side of my mouth.

She turns my body away from the men sitting behind the car watching us. "My mom once told me that men buy corvettes to compensate for having a small..." She shifts her eyes back and forth to make sure we are out of earshot. "Package." She tells me in a low voice. "I obviously don't know if it's true, but I remember that every time I see one and it makes me laugh."

Avery's mom has always been an infinite source of wisdom when it comes to things like that. Luckily for us, as soon as we became teenagers, she began to share all of those nuggets of advice with us regularly. Much to my mother's dismay, of course.

We turn back towards the car and the owner is watching us intently under the brim of his worn straw cowboy hat. Never in my life would I have thought about this mans package, and I almost wish I could wash my brain out. I'll never look at a Corvette the same again.

Luckily, the awkward silence is interrupted by my name being shouted through the crowd. My eyes search the crowd for the culprit. Just two cars to my left, under a shade tree, stand Cassidy and Sierra. Sierra is waving excitedly.

"Sierra, hey!" I shout, as I move towards her. As the distance closes between us, I almost can't believe it's her. When I left Fawn Creek, she was still just a kid. Now, she's a woman and I just can't believe how much time has passed. She squeezes me into a hug and then I stand back to look at her. Her long red hair nearly reaches the waistband on her jean shorts. Her face has changed very little since she was a kid. But at least the splatter of freckles across her nose and cheeks hasn't changed. "How are you so grown up?" I sigh.

"Right?!" Cassidy agrees. "It's awful. I can't believe it. She's a full-time hair stylist at the salon and she's getting married soon." She puts an arm across her daughter's shoulder and hugs Sierra close to her. "It all happened so fast."

"Agreed." I say. "When I left, you weren't in high school

yet."

"Okay, you two old ladies. That's enough." Sierra rolls her eyes at our remarks. She turns to me. "Mom tells me you moved back. That's so exciting." Sierra interjects, changing the subject.

"Temporarily moved back." I correct her, although I feel like I'm reminding myself as much as everyone else these days.

"How long are you going to be in town?" Sierra asks.

"Um, through the end of summer, probably. I'm trying to get Hazel's house ready to go on the market before I leave town again."

She nods thoughtfully. "So, you'll be here for my wedding? It'll be at the end of July."

"As of right now, yes." I tell her.

Sierra grins. "Okay, well, then you have to come. I'll leave an invitation for you in the mailbox at Hazels."

I smile back at her. "I would love to. Count me in."

Behind me, Juliet fusses in her stroller, wriggling back and forth. Avery attempts to calm her by rocking the stroller back and forth, but it's obvious that Juliet's bored and ready to continue her stroll.

"We better get going." I say to Sierra and Cassidy before leaning in to hug them both goodbye. "It was good to see you."

"You too." She whispers, hugging me tighter. "Let's get together sometime, okay?"

"You got it."

* * *

Avery and I spend the rest of the morning grazing through the vendor booths before stopping at the food trucks for lunch. We take a seat at a picnic table in the park with our food and wait for the local dance class to start their performance in front of the gazebo. I smile down at Juliet as she drools all over a French fry.

"She's just like her Aunt Tyler." Avery jokes.

"I've never met a French fry I didn't like." I agree with a shrug. "Well, what else is on the docket for today?" I ask, just as a group of tiny ballerinas take their positions.

Immediately, I recognize Piper, the little girl from daycare that was so worried about my messy hair. I smile at the quirky little girl. While all the other ballerinas have their hair all neat and their smiles frozen, Piper is dancing on the makeshift stage with face paint she obviously got from one of the local booths. The black and orange tiger face she's rocking makes her even more of a star. I hope if I ever have a daughter; she grows up to march to the beat of her own drum like Piper does.

"Nap time for both me and Juliet." Avery yawns. "This is pretty much it for me, unless you want to do something else."

"So, I'm off the hook for the rest of the weekend?" I ask with the largest grin I can muster.

"I suppose so." Avery shrugs.

Once the little dancers finish their routine, we clap and get to work at picking up our mess. I don't know what I'm more excited about, to get home and get back to work on my house? Or to spend the rest of the weekend possibly running into my neighbor.

# Chapter 16

I step into the house and close the door behind me. This weekend has been exhausting, but also more fun than I've had in a long time. It's been nice to spend time with Avery, like we used to when we were kids. I love how low maintenance our friendship is. Some weeks we talk every day, sometimes we go weeks without talking, just sending Tiktoks back and forth. But when we do finally connect, it's like we don't skip a beat. We just fall into our regular groove like no time has passed. It's nice to have a friend close by. This is the friendship I was missing in the city.

Ugh, Oklahoma City. I've sat down a few times this week and scrolled through apartments, but it's been unsuccessful. The only places that I can afford to live are in the more sketchy parts of town. I may love living in the city, but my small-town girl heart knows that feeling safe is a priority of mine. I can't live just anywhere, especially if I'm living alone. Wherever I go next has to be just right.

The last few days, I've stayed busy moving from room to room decluttering and sorting, all while in between working, of course. Piles of yard sale items, and the clothes that I still never finished digging through, have officially taken the guest bedroom over. I'm sure the city workers are already tired of the amount of trash I piled in and all around my trash can. I just feel like I'm drowning in stuff. It's almost like I'm paralyzed by the amount of crap around me. But Avery and I decided to go through with the garage sale next week, and that means I have to get things ready in the next 6 days. My only choice is to get to work.

I work for hours and before I know it, I'm out of energy. While the guest room is still full, it's at least organized and ready for our sale. I slowly drag myself to the living room and collapse onto the couch. The living room is basically empty of clutter and ready to paint, and that scene practically gives me whiplash after spending the day in the guest room. Suddenly, it doesn't feel like Hazel's house anymore. It feels like a blank slate. I thought this was exactly what I needed and I know it's what I need in order to move forward with my plan. However, for the first time since I've started this project, it really hits me she's gone.

I hate that she isn't here. She won't see me get married, if I ever do. She won't meet my babies or ever hold them. There are so many memories I wanted to make with her, and I hate that we ran out of time. I hate that I'm blaming myself for not being here and I hate that I can't get that time back.

I look around again. This isn't even her house anymore. It's an empty, neutral shell of what once was my safe place. This is the place where I felt loved and wanted. Where I knew there would be cookies waiting for me after school and a puzzle for us to work on while we watched Wheel of Fortune and Golden Girls. This house is more ingrained into my soul and more a part of me than I had ever realized it was. With this realization, I finally break and have the cry I've been needing. The cry I expected at the funeral. This is the cry I needed when I stuck out like a sore thumb with my city friends and the cry I needed when Elliott and I split up. This is the cry I thought I got last night at the concert. In reality, last night was just when I broke the seal.

Every shitty thing that's happened in the past week has been resting on my shoulders, but now the dam is open. I don't see it stopping soon. The only thing left to do is lay down on the couch, cover up with a blanket, and cry myself to sleep.

* * *

What feels like hours later, I wake up to the sound of knocking. I open my eyes and glare at the door, trying to will it to become see through so I can tell who is standing on the other side.

As if the visitor reads my mind, they call out "Tyler? Are you in there?"

The voice is vaguely familiar. *Andrew? Why would he be here?*

"Be right there!" I yell out before rolling myself off the couch. I pause in front of the mirror hanging on the wall and assess myself. My eyes are still a little red, but I've definitely seen worse. I can only imagine how bad they were before my nap.

I stand on my tiptoes to check the peephole, and there stands Andrew with a pizza box and a six-pack of beer in hand.

"Hey." I say, opening the door, eyeing him suspiciously. "What's up?"

"I just went to grab some pizza and well...have you eaten yet?" He asks, almost sounding nervous.

"I have not." The savory scent of the pizza meets my nose and my stomach growls audibly.

"Sounds like I was just in time." He says with a grin, pushing past me into the house.

"Sure, come on in." I say, following his lead to take a seat on the living room floor.

By the time I sit next to him, he already has the pizza box open.

"Beer?"

"Uh.. sure."

He opens a bottle for me and passes it over before handing me a slice of pizza on a napkin.

"Thank you." I say with a crooked smile.

He takes a drink of his beer and then leans his back on the couch while he takes in the room. "This looks a lot different from when I was last here."

I scrunch my nose. "When were you here?"

"When I removed your pet snake."

"Oh, yeah." I say, my face turning red. "For about half a second, I was concerned that you've been sneaking into my house when I'm sleeping."

"No, I only do that when you aren't here."

I roll my eyes, and we eat in silence for a few moments. "What's up with the impromptu dinner?"

He shrugs, taking another bite. "I don't know. I'm tired of eating alone every night. It's nice to be around another human every so often. Is this okay? I guess it was pretty forward of me."

My stomach flutters. I think I might like 'forward'. It's more than okay. I really like him being here, and the more time I spend with him, the more time I crave our next encounter. I shake my head, trying to clear those thoughts. Surely, he is only interested in friendship. He and I are going back to separate lives soon. There's no point in starting something that is just going to fall apart in a week or more.

"So, tell me about your ex," Andrew says, turning towards me, looking genuinely interested.

I sigh. "I'm not sure where there is to tell." I say before taking a bite of my pizza.

"Well, it sounds like the breakup was pretty abrupt. What happened?"

"Basically? He and I had been together for three years. We lived together, and somehow, over that time, he decided that he suddenly has no desire to get married or have kids." I shrug.

"And you do?" Andrew asks with a raised brow.

"Yeah. At least some day." I pause for a second to ponder on my life. "In hindsight, I think I knew for a long time that he wasn't really the one. We were kind of just living separate lives in the same house there at the end. Unbeknownst to me, while I was dreaming of a family, he was more focused on his Tesla and his golf game." I say, shaking my head.

"His loss." Andrew says with a smirk, before taking another sip of his beer. "So, what's next over here?" He adds.

"Huh?" I ask, puzzled by his question.

He waves a hand around the room. "What are you planning to do to the house next?"

"Oh." I laugh nervously. Why am I so freaking awkward? "I think I'm about ready to paint."

"What about this amazing carpet?" He asks with a raised brow.

I scoff. "Do you mean to tell me you have a problem with shag carpeting?"

He takes a bite of his pizza and laughs. "No, not at all."

I frown. "I'd love to rip it out, but I know nothing about putting new carpet down."

He stands up and wipes some pizza grease on his jeans. "I'm willing to bet there is hardwood under this carpet. Want me to look?"

"Um, sure!" I agree excitedly. "You could probably eat first."

"Eh, it'll just take a minute." He says with a shrug. Leaving his pizza crust resting in the open pizza box, he opens the hall closet. "Will you come hold this flashlight for me?" he asks.

"I don't know. It seems that I still have some PTSD from being my dad's flashlight holder, so just try to be nice to me." I joke.

He rolls his eyes and hands me the phone. "I'll try, Princess." He says with a roll of his eyes.

Seconds later, I watch him peel back a corner of the carpet. He turns to smile at me. "Bingo! Come check this out."

I lean around his body to examine the exposed hardwood floor, illuminated by the light of his phone flashlight. "It's beautiful." I whisper.

"Now, that's not to say it'll be like that throughout the entire house." He warns me as he stands back up and turns to face me. "You won't really know until you pull it all up. I can come over and help you tomorrow if you want me to."

I nod. "Okay..." is all I can get out before it happens.

I couldn't tell you who made the first move; who kissed who? Hell, we might have actually both moved at once. It's all a blur in the moment, but what I know is that when our mouths crash together, I feel electricity that I've never felt before. It starts off softly, but neither of us pulls back. Slowly, he wraps his hand around the back of my neck and laces his fingers through my hair, tenderly pulling me closer to his body. We kiss as though we've been doing this for years. We kiss like he knows my mouth and I know his. The familiarity of it all is astounding.

Once we finally come up for air, I take one step back and smile at him sheepishly.

"So." He says, breaking the awkward silence. "I'll see you tomorrow, then?"

"Yeah, sure. That would be great." I say with a nod, still trying to wrap my head around what had just happened.

And with that, he's gone, leaving me standing in the middle of my living room dazed and confused and anxiously awaiting tomorrow.

\* \* \*

Sunday morning, I wake up with my head spinning from the night before. I lay in my bed and think back to Andrew in my house, sitting on the floor next to me eating pizza. I think of the kiss and the awkwardness that followed, and that he's coming back today.

I climb out of bed and march to the kitchen to start the coffeepot. While my coffee is brewing, I stand in front of my closet and carefully choose my outfit for today. Obviously, I need something I can get dirty, but also; I want to look cute. Eventually, I settle on a pair of skinny jeans and a mustard yellow t-shirt. I put my hair up into a ponytail that is supposed to look effortless, but in reality I have to put it up and take it down a few times to get it exactly right. I put on a light coat of makeup and shiny pink lip gloss before standing in front of the mirror to assess myself. It's probably silly to get all dolled up to do work on the house, but I'm working on the house with a cute boy. One that I have to admit that I like. One that happens to be a great kisser.

I sit down with my cup of coffee, just as I hear movement coming from the house next door. I peek through the window just in time to see Andrew climbing out of the bed of his truck. He looks at my house and catches me watching him and gives me a small wave.

*Busted.*

I wave back and then make my way to my porch, coffee in hand. "Morning." I say to him with a smile.

"Hey. I was just getting the bed of my truck emptied so we can fill it with your carpet. I can take it to the dump tomorrow."

"Oh." I look at the truck nervously. I hadn't thought about what to do the carpet after pulling it out. "Thank you. It never crossed my mind that I would have to throw all of that away. I guess it won't fit in my trash can?"

Andrew chuckles and shakes his head. "No worries. I have some things around here that I need to take anyway. You ready to get to work?"

"Let's do it."

* * *

Hours later, Andrew and I plop down on the couch in exhaustion and survey our handiwork. Every piece of carpet has been drug out of the house and piled in the back of Andrews' truck. The floor is swept and gorgeous hardwood floors can be seen throughout the house.

Andrew stretches his arms over his head and yawns. "You got lucky. I can't believe this floor is in such good shape." He says as he turns to me. "Most places have an old floor heater that's been covered in plywood or water damage. Honestly, I don't think you even need to clear coat it. Just mop the floor and move on."

"It looks so much better in here already."

"It really does." He agrees. "I will never understand people that cover gorgeous floors like this."

"Me neither." I shake my head. "Thank you for your help today. There's no chance this would have happened without you." I pause, suddenly feeling shy again. "Can I make you dinner tonight? Return the favor from last night?"

"You don't have to do that." He stands and stretches again, taking a drink of his bottle of water.

"I know, but I want to." I smile. And it's true. I want to return the favor, but also I want to spend more time with him. "Do you like chicken fajitas?"

"I'll never turn down Mexican food."

"Be here at 6:30 then."

"It's a date." He says with a smile.

# Chapter 17

*It's a date.*

The words ring in my head over and over all day. While I'm driving to the grocery store for ingredients and the hardware store for painting supplies.

While I paint the living and dining room, I keep hearing the words. *It's a date.*

While I shower and scrub the paint from my hair and skin. *It's a date.*

All day, I have felt anxious, yet excited. It's been a long time since I've felt like this. Elliott and I were together for three years, which means it's been at least that long since I went on a first date, let alone kissed another man, or even wanted to. But with Andrew, I definitely want to do that again.

I know I shouldn't get my hopes up, of course. He and I are from different places and have different lives. He's leaving soon, and who knows if I'll ever see him again? The last thing I need to do is get involved with him, or anyone. But what's wrong with two adults enjoying each other's company while we are both here?

By 6:00, I've changed my clothes four times and done my hair twice. I settle on a pair of jeans and a flowy tank top, with soft curls in my hair. Then, I awkwardly move around the house fluffing pillows and cleaning the dining room table for the fourth time.

At 6:27, a knock at the door startles me, and I jump off the couch. I had been rereading the same page in my book for the last ten minutes, and I don't remember any of the words I read. I sling the door and there stands Andrew. He definitely put some extra effort into tonight, just like I did, and that's a relief. He's wearing dark wash jeans with a pearl snap button down flannel. (Not the one I dumped coffee on.) Instead of his usual baseball cap, his jet black hair is combed and slicked back. He smells woodsy and squeaky clean and I just want to breathe him in.

"You look beautiful," He says softly.

"Thanks. I hope you're hungry." Looking back towards the kitchen.

He smirks. "Starving."

For some reason, I'm not entirely sure he's talking food.

* * *

After we finish eating, I refill our margarita glasses and then get to work on cleaning up the kitchen. As I fill the sink, Andrew immediately jumps up to rinse plates and loads them in the dishwasher alongside me. "You don't have to do that." I say.

"You did all the cooking. I can at least rinse a few dishes." He says with a smile. "That was fantastic. I haven't had a home cooked meal in a long time."

"Thanks, it's one of my favorites." I say, taking another drink of my margarita.

"These are good too." He laughs, picking up his own glass.

"Maybe too good." He says with a pause.

The way he's looking at me sends a shiver down my spine.

"You got a lot of painting done today." He observes, as he takes his glass and moves back towards the dining room. He pauses in front of the wall of shelves next to the dining table. "You like to read?"

"Like is a bit of an understatement." I laugh. "If reading were a sport, I'd be an Olympic athlete." I run my finger across several of the book spines on the shelf.

"Quite a collection you have here." He says, admiring the wall full of books. "Almost enough for a library or a bookstore."

I smirk. "Most of these actually belonged to Hazel. I didn't have a lot of space to collect many books at my last house." I pause. "It's funny you say that though. When I was a kid, I used to dream about owning my own bookstore."

He raises a brow. "Is that still your dream?"

"I don't know. Maybe." I shrug. "In a perfect world, I think it would be fun to own a cute little bookstore downtown, but I'm afraid bookstores are a dying breed. It could never be profitable and surely not enough to support me."

He smiles softly. "I bet you could do anything you put your mind to. You're a determined woman, and I think you could make it work." With that, he reaches out and squeezes my hand. I melt immediately.

*How can he have so much faith in someone he doesn't really know?*

"Hey," Andrew interrupts my train of thought. "What do you think about going over to my place and lighting up the fire pit? It's full of branches I picked up all over the yard and I need to get them burned up before I leave."

The mention of him leaving sends a wave of sadness over me,

147

but I try to quickly bury it. This is not the time to get emotional. We're just having a good time. I remind myself. "Sure. That sounds fun." I agree, relieved that he isn't ready for this night to end either.

We step through the privacy fence into his backyard and he uses his phone as a flashlight to lead the way. I take a seat on the patio sofa and he quickly gets to work on starting the fire. Once the flames are going, he steps through the backdoor of the house and comes back with a woven blanket. I look up at him just as he lays it across my lap and I feel my stomach flutter.

"Just in case you get chilly." He whispers, his words cause goosebumps to rise on my arms. He settles in close to me and puts his arm around my shoulder, pulling me in close.

I share the blanket with him, extending it over his lap, and we sit in a comfortable silence for a long time, sipping the rest of our drinks and watching the orange and yellow flames. I finish my drink and place the glass on the ground and he follows suit. His hand slides across my thigh and squeezes my hand gently. I must admit that I like all of this, especially the simplicity and the calm. I love that he and I just sit here without phones and books and televisions. Just as I look up to him to offer him a gentle smile, he moves in for another kiss.

What starts as slow, light kisses quickly builds into a faster rhythm. Once our mouths meet, it's like we can't get enough of each other. And like last night, it's like we've been doing this for years. I don't want him to quit and from what I can tell, neither does he.

When we finally come up for air, he leans his forehead against mine and whispers, "Hold on for one second, okay?" He picks up the blanket that has since fallen onto the ground and lays it in the grass near the now roaring fire.

Gently, he tugs my hand and pulls me towards him. Suddenly, I find myself straddling his waist as we go back to fueling the hunger that is burning inside of us. Just as he slides his calloused hands under the hem of my tank top, my phone rings.

I let out an exasperated sigh and throw my head back. "Dammit." I mutter softly.

I stand from my position on the ground and grab my phone from the arm of the patio couch. The display tells me it's Avery.

"Hey. What's up?" I ask into the receiver.

Andrew sits up behind me and gently brushes my hair out of the way while he kisses my shoulder. Electricity runs down my spine.

"Tyler?" Avery says with ragged breath. She sounds like she's crying. "Can I come over?"

"Of course." I say, straightening up my body. I turn towards Andrew with a frown. "Are you okay?"

"Yeah. I just can't be alone right now."

"See you in a few."

* * *

I wake up Monday morning with a dull headache pounding behind my eyes. Undoubtedly it's from the half pitcher of margaritas Andrew and I shared last night before our make-out session in his backyard. The second half of the pitcher that Avery and I downed after she got here didn't help matters, either.

I climb out of my bed and pad to the kitchen to start the coffeepot and down a couple of aspirin. While I wait for the magic bean juice to be ready, I reminisce about last night before we were interrupted. A shiver runs down my spine when I think of what might have happened had Avery not called.

Honestly, it's probably a good thing. The last thing I need to do is have drunk sex with my neighbor in his yard and then not be able to look into his eyes again until he leaves. But boy, did I want to.

Regardless, I'm glad I could be available to Avery when she needed me. Single mom life is wearing on her and the constant fighting with Cory isn't helping either. I hate this for her and wish I knew how to make it any better. Hell, I wish I could relate at all. I don't even have a houseplant relying on me right now since I haven't yet replaced the dead cactus. The idea of supporting a baby feels like something from another planet, yet something I'm yearning for so much.

Juliet was with her dad last night. Well, her dad and grandma. Dad lives with his mom right now, and that means Juliet basically stays with Grandma while Cory visits. He's only involved with her when he feels like it, and that's not very often. This is the only way Avery feels even a little safe about Juliet seeing her dad, not that she has much of an option.

When she dropped Juliet off last night, Cory started yelling at her about the concert again. His mom broke up the argument before the police had to be called, but Avery's feelings were already hurt. He left pissed off, and she was afraid he would show up at her house for round two. I'm just thankful that she was calling to tell me she needed to come over and talk, instead of calling me to visit her in the ER again. We've been there before, so when Avery calls me crying, I assume the worst. I don't know if that feeling is ever going to go away.

I take a seat in the recliner and slowly sip my coffee, willing my body to wake up, just a few moments before shuffling into the room from the guest bedroom.

"Good morning, princess." I say with a yawn.

"What was in that pitcher of margaritas?" She asks, covering her eyes with her hand, trying to shield them from the light.

"A lot of tequila." I moan, taking another sip of my coffee.

"I can still taste it." She says, making a show of smacking her lips with a disgusted look on her face before disappearing to get a cup of coffee.

The sound of metal hitting metal outside rings through the living room, and I move the curtain to look outside. Andrew is throwing things into the bed of this truck, onto the pile of carpet and padding we already filled it up with. Suddenly, he looks up and once again catches me watching him. I wave at him sleepily before I let the curtain fall closed.

"Sorry I ruined your date last night." Avery says, reappearing into the room, catching me in the act.

"It wasn't a date." I tell her with an eye roll, moving my way back to the spot on my couch. Although, it definitely was. I'm just not quite ready to talk about it yet.

"Yeah, the dead grass in your hair looked like your 'not a date' was going rather well." She says, making her way down the hall, coffee cup in her hand. I hear the bathroom door click shut.

I open my mouth to shout an argument, but I'm interrupted by a knock on the door. I open the door to find Andrew standing on my porch. He's wearing faded jeans, a black t-shirt and a blue unbuttoned flannel shirt. "Hey." He smiles at me.

"Hi." Suddenly aware of my messy hair, morning breath and lack of pants while I stand there in my oversized sleep shirt. "I bet I'm a sight to see." I say, embarrassed. Truthfully,

I don't like anyone to see me without makeup on, especially the hot guy next door. It was years before Elliott saw me not completely put together and that would have never happened if it were up to me.

"You're beautiful." He smiles and reaches out to squeeze my hand, and I blush in response. He pulls me in for a kiss when we're interrupted.

As if on cue, Avery walks out of the bathroom and sees that I have company. "Oh, hello everyone. Don't mind me." She's dressed and looks like she didn't wake up five minutes ago with a hangover. "I have to go to work." She looks at us. "And you two can get back to whatever I ruined last night."

I roll my eyes at my friend as she steps past us and onto the porch.

Andrew turns to me. "Do you have some free time this morning?"

I glance at the clock on the wall. "I have a couple of hours. I just need to get clocked in by nine."

"Want to go for a ride?" He asks with a grin.

"Um... sure." I look down at my naked legs again. "Just let me get dressed real quick?"

"Or don't." He says with a wink. "What you're wearing is great, too."

I roll my eyes and turn towards my bedroom. "I'll meet you in five minutes."

* * *

Five minutes later, I emerge from the house wearing leggings and a t-shirt, a messy bun and a quick layer of makeup. I'm carrying two travel cups of coffee when I meet Andrew at his truck bed.

"Is that for me?" He asks, motioning towards the cup.

"Yeah. I wasn't sure how you liked it, but I had a feeling you were a black coffee kind of guy." I say, handing the cup over.

"You would be right." He grins and motions towards the truck. "Let's go."

"So?" I ask as we pull out of our neighborhood. "Are we going to the dump?"

He laughs. "You can't take a girl to the dump on your second date. Who do you think I am?"

I scoff. "Sorry, I didn't realize this was a date." I take a sip of my coffee. "So, where are we headed then?"

"You'll see." He says with a soft grin.

Ten minutes later, we turn onto a dirt road outside of town. A few minutes after that, we enter a driveway with a large iron gate and a for sale sign next to it. I look at Andrew as if to silently ask what we are doing, but he ignores me and just keeps driving.

He goes through the gate and follows a long gravel drive, stopping at a sad little house hidden among a patch of over-grown grass. The house is white, with an old wooden porch that is on the verge of collapsing. One wooden pillar appears to be supporting the entire roof, and the stairs leading to the porch are broken. The shutters are falling off; the paint is peeling and the windows are boarded closed with KEEP OUT spray painted across them. I feel uneasy, to say the least. What have I gotten myself into?

Andrew notices my distress and reaches over to squeeze my knee. "You okay over there?"

"Yeah." I answer, slowly nodding my head. "Just thinking

that every movie I watched growing up told me not to go to the middle of nowhere with men that you hardly know, especially when no one else knows where you are."

"Did they also teach you not to get tequila drunk and make out on a blanket in your neighbors' backyard next to an open fire?" He teases.

I blush. "You got me there."

"Well, I promise not to murder you here. People may not know where you are, but they know where I am." He puts the truck in drive again and drives past the house.

"Whew, that's good, I guess." I say, looking out the passenger side window as we drive along a path through the pasture. "So, where are we exactly?"

He rolls down both windows as he creeps along. "My brother is trying to convince me to buy this place with him."

Crap. So much for us both leaving Fawn Creek.

I bite the inside of my lip gently. "So, are you going to?" I turn my body to look at the surrounding land.

"I'm undecided." He says, talking to the windshield. "I keep coming out here, driving around, trying to feel inspired and so far I just keep coming up empty."

"So, you were hoping I'd inspire you?" I tease him and gently elbow his side.

He gives me a half smirk. "Something like that. I just thought maybe I could get your opinion on it. You know, fresh eyes and all."

"Well." I say, repositioning myself in the seat to turn towards him, folding a leg under my body. "What would owning this look like? Would you guys redo that little house that we passed and live in there?"

He shakes his head and laughs. "No, I don't think I want to

share a house with my brother and his new wife. We would both build our own houses, just far enough from each other so that we can each have some personal space. That house would probably get torn down."

"Well, that's sad. I bet it has a lot of potential."

He snickers. "Give a girl one house to repaint and strip carpet from and suddenly she is a professional. Maybe you could get a show on HGTV."

I smack his arm playfully. "Maybe I will. I mean, as long as all I have to do is clean, paint and change a doorknob, I'm practically a house flipper already."

"Sounds to me like you could land a ten-year contract, at least." He laughs.

I shrug. "I'll contact the network as soon as I get back to the house."

We ride in a comfortable silence for a few more moments. "So, how many acres is this? Will you split it in half?" I ask, gazing out the window.

"It's 80 acres. From what we've discussed, we will use ten acres to build our houses and then use the rest for cattle. That will give us another source of income."

He parks next to a pond and motions for me to get out with him. I follow suit and we climb onto his tailgate with our drinks in hand.

"So, what's keeping you from pulling the trigger?" I ask, sipping from my cup while I enjoy the stillness of the pond.

He shakes his head. "I don't know. I guess the thought of moving back home and building my business all over again scares me a little. To be honest, I never thought I'd come back to this place until he did, and now I feel like I need to. Grandpa left us some money, and I think this is probably the best thing we could use it for."

"Do you and your brother get along?"

"Yeah, we do. He's quite a bit younger than me, but we've been through a lot together." He pauses as his face turns soft, as if the pain is still fresh. "When he was a baby, and I was eleven years old, my mom dropped us off with my grandparents for an afternoon. She told them she had a doctor's appointment in the next town and she would be right back." He pauses and looks out over the water. "She never came back. I still don't know where she went. My grandparents ended up raising us and we never heard from her again. It made Cody and I pretty close."

I reach over and touch his leg, rubbing at his knee with my thumb. "I'm sorry, Andrew. That's awful."

He continues. "My dad was in jail for most of my life. We've never had a relationship. My brother doesn't know who his dad is. Our grandparents are both gone now." He lets out a breath. "He's all I've got and aside from his fiance, I'm all he's got. I'd love to be close by, so when he has kids of his own, they will know what it's like to have an actual family. Hell, I'd like to know what it's like to have an actual family myself."

"It sounds to me like you know exactly what you want to do." I say and nudge him with my shoulder.

If only it were that easy for me.

# Chapter 18

I climb out of Andrews' truck and say goodbye as we part ways. We've been parked in his driveway for ten minutes now, but as soon as he put the truck in park we became... preoccupied, for lack of a better word.

What I thought was going to be a gentle kiss goodbye ended up turning into a full on make-out session in his truck. If he didn't have work to do at Drip this morning, and I didn't have to get clocked in for my own job, who knows how much further it could have gone.

As I cross his front yard to my house, I can feel him watching me. Just as I open the front door, I turn and look back at him with a smile, and confirm my feeling.

Last night, I thought that our steamy session was only because of convenience and liquor. I'm right next door. We're both available and lonely. Of course, it would make sense for the two of us to enjoy one another's company. Today, however, was different. We held hands in his truck; we chatted, and he took me to a special place for my opinion on a tough decision. It's almost like... we could actually become something.

I have to admit; I like this guy. A lot. Is it a good idea? Absolutely not. While he may live back in Fawn Creek soon, I am still not convinced that I want to stay here. Sure, this short time since I've been back has been great. However, do I really want to make Fawn Creek my permanent home all over again? Do I want to be intertwined with my parents again? I shake my head. It just makes so little sense. But what does anymore?

I step inside the house and head straight to the dining room. When Hazel moved in, one wall of the dining room already had floor to ceiling shelves. I'm sure they were actually made for holding fine china and knick-knacks, but Hazel used them to create her own library. She wasn't exactly a fine china kind of woman after all.

I run my hand along the books on the shelf until I land on one that just seems to stick out to me. The book's spine proclaims the title, "The Bookshop on Main." I smirk at the book and pull it towards me, quickly discovering that it isn't a novel at all. I open the cover and discover that it's a box painted to look like a book. The detailed paint job on the outside makes it look remarkably like worn leather. Inside, I find a note and an envelope. I quietly unfold the paper and find that it's addressed to me. Seeing my name in her handwriting brings back a rush of emotions that I wasn't quite expecting, but again Hazel always seems to know exactly when I need her the most. Through blurry eyes, I unfold the paper and read.

*Tyler,*

*If you're reading this, I can only assume that I have gone to heaven to be with Grandpa Karl and you are the new owner of my house.*

*I know you left Fawn Creek some time ago, and I'm sure you are wondering why I left this place to you. No, it wasn't some elaborate scheme to get you back to your hometown, but more so because I want you to always have a place that you can call home. Maybe you want to fix it up and keep it as a place to stay when you come home to visit. Maybe you'll rent it out to someone else in town. Perhaps you'll sell it and use the money to buy a house somewhere far from here.*

*What you do with this place is completely up to you, but I hope that this house at least brings you back to this town I love so much, even if just for a little while. I hope you can spend some days enjoying the simplicity of a small town, surrounded by the people that love you. Allow this town to slow you down and find you some peace.*

*And, just in case you have any inkling to do so, I want you to know that I still think you really need to open up your bookstore. While I can't be your first customer anymore, I'll still always be cheering for you from above.*

*I left half of my savings to you, and I feel like that should be more than enough to get started on your dream. You could open one in Fawn Creek, your new town, or somewhere you've never been before. It's all up to you.*

*Whatever you do with it, I hope you use it to follow your dreams. You were made to change the world. You just might need a little push to do it.*

*Love,*

*Hazel*

*P.S. I found your old business plans and sketches for your shop and included them with this letter. Maybe they will inspire you to open your store after all these years. I hope if nothing else; it gives you a smile. I love you, kiddo.*

I fold the note back to the way I found it and remove the yellowed papers from inside the manila envelope. The image almost takes my breath away. I don't remember drawing this photo, but it becomes so familiar once its in front of me. I had drawn the small brick building downtown. The windows are covered in signs proclaiming, "BOOK SALE!". The banner across the front door declares the name of the business as "The Bookshop on Main." Just like what was written on the faux book I found it in. The second page was full of business information, as dreamt up by a ten-year-old, of course. I wrote the different sections the store would have (non-fiction, fiction, kids, religious, cookbooks, etc.) and I had detailed drawings of the kids' area complete with plenty of bean bag chairs for comfortable seating. I had it all figured out at ten years old. If only I knew I could make it work as an adult. Even with the money that's coming to me, is it worth the risk? What if I fail and lose everything Hazel worked so hard to save for me?

Right now, I can only put my predicament to the side and clock in for work. The rest of the day goes by in a blur. When I'm not busy assisting customers, I find pockets of time to work on painting the house. As the evening draws near, and I'm just finishing up the second coat in the bathroom, I'm interrupted by a knock at the door.

I can't help but immediately feel excited. While Andrew didn't tell me he was coming over tonight, I have a feeling it's going to be him, anyway. Who else could it possibly be? After spending the last few evenings together, I'm enjoying our new little routine.

"Who is it?" I call out across the room, as I head towards the door.

"Uber Eats." Andrew yells back from the porch.

I grin and pull the door open. I'm half expecting him to pull me in for a kiss, but his hands are full. He walks right past me to the kitchen with a cast iron pot in his oven mitt covered hands.

"I didn't know this was a daily thing." I say, following him into the kitchen. "Good thing it was your turn, though, otherwise you might have starved tonight."

"You had a busy day." He says, looking around the room. "It looks so good in here." He puts the pot on the stove and finally leans in to kiss me lightly. He presses his forehead against mine and kisses my nose. "Be right back." He whispers, before turning and heading right back out the door.

I move to the sink to wash my hands and as I'm drying them on a floral dishtowel; he comes back in with a cake pan full of cinnamon rolls.

"Are we having breakfast for dinner?" I ask, moving towards the covered pot on the stove. But once I lift the lid, a savory scent hits my nose, catching me off guard. "Chili?" I ask, confused.

"What, you don't like chili?" He asks, leaning against the counter, arms crossed over his chest with a raised brow.

"I like chili." I scrunch my nose. "But I'm confused about the cinnamon rolls."

"Don't act like you've never had chili with cinnamon rolls."

"No." I shake my head. "That's not a thing."

"You went to school here in Fawn Creek, right?"

"Yes."

"We used to eat this in the cafeteria like once a month." He says.

"I most certainly did not eat chili with cinnamon rolls in the cafeteria. Maybe only old people like you were served that." I say, scrunching my nose.

"What a minute. How old do you think I am?" He asks as he

works on pulling bowls and a plate from the cabinet.

"Based on your food choices, I'm thinking at least 87," I respond, crossing my arms.

"I'm 33! How old are you?" He asked, backing away from me suspiciously.

"I'm 28." I ponder for a second. "So, maybe they stopped the chili and cinnamon roll thing after your class."

"Nope, my little brother is 22. They definitely served it to him, too. I remember Grandma used to make it for us all the time and we talked about it. I can't believe you don't remember this."

"I definitely never mixed the two together, if they served them this way." I take a seat at the table.

"Well, try it." He sets a bowl in front of me and takes a seat. "It's a Midwestern delicacy."

I roll my eyes. "Since you have such strong feelings about this combination, I will try it just for you, but I will not like it."

I tear off a piece of roll while scrunching my nose. Cautiously, I dip the bread into the chili and bring it to my mouth. However, I am pleasantly surprised once the flavors hit my tongue. The sweetness of the cinnamon roll mixes with the spicy flavor of the chili, and I don't know why, but the combination works. It works really, really well actually. "Holy crap. That's fantastic." I say, before scooping another spoonful of chili into my mouth. "Who would have thought that those completely different things would be so good together?"

"Kinda like me and you." He says with a wink.

His words make me melt, deep at my core and I know for sure that I'm in a lot deeper than I ever planned to be.

* * *

*Cock-a-doodle-doo!*

"Is that a rooster?" Andrew mumbles into my hair. A small sliver of light peeks into the room between my bedroom curtains, awakening us from our first night together.

"His name is Fernandez. I've been wondering where he is." I say, rolling over and snuggling in close to Andrew's chest, breathing in his scent.

He leans down to kiss my forehead. "Friend of yours?"

"More like frenemies." I scoff. "He woke me up on my first morning here, and I haven't seen him since. I've been worried about him."

"Worried enough to name him, I see," He jokes.

"It makes it harder to hate him if he has a name. I have no idea where he belongs. I didn't know you could have chickens in city limits, actually."

"I don't think you can," he answers, pulling me in tighter. "If I remember correctly there was a fight about that at a city council meeting."

I look up at him. "Do you think he's lonely? Maybe we can find a farm to take him to, so he has some friends."

Andrew rolls me onto my back and lies on top of me, kissing my nose. "You're really worried about him, aren't you?"

I nod. "I am. Life is really lonely when you don't have a community. I don't want Fernandez to be alone."

He kisses my lips gently. "You are so freaking weird." He says with a sigh. "But I really like that about you. I'll see what I can do about finding Fernandez a place to go."

"Thank you."

He rolls over next to me and pulls me close. "I could get used to this."

As soon as I hear those words, my heart drops into my stomach. As much as I enjoy what is happening at the moment, I really enjoyed last night even more. After dinner, we sat down on the couch to talk. Except there wasn't much talking at all. We quickly picked up where we had left off the night before, this time with no interruptions.

Shivers run down my skin as I remember him carrying me to my bedroom, where we had some of the most incredible sex of my life. It's insane to me because usually there is something awkward about your first time, but not with him. Everything was just so natural. There was no learning curve. Almost as though we already knew one another's bodies. Afterwards, we fell asleep in each other's arms like we've done it a million times over. I'm not afraid to admit that I would love to replay last night over and over at least a million more times. It's clear that I'm falling for him, and it terrifies me.

Once again, I'm facing the fact that I'm going to have to give up what I want for the man I want to be with. He's most likely going to settle in Fawn Creek, and live out the rest of his days alongside his family. Which means, if I want him and we make it work, I will be right here too. It's crazy, isn't it? All these years I couldn't wait to get out of this town, to build a new life. Now, everything I want in life could be possible right back in this same old place. The only question is, am I ready to be back here?

We lay in silence, staring into each other's eyes for a few moments. He runs a finger along my jawline and smiles softly. His eyes hold a bit of a sparkle that I haven't seen since the day we met. I hate thinking that in a few days this will all be over and who knows what will happen between us? I wish I could freeze time.

When we finally separate, he rolls over to check the time on his phone. "I hate to say it, but I'm going to have to go. I'm doing some more work at Drip today." He slowly climbs out of bed to get dressed. As he pulls on his jeans, he looks down at me with soft eyes. "Can I see you this afternoon?"

"Yes, please." I whisper as he leans down to kiss me goodbye. I let my fingers graze across his torso. The touch of his skin under my fingers sends shivers down my spine.

"I can't wait." He whispers back.

My stomach turns again as I watch him leave.

*Me too. And that's what I'm afraid of.*

# Chapter 19

**Avery: Hey, can you see if your parents have any folding tables we can borrow for this weekend?**

**Me: Way ahead of you. I'm about to go over there and see what they've got.**

**Avery: Perfect!**

Just before I walk to my car, I open the mailbox and find an envelope addressed to me from Harrison Law Firm. I frown down at the return label, confused as to why I'd be receiving anything from a lawyer's office. For a second, I consider not even opening it yet. It's been an incredible morning, waking up next to Andrew, and whatever is in this envelope would surely ruin it, right? Fortunately for me, I have just enough anxiety that I couldn't possibly move on with my life without knowing what is inside.

I take a deep breath and open the seal, preparing for the worst. However, inside, I find a letter regarding Hazel's estate. The letter reiterates the fact that I was named as her sole beneficiary, as far as her house and half of the contents of her bank account. I had fully expected it to take another six to eight months before the funds were going to be available to me. However, because all of her bills had been taken care of, including funeral expenses, there was nothing else to wait for. Enclosed with the letter is a check. A check for one hundred and twenty thousand dollars.

I gasp for air, shocked at the number I'm reading in front of me. Surely, I'm reading it wrong. Hazel couldn't have had this kind of money just sitting around, could she? After I scan over the check and the letter once more, I realize that I'm not just seeing things. Hazel blessed me even more than I had ever expected. I make a note to ask my mother about this after I get to their house. Did she even know that Hazel had this kind of money? If she did, why hadn't she told me? What a whirlwind of a day this has turned out to be.

As I pull out of the driveway, I decide to run by the bank first. The last thing I need is to lose this check. Thankfully, I've been able to use the same bank since I was sixteen, thanks to there being a branch in the city not far from my old house. I pull up to the drive-thru window. The teller, Chloe, a girl I went to high school with beams at me from behind the glass. "Tyler! I heard you were back in town. How are you?" She asks, as I place the signed check and a deposit slip into the drawer.

"I'm doing great. How are you?" I ask in return.

She pulls the check from the drawer and flips it over to read the amount. "Oh, yeah, looks like you are doing pretty good." She jokes.

I frown. Chloe was one of the biggest gossips when we were in school. I can only imagine that she didn't outgrow that. The news about my deposit will surely be all over town by the end of the day.

"Yeah." I answer dryly. "It's from my dead grandma, so I wouldn't say I'm that excited about it."

The color drains from her face. "Oh. My gosh. I am so

sorry. I'll be right back." She says, before taking the check and disappearing around the corner.

For a second, I feel bad about being rude to her, but then I remember when she told everyone that I had a crush on Kevin Peterson in the third grade. It was so embarrassing and I would have changed schools if I could have without moving to another town. I'm not saying I typically hold grudges, but, okay, maybe I do.

Sure, getting this inheritance from Hazel is incredible. Between that and her house, I could really do anything I want in life. But I'd still rather have her here instead. It's crazy how the grief seems to come in waves. One moment, I'm fine, and the next my heart is yearning for the days when she was here. All I can do is hope that it'll get easier in time, but I have a feeling it won't.

When I leave the bank, I drive to my parents' house, reeling from the events of this morning. Per usual, I need something to distract myself with. Gathering things for the yard sale will work just fine, and I plan to spend all day pricing and organizing merchandise between customers at my day job.

Much to my surprise, when I get home I find mom's car missing. Dad's truck is sitting in the driveway, though. I knock on the door and when it goes unanswered; I open the unlocked door and stick my head inside. "Dad? Mom? Anyone here?" I yell.

I'm met with no answer. Weird. If they were both gone in Mom's car, the door should be locked. Actually, the door is normally locked all the time, anyway. I think they are on the few people in Fawn Creek that lock their door during the day.

I step inside and walk through the house quietly. Dad's full coffee cup is still on the kitchen counter, and at the risk of sounding like Goldilocks, it's still warm.

I quietly step through the kitchen to the laundry room and then out to the garage when I find him. I almost miss seeing him, but I hear a gasp and it catches my attention.

"Hello? Dad?" I ask, carefully creeping around his project truck, parked in the middle of the two-car garage. That's when I find him on the other side of the truck, laying on the ground. The panicked look in his eyes and the limp state of his body cause my heart to pick up speed.

"Dad! Are you okay?" I ask, rushing to his side. He's breathing, and he's conscious, which is good news, but he's clutching his chest and can't respond. My eyes search his and I try everything within me to keep him calm. "I'm going to call 911, okay?"

His eyes almost look as though he's begging me for help. I sit down on the floor, gripping his hand while I dial the number.

"9-1-1, what's your emergency?" the dispatcher asks.

I have to steady my breathing to respond to her. "I think my dad is having a heart attack." I tell her, my voice shaking. Anxiously, I look again at my father while I grip his hand. All my life he has been the strong one. He has been the one that can fix anything and handle any problem, the one I can turn to no matter what. But today, it's up to me to be there for him and I am scared to death.

"We will get help there immediately. What's your address?" She asks.

I rattle off their address, dad's name, his age and the fact that he is conscious to the dispatcher.

While we wait, I can't do much else other than try to keep him calm. His skin, which always looks like he's fresh off the beach with a tan, has a paleness that I've never seen before. He looks as terrified as I feel. His body looks broken and all I want to do is cry out, but I resist, knowing I need to keep him calm.

Within minutes, I hear sirens approaching, and I open the garage door for the EMTs. My entire body is shaking and I'm having trouble deciding what to do next. I've never been great at handling stressful situations, and mostly I feel like I black out for the entire event.

As soon as they get dad on the stretcher and into the ambulance, I call my mom. She's at the salon getting her hair done and I have to try twice to get her on the phone. I quickly tell her what is going on while I follow the ambulance out of our neighborhood. The entire drive to the hospital, I only have one thought. I've already lost Hazel. Please, don't let me lose my dad, too. Without him, I really may fall apart.

Who knew this day would take a turn so damn fast?

\* \* \*

I'm sitting in a chair in the waiting room, scrolling through my Facebook feed in an attempt to occupy my mind when my mother enters the room. Her hair is still wet and from the look of her red blotchy face, she cried all the way here. Owen, the neighboring town where the hospital is located, is about half an hour away from Fawn Creek.

"Any news?" She quickly approaches me., while looking anxiously around the waiting room.

I shake my head and pull her in for a hug. "Nothing yet." I say, trying to fight back the tears. "Mom, I'm so scared." I whisper. "Seeing Dad like that, that was the worst thing I've ever seen in my life." The tears are flowing freely now, with no sign of stopping.

Mom raises her hand to my cheek and brushes a tear away. "I know, baby. I am too." She grips both of my hands with hers. "But he's going to be okay, you hear me? We are going to be strong and we are going to have faith that our time with him is far from over."

I sniffle and brush away the remaining tears. "I love you, Mom." I whisper.

"I love you, too. And so does your dad."

Just then, a doctor makes her way into the waiting room and calls for the family of Jerry Burris. Mom and I get up together to move towards her.

"I'm Dr. McIntosh," the tall, redheaded doctor introduces herself and shakes our hands. She turns to my mom and speaks. "Your husband suffered a heart attack today. He is very lucky that your daughter found him when she did and quickly called the ambulance." Mom turns to me with misty eyes and squeezes my hand. "He's stable, but he is going to require surgery. We are going to need to place a stent to make sure this doesn't happen again."

Mom remains silent, but the squeeze of her hand feels incredibly reassuring.

"Do either of you have questions?" The doctor asks, looking back and forth between the two of us.

"When can we see him?" I ask.

"You can see him now, but it needs to be quick so that we can prepare him for surgery."

"Thank you, Doctor." My mom says quietly, a tear running down her face.

The doctor's words ring in my ears. "He is very lucky that your daughter found him when she did."

*What if I was still in OKC? Would I have lost my dad today?*

\* \* \*

While Dad is in surgery, I run back to Fawn Creek and pack a bag for the two of them. I know mom will be at the hospital with dad for at least one night, if not two. The thirty-minute drive there and back gives me plenty of time to think, probably more time than what is actually good for me.

Once I walk into my parents' house, I quickly get to work on packing. I'm on autopilot, handpicking their clothes, mom's makeup bag, phone chargers, and medications as per mom's list. Once I have everything they need, I stop at home to grab my phone charger, a cardigan and my Kindle. I don't know how long I'll be there, but I want to be prepared just in case.

Andrew's driveway is empty. Part of me had hoped I could catch him while I was home, but another part of me is relieved. I'm not ready to have the "what are we?" talk with him that I am fully aware I need to initiate. It's inevitable, but I'll happily put it off for another day. I'm terrified to ask him what is going to happen on Sunday when he goes back home. Trying to figure it out is too overwhelming. I can only handle one disaster at a time, and right now, my focus has to be on my dad.

I can't stop picturing what he looked like when I found him today. All my life, he's been immortal, as far as I was concerned. If something needed fixed, he would take care of it. If I needed help with anything, he would figure it out. He's my lifeline. I could always rely on him, and I knew he would be there. Today, however, he looked so fragile and it scares me. Life without him here is something I've never imagined. I don't know what we would do. Especially my mom.

At this moment, I feel my heart change. This settles it for me. I can't leave Fawn Creek. It doesn't matter what I wanted in the past, or what I thought the plan was for my life.

My life is here. My family is here. I want to be close to my parents in case they need me and to see my best friend more often than just once or twice a year. I want to spend more time with my loved ones outside of funerals and holidays. The community I want is right here. This is home and I'm staying.

That settles it. When I finally talk to Andrew, I can tell him I'm staying. The ball can be in his court. Maybe we have a chance at a happily ever after, after all.

# Chapter 20

It's after ten o'clock at night when I pull back into my driveway and kill the engine on my car. I take a moment to rest my forehead on my steering wheel. I'm exhausted. Honestly, I still can't believe everything that's happened in the last twenty-four hours. Was it really just this morning that I woke up in Andrew's arms? It feels like a lifetime ago.

But, at least all is well, for now. Dad did great in surgery and he's going to be okay. My mom is calm now, knowing that he is alright. Me? I'm just relieved to see everyone I love in one piece.

I glance next door to Andrew's house. His truck is home, but the lights are all off. I completely forgot until I got back to the hospital that we had plans for tonight. By then, there wasn't much I could do. I don't have his number. Honestly, I've never needed it until now. I tried looking him up on Facebook, but he apparently doesn't have social media. Who in the world doesn't have a social media account these days? Andrew Hayes, that's who. Eventually, Dad was out of surgery and I got distracted by that, giving up my search. I decided I'd catch him when I got home. Now, it appears that will have to wait until tomorrow.

I wearily drag myself inside the house and after a quick shower, I succumb to the exhaustion of the day. Falling asleep as soon as my head hits the pillow.

I must have been exhausted because I don't even stir until just after nine in the morning, when someone wakes me by banging on my front door. Assuming it's Andrew, I climb out of bed and quickly rush to answer, not bothering to put on pants or even check out the peephole before I fling open the door. The person on the other side is far from who I was expecting.

"Elliott?" I step back, taking in the sight of the man standing on my porch. Of course, he would show up as soon as I really feel like I'm figuring things out. The last thing I need is for him to try to get back together with me. "What are you doing here?" I ask, bracing myself for his answer.

He snarls. "Why are you answering your front door dressed like that? Especially if you didn't know who it was?" He asks, arms crossed over his chest and a judgmental look across his face.

I stare down at my naked legs, sticking out from under an oversize T-shirt. "Listen, it's been a long couple of days." I say as tears start building in my eyes.

His judgmental expression turns remorseful. "What's wrong?" he asks, with genuine concern. That is enough to cause my tears to fall once again.

"Dad had a heart attack yesterday." I respond through my sniffles.

Without warning, Elliott moves towards me to give me a hug. I don't fight it. We may not be together anymore, but this man was my life for three years. I don't hate him. I hate how much time we wasted, but neither of us is the bad guy. Sometimes things just don't work out, right?

Honestly, a hug feels good after what I went through yester-day, and for just a second, I melt into his embrace. Finally, I step back, inviting him into the house, and he closes the door behind us.

I excuse myself before padding to the kitchen to start the coffeepot. Then, I move to my room to get dressed. I throw on sweatpants and a bra because even though he's seen me millions of times in much less; it feels weird now to allow myself to be so exposed to him. It's strange how much can change in such a short time. The entire time I dress, my mind jumps to conclusions about why he's here. Is it to argue? Or what if he changed his mind? What if the time apart made him realize he loves me and he wants to settle down and give me the life I wanted?

How in the hell am I supposed to tell him I am falling for someone else so quickly?

"Coffee?" I offer Elliott when I reappear in the living room.

He declines, so I make myself a cup and then join him. I take a seat across the room to put plenty of space between the two of us.

His head swivels around the newly painted space. "It looks so different here. Did you do all this yourself?" He asks, in what appears to be an attempt to make small talk.

I nod, "I did. How'd you know where to find me?"

"There's only so many places to look in Fawn Creek." He smirks.

"I guess so." I pull a throw blanket over my lap. Even fully dressed now, I feel more exposed sitting here with him, knowing that he's been watching my every move from afar.

"How's your dad?" He asks casually, as though driving to Fawn Creek and showing up in my doorway unannounced is a regular thing for him.

"He's okay." I nod. "He had surgery yesterday and they are

just watching him now. Hopefully, he will be home soon." I turn to look at him and sigh. "Elliott, why are you here?"

He shrugs, casually. "I found some of your stuff after you left. I thought maybe you'd want it back."

I shake my head. "So you just decided to just drive three hours up here to give me stuff that you could have shipped? That makes no sense. You always hated driving down here."

Elliott lets out a deep sigh and drags the palms of his hands down the sides of his face. I watch him wearily and wait for him to speak. I have not had enough coffee for this beating around the bush business and my patience is wearing thin.

"Well, I also came to talk to you." He pauses for a beat. "Tyler... I'm so sorry."

I take another sip of my coffee and put a hand up to interrupt him. "Elliott, we don't need to do this. You and I are not meant to be together." I say, feeling almost bad for the guy. Obviously, he's here because he misses me and I just have no feelings for him anymore. "This was best for us."

He fidgets in his seat. "That's actually not it." He looks down at his hands that he is wringing over and over. "I....." He looks up into my eyes again. "Kinda met someone."

His words knock the air from my lungs and it makes no sense to me. I've met someone too. This shouldn't hurt the way it does, but I can't ignore the sting of it all.

"I know it's soon.... but I think I'm going to propose to her." He whispers.

In an instant, my hurt turns to anger. "Wait... what?" I say. "Surely I didn't hear you right. Last I knew, you would never get married."

Two weeks ago, we were living together, and he was content with me being his live-in girlfriend for the rest of his life. He had no desire to get married, but now he does? What kind of asshole comes all the way up here to tell me this?

"I know. I'm sorry, I just can't explain it." He says.

I stare down at the floor, trying to channel my feelings. "Who is it? Do I know her?"

He shakes his head. "Her name is Jessica. We work together."

I rack my brain. Why does that name sound familiar? Did we meet at a party or a company picnic? That's when it hits me, the girl I met after hot yoga. "Is she friends with Mandy and Caroline? Pretty thin brunette?" I ask with a furrowed brow.

He swallows hard. "Yes. How do you know her?"

"I met her when I went to hot yoga with them, the weekend before we broke up." I say, blinking back my tears. But this time it's because I'm livid, not because I'm hurt. "So, how long were you messing around with her while we were together? I never pegged you as a cheater, but not much surprises me about you anymore."

Elliott stands immediately from the sofa to defend himself. "I know it looks bad, but I swear there was nothing going on until you left. She and I were just friends."

"Well, how convenient for you that as soon as I was gone, she was there." I say rolling my eyes, and pointing to the door. "Please get out of my house. We are done here."

"Tyler, I'm sorry for hurting you. This is exactly what I didn't want to happen." He pauses, as though waiting for a response. When I offer none, he makes his way towards the door. "I'll leave your things on the porch." He mutters before walking out my door for what will hopefully be the last time ever.

As soon as he's gone, I race across the room and turn the deadbolt. I then watch through the window as he leaves two boxes on the porch and backs out of my driveway.

I lean my back against the door and try to comprehend what just happened here. My feelings are all over the place and it's hard to make sense of them. I'm hurt and angry. I want to throw something and cry and scream. But also, I'm mad at myself for even being upset? I don't want him. I don't miss him and I haven't missed him at all since I left, but damn, what a punch in the gut. He may as well have gotten me a card that said, "Like always, you'll never be enough."

I admit, though, it hurts. For three years, I really tried to be what he wanted. I tried to make him happy. All I wanted was for him to want to spend his life with me, but in the end; I wasn't enough. Then suddenly, she came along and she was everything I couldn't be. He had no desire to marry me, but he can't wait to settle down with her. I can't believe I was willing to give up my chance to be a mother for a man that saw nothing in me.

I move my eyes toward Andrew's house. His driveway is empty. I try to remember if his truck was there when Elliott arrived, but I don't think I even looked that way. Elliott's appearance had me too shocked to even notice.

My brain is swimming and I don't even know how to feel anymore. I wish I felt like I was enough for anyone, or anything. But, just like my mother and Elliott and his stupid family and friends, I feel like maybe I am only meant to be mediocre. I lay down on the couch and curl up with a blanket, and cry myself to sleep.

# Chapter 21

After a long nap, I wake up to the sound of Fernandez screaming outside my window once again. Immediately, I run to the window but find that Andrew is still not home. Disappointed, I grab some bread from the kitchen and walk out to the porch to try to make friends with the neighborhood rooster.

I lean over the porch railing and find the Fernandez waiting for me. "Hi, Fernandez. You hungry?" I ask, before I throw crumbled pieces of bread towards him. When the first piece of bread lands on the ground, he jumps, but after cautiously approaching the food, he devours it. He slowly makes his way towards me and I throw another piece of bread down at his feet.

"You know what, Fernandez? You have quite the life." I say with a shrug. "What I wouldn't give to just be able to scream at the top of my lungs whenever I feel like it." I confess.

Fernandez cocks his head sideways and stares at me. He's obviously not amused by me.

"Who do you belong to?" I ask him with a frown. My eyes scan the street, reminding myself to ask my neighbors about him. If he's someone's pet, I shouldn't just ship him off to a farm. Someone might miss him. The last thing I need is to be labeled as a rooster thief.

With sad eyes, I look towards Andrew's house again. Something isn't right, and I wish I knew what was going on. I'm trying to remain hopeful that he will be back later tonight, but the longer he's gone, the more I worry he won't return. It's not like him to just disappear.

In an effort to distract myself, I decide to make some comfort food for dinner. Making lasagna from scratch, paired with garlic bread and salad, is just enough to keep my mind and hands busy. But, unfortunately, when I get done building the pan full of food, Andrew still isn't home. Still nothing by the time I pull the lasagna from the oven either. I place the food on the stove to cool, and decide to call mom to check in on dad, another distraction tactic.

"Hello?" Mom answers on the first ring. I can hear the beeping of hospital equipment in the background, telling me that dad is still hooked up and being monitored. She sounds exhausted.

"Hey. Just checking in." I say, "How's it going there?"

"He's doing good. I think we are going home tomorrow morning." She says, groggily.

"Good. I'll be glad to have you guys at home. You sound exhausted. Anything I can do to make your transition back home easier?"

"Oh, no. The ladies from the church have already organized a meal train, not that we need anymore food after Hazel's funeral." She adds with a bit of a groan. "We will be just fine. Dad's just getting restless and ready to get out of that bed."

"I bet he is." I say, thoughtfully. Dad has never been good at sitting still for long periods of time and being fussed over is his least favorite thing. "I'll be ready to see you both get back to normal."

"Us too." She pauses for a beat. "Tyler, thank you so much

for being there for your dad. I hate to think of what would have happened had you not been around."

"Me too, mom." I agree with a nod, as if she can see me. "I'm so glad I could be there."

"It's been so good having you home. We're going to miss you when you leave again..." she trails off, letting the sentence hang in the air.

"Well, I don't think you'll have to worry about that." I pause. "Mom, I think I'm going to stick around here for a while. Maybe plant some roots." I let out a deep breath as soon as the words leave my body. This is the first time I've admitted it to anyone, and I'm still having a hard time believing it myself.

My mom's voice immediately perks up. "Really?"

"Yes. I just hate the idea of being anywhere else in case you guys need me. Besides, I'll admit, this town has grown on me over the last couple of weeks."

"That makes me so happy." She says, with obvious joy in her voice.

"Me too." I say as I glance towards the window and notice movement in Andrew's driveway. My heart picks up speed. "I'm going to let you go. Let me know when you guys are home, okay? Love you."

"Love you, too." She answers with a pep in her voice that she did not have when I called a few minutes ago.

Having that conversation takes a load off my shoulders, but now I need to focus on what's happening next door.

I move to the window to peek out the curtain, expecting to see Andrew's truck. Instead, I see a royal blue SUV parked in his place. I watch as a woman steps out of the car. Instantly, I feel a small wave of jealousy come over me. I'm sure no one could blame me. The woman's a knockout and can't be much older than twenty-one. She's dressed in business casual, wearing jeans, a white top, and a blue blazer that matches her car perfectly. Her long dark hair is in soft curls and falls to the center of her back. Quickly, she climbs the steps, unlocks the door and disappears inside.

The rational part of my brain kicks in just in time, and I realize there has to be some sort of reasonable explanation. But who is she? Maybe his soon to be sister-in-law? I can't think of anyone else that might be there, especially when he's not. I don't know if he really has any friends here other than me and his brother. But then, how much do I really know about him? In silence, I continue to stand behind the curtain, watching for movement. It doesn't take long before she is outside again. She immediately moves to her car and pulls a For Sale sign from the back.

Before I can stop myself, I open the door and walk outside, waving to her. "Hey! Hi. I'm Tyler." I say, making my way towards her.

"Hi, I'm Ava Montgomery. Nice to meet you." She sticks out her hand to shake mine, while leaning the sign against her torso.

"You too!" I pause, rocking back on my heels, trying to think of the least invasive way to ask for information. "I didn't think he was going to list the house until later this week. You caught me by surprise."

She stands on the bar at the bottom of the sign, causing it to slowly work itself into the ground. "Yeah, same." She says, stepping backwards to survey her handiwork. "He stopped by the office and said that he had an emergency and had to get back to Texas immediately. We did all the listing paperwork virtually and now here we are." She dusts off her hands onto her jeans. "Hopefully, selling it will be just as quick and painless as the listing."

I hold up my hand to make the universal sign and say, "Fingers crossed."

"Speaking of, I heard you're planning to sell soon, too." Ava says with a smile. Quickly, she hands me a business card she pulls from her back pocket. "Call me when you're ready. I'd love to help you."

"Yeah, I'll do that." I take the card and hold it carefully, not seeing any reason to tell her that I'm planning to stick around. "Have a good night." I say with a wave as I make my way back to my house.

What kind of emergency could have come up? Why didn't he leave me a note at the least? When will I hear from him again? I feel like an idiot. I slept with him last night and then he just up and left with no warning. Maybe he's not that great of a guy after all.

I walk to the mailbox to check the mail, hoping to find a note from Andrew inside. But there's nothing other than a wedding invitation from Sierra. I toss it on the entryway table when I walk back into the house and shuffle to the kitchen to quiet the beeping oven timer.

No matter how good it smells or how hard I worked on it, I've officially lost my appetite. Who knew you could have your heart broken twice in one day?

* * *

"Enjoy." I say, as I hand a plastic bag full of Hazel's old clothes across the table to one of my neighbors.

184

"Oh, I will." The grey-haired woman says with a smile. "Hazel always had the best sense of style. They will have a good home."

"I'm so glad." I tell her and watch as she makes her way back to her house. As soon as she's gone, I pick up my phone and find that I still have no notifications.

"Still nothing?" Avery asks with a frown as she refolds some clothes on the table.

I shake my head. "Nope. Maybe he really is just an asshole, after all." I say. It's been three days since Andrew disappeared with no warning. Thanks to Avery, she was able to get his number from her brother, Bryan. I sent Andrew a text asking if he was okay, and it's been sitting on read ever since. He hasn't even bothered to answer me. "I mean, he slept with me and then disappeared the next day with no warning. Typical guy." I tell Avery.

"I don't get it." She says. "That is so not like him."

I sigh. "That's what you keep telling me. Maybe you don't know him all that well after all." I say.

"I'm sorry, friend. I really thought you guys had something."

I give Avery a tight-lipped smile. "Me too."

# Chapter 22

*Two Months Later*

The Blackledge Event Center is the focal point of downtown Fawn Creek and one of the city's best hidden gems. As Avery and I approach the building, I can't help but be in awe of its beauty. Especially when it's all lit up after dark. The glass chandeliers hanging from the tin ceiling on the third floor sparkle as they reflect the dozens of rows of string lights that hang around the room. I smile as I watch figures moving in front of the windows, hugging and laughing. It's the perfect night for a wedding reception.

I stop as we reach the building and I lean against the sandstone wall, to quickly change from my flip-flops to my heels. I refuse to walk on brick streets wearing three-inch heels. The lace cocktail dress Avery talked me into buying for this occasion just doesn't work with sandals, though. Plus, the heels make my legs look incredible, if I say so myself, so I opted to carry my party footwear until we arrived.

"When did Friday night weddings become a thing?" Avery asks me, looking up at the massive building.

"Apparently, ever since this place is booked for every Saturday of the summer. Cassidy said they had to book for a Friday or choose another venue." I shrug.

"There can't be that many weddings happening in Fawn Creek."

I shift my gaze to my reflection in the building's window and absentmindedly tousle my hair. "It's probably a mixture of reunions, weddings, baby showers and who knows what else. I guess it's a good problem for them to have. Seems like everyone around here is celebrating something right now." I frown, feeling instantly aware of the lack of forward motion in my own life.

"Our time is coming, I just know it," Avery says with a smile. "You look smoking, by the way. We will have to fight eligible bachelors off of you all night." She says, fanning herself dramatically.

I smile softly. "Thanks for being my date."

"Only a fool would turn you down." She laughs, linking her arm in mine and leading me towards the entrance.

We round the corner and enter through the double glass doors that are propped open, welcoming in the guests. The family had a private wedding ceremony outside of town earlier tonight and then invited everyone to join in on the reception downtown. There's something sweet about the idea of an intimate ceremony with just your family that makes me want that one day, too. That is, if I ever get that far. Hell, at this point, I'm wondering if I'm just meant to be alone.

Stepping into the entryway of the building, we pause at the guest book resting on a wooden pedestal. After signing in, we follow a chalkboard sign with a handwritten message proclaiming 'This way to happily ever after'.

I roll my eyes and shoot Avery a look. "So cliche." I mutter.

"Love is supposed to be cliche." She responds with a shrug. "I think it's cute."

"I suppose." Is all I can respond with.

At least someone around here is getting a happily ever after. If it's going to be anyone, I'm glad it's Sierra. It's certainly not going to be me at this rate. My recent track record is solid proof of that. Ever since Andrew disappeared without so much as a goodbye nearly two months ago, I have avoided men like it's my full-time job. I think I've given up on love, at least for now.

Instead, I'm just focusing on myself, which is exactly what I should have been doing all along. I've picked up running, something I always thought I hated, and I do it almost daily. The house is taking shape thanks to YouTube and the help of my father. I've been able to make some actual progress in the last few weeks. Who knew I could change out my light fixtures and electrical outlets all by myself? Not me. The house looks better than I ever imagined, and while it's not my dream house, it finally feels like home. Fawn Creek finally feels like home, too. My time here has really opened my eyes to what I've been missing for the last several years. Community, friendship, and a sense of belonging. All of those have been given to me right here.

We follow the carpeted staircase and pause at the second story. Quickly, I open the door to the coat closet next to the bathroom and place my sandals inside. It's unlikely that anyone else will need to use the coat room tonight since it's July in Kansas, and I don't want to carry my shoes all over the place for the rest of the night. Hopefully, I'll remember to grab them later.

Once I'm done, we proceed to the third floor. We are still early, so Avery and I grab a table in the back of the room before anyone else can claim it. After getting some charcuterie cups to snack on, and ordering the signature drink, a blueberry basil margarita, we meet back at the table to people watch. It's not long before the room fills with familiar faces.

"Ladies and gentlemen..." The DJ's voice booms from the speakers across the room. "Please let me introduce to you, for the very first time, Mr. and Mrs. Hayes."

The room fills with applause as Sierra and Cody enter the room and I feel the color drain from my face.

Hayes. Sierra's new last name is Hayes. As in, Andrew Hayes? Surely, Cody and Andrew aren't related.

Perhaps it's just a strange coincidence. I mean, if his brother was marrying my friend, then I surely would have put the pieces together long before now, right? Except, I probably wouldn't have. My life has been a bit of a blur since the day he left and I've done nothing but constantly attempt to distract myself. It hasn't been lost on me that I've been more heartbroken over Andrew than I was over ending my three-year relationship with Elliott.

I think back to the day that I received the wedding invitation. The day Andrew disappeared. I can't even say for sure what happened to that envelope. It might be buried in a pile of papers in the guest room and hell, it could have gotten thrown away by mistake. I wouldn't have even known when this event was if Cassidy hadn't reminded me constantly in the days leading up to the celebration.

I look to Avery. "Are Andrew and Cody related?" I ask, raising a brow.

Her face goes pale. "Well, maybe?" She pauses for a second before turning to me with wide eyes. "I swear, I didn't know. They are so much younger than us and all I knew was that she was marrying some guy that moved here from Texas."

Frantically, I scan the room for Andrew. Hoping I'm wrong, or maybe he just didn't come. But, in my heart I know that family is the most important thing to him. There's no way he was going to miss being here, even if it means avoiding me and sparing my feelings. The DJ plays the ChaCha Slide, and just as I think maybe he isn't here after all, I spot him.

When he enters the room, the rest of the world fades away. I can't see people dancing. I can't hear the music. Hell, I can't even remember what I'm doing here. Our eyes meet and I immediately feel my heart fall into my stomach. Now, it's my turn to run.

* * *

Just as I turn and make a dash for the hallway, I hear him call out to me. The sound of my name on his tongue cuts me deeper than I ever imagined it would. It's almost enough to make me turn around, but the tears welling in my eyes urge me to keep moving.

I lean against the stairway banister and remove my heels before descending the stairs. Once I reach the second story, I make my way to the coat closet and close the door behind me. By now, the tears have broken free and are running down my face. I use my phone as a flashlight to look for the light switch and then once the room is illuminated; I make my way to the back of the room and take a seat on a bench against the wall. Once I'm situated, I sit back and let the tears fall. One at a time they drip down, starting off slowly, but gradually building up speed as they fall against my thigh and then hit the floor. I grab my phone and set a timer for three minutes.

Hazel always told me it's okay to cry. It's good for you to get it out and sometimes you just need it. However, you can't cry forever. Eventually, you are going to have to get up and deal with whatever made you feel this way. So, you get three minutes to be emotional, and then you have to move on. Dwelling won't do anything for you, anyhow.

By the time I have one minute left on the timer, my tears are subsiding. My breathing steadies and heart rate is slowing down. My panic attack is ending. I wipe my eyes and turn off the timer, placing the phone next to me on the table once again. And then the doorknob turns.

My eyes move to the door as it slowly opens into the space. There's nowhere to hide, and my only option is to have an awkward interaction with whoever is on the other side. Never in my wildest dreams would I have assumed that Andrew would make his way into the room.

"There you are," He says, with a solemn expression on his face. "Hey. What are you doing in here?" He closes the door behind him.

I wipe my eyes and will myself to be strong. No more crying. Now we have to handle this mess. "Go back to the party, Andrew. I'm fine."

His face drops. "Tyler, just talk to me. Are you okay?"

I scoff. "When you put your house on the market and disappeared without a trace, you lost all rights to knowing how I feel."

He grimaces. "I deserve that. Tyler, I'm sorry I hurt you."

I shake my head and direct my eyes to the corner of the room to avoid eye contact. "It doesn't matter anymore. I gave you the opportunity to tell me what was going on. I texted you and you left me on read. Obviously, you got what you wanted by sleeping with me and then ghosting me. I'm over it."

He moves closer to me and then hesitates. "You're not over it and that's not what happened. Obviously, you wouldn't be crying in a coat closet at a wedding if you didn't still have feelings about this." When I don't respond, he continues. "I'm sorry, Tyler. I panicked. We slept together, and then the next day you just disappeared all day long. Then, after, your car was home as if nothing had ever happened, and so was a Tesla with Oklahoma tags. I know that was your ex."

"So, you just took off because you saw my ex's car? I could understand it if you saw me making out with him, but not a hug."

He throws his hands in the air. "What was I supposed to think? You were out on your porch with him half dressed. It looked like you two were awfully cozy."

I take a deep breath and explain. "Yes. That was my ex-boyfriend, Elliott. I didn't ask for him to show up. Truthfully, I didn't even know he was coming, and hell, I didn't know that he even knew where I was." I search Andrews' expression and the lines around his eyes soften. "I opened the door without getting dressed because I thought it was you knocking. Seeing him was just a smack in the face. It had been a rough 24 hours." I stare down at my dress. "My dad had a heart attack the morning before. I had gone to their house to get tables for the yard sale and I found him on the floor. When I told Elliott about it, I started to cry and he pulled me in for a hug. That's all."

He runs a hand through his hair and shakes his head. "I'm such an asshole. When I didn't see you all day and then I saw you with him the next morning, I assumed...."

"You assumed the worst." I interrupt him. "And that's not

fair to me. I gave you no reason to think that's who I am as a person." I pause. "Elliott came by to tell me that he had met someone and to drop off the last of my things. He's probably engaged by now to a woman that he started seeing four minutes after I walked out of his door. And I didn't care because I had found something better, you." I huff. "Or so I thought."

He moves to the bench and sits next to me in silence.

I begin again. "I liked you... a lot. And I thought we had something that could go somewhere."

"I liked you, too. I still do." He pauses. "Sorry, I know I should've talked to you first. I guess I just thought that maybe I was more into it than you were," He admits with a shrug. "I know you are planning to leave Fawn Creek and I thought maybe you decided to just get back with him after I saw his car parked outside your house. I panicked, and I left. When you texted me, I just didn't know what to say, so I said nothing. I figured you'd be gone by the time I came back here."

"I'm staying here." I respond quietly.

He turns to me, puzzled. "You're staying where?"

"Here. In Fawn Creek." I shrug. "I'm not selling the house. Summer is almost over and I've decided to stay put." I stand up from my seat and move towards the door. "So, I guess I'll see you around. Have a nice life."

I leave the room, carrying my extra shoes, and don't stop walking until I make it home.

# Chapter 23

Saturday morning I wake up with my head still swimming from the night before. I move through the house, just going through the motions. After the way I walked out on Andrew last night, I feel even more unsettled than I have in months, if that's even possible.

It's the end of July, and the hottest time of year in Kansas, but it's early enough in the day that the temperature is at least tolerable. If I'm going to get out for a run, now is my only chance.

Within minutes, I'm locking the door behind me and jogging towards the downtown area. After a lot of practice, I've figured out how to jog three miles in this place that's just under a mile wide. It requires quite a bit of zigging and zagging through almost every neighborhood.

Once my run is complete, I make my way into the business district. Just as I am approaching Drip, my eyes wander towards the building next door, like usual. I have to do a double take to catch that the "For Sale" sign is now topped with the words "Under Contract."

It shouldn't upset me. Realistically, I'm aware of that. The building needs more work than a coat of paint and some cleaning. Even with the chunk of money Hazel left for me, it'll surely never be enough to turn that place into a storefront on my own. Still yet, it stings knowing someone else will move in there. It hurts even more knowing that I'll have to see someone in the building I loved so much every time I come downtown. I shake my head, trying to clear the negative thoughts.

Was I going to buy that building? No, of course not. If I was going to, I would have done it by now. The sale means good things for Fawn Creek because that means that another business will be eventually opening in town. I need to focus on myself and what I can do with my life.

I push the door open to Drip and step towards the counter to give Devin my order. The sound of Cassidy's voice makes me jump.

"Hey girl! That was some party last night, wasn't it?"

I feel the color drain from my face. The wedding reception. I missed all of it and it's because I couldn't stand the thought of spending the evening in the same space as Andrew. At least Cassidy didn't seem to notice my absence.

"It was great!" I agree, hoping she won't call my bluff. "What are you doing at work, though? Shouldn't you be recovering?"

"Oh, I plan to! I just need to make sure the event center was cleaned up and then I'm turning the keys back in. We hired someone from Owen to take care of it, but you know me. I have trust issues." She laughs. "I'm going to make sure it's up to my standards and then I'm going to put on my pajamas and stay that way until Monday."

I pick up my coffee from the counter and stuff some cash in the tip jar. "That sounds like a good plan." I move towards the door and wave behind me. "I'll see you next week! Get some rest."

Half a block away from my house, I can see the floral arrangement on my porch. All morning, I've told myself that Andrew and I are done. I've worked to convince myself that I don't care about him and what he does next. I tell myself that I don't care if I ever speak to him again. But those flowers... Those stupid flowers make my heart flutter and I feel excited and I want nothing else in the world but for them to be from him.

I pick up the arrangement and eyeball the card, while unlocking my front door. The overwhelming scent of the pink lilies reach my nose and I pause for a second to enjoy it. Once inside, I place the flowers on the table and reach for the card.

*Tyler,*

*I'm so sorry about everything. If you'll forgive me, I'll spend the rest of my life making it up to you.*

*Love, The Asshole of Fawn Creek*

*P.S. Text me if you're willing to give me another chance.*

I sit the card down on the table and look back at the flowers. In my heart, of course I want to try again. But what if I get all wrapped up in him, only for him to leave again? Is it worth the risk?

I decide to talk things through with Avery, hoping she will have some insight for me.

**Tyler: Andrew left me flowers today while I was out on my run. He left me a note to text him if I am willing to give him another chance.**

**Avery: Did you text him?**

**Tyler: No. I'm not sure if I'll be making a huge mistake by giving him another chance.**

Avery: Do you still have feelings for him?

Tyler: Yes.

Avery: So, what's the problem?

Tyler: What if he disappears again? What if he waits until we've been together for six months and he just ghosts me?

Avery: Or what if it works out? What if you guys get married and have babies and live happily ever after?

Tyler: So, I just forgive him?

Avery: Maybe? I know he isn't going to want me to tell you this, but I'm going to. A couple of years ago, Andrew was engaged.

Tyler: Oh, to who? Someone from here?

Avery: No, he met her in Texas. They were engaged for a long time, but he could never get her to commit to a wedding date. Then suddenly, he came home to visit his grandpa and when he got back there earlier than expected; he caught her in his bed with another guy.

Tyler: Oh no. I bet that broke his heart.

Avery: It did. I shouldn't even know about it, but you know he was friends with my brother growing up and word got around town pretty quickly.

Avery: So, I'm not saying it's an excuse, but maybe that explains why he jumped to conclusions. I think you should go for it, cautiously. Talk through things with him and let him know you will not stand for him ever pulling that shit again. I think when he knows you are all in, that will help him to not run at the first sign of trouble.

Tyler: I guess I have a lot to think about.

* * *

I spend the rest of the day avoiding the card on my table. I clean the house, do laundry, bake some cookies, and then finally, I settle into the bathtub with a can of White Claw and a book to relax. It's no use. The only thing I end up reading are the same few lines repeatedly.

After several minutes of failed attempts at relaxation, I give in. I grab my phone and fire off a text before I lose the courage.

**Tyler: Hey.**

I don't even have time to put my phone down on the floor next to the tub before he answers.

**Andrew: Hi, beautiful. I was thinking I would not hear from you. How was your day?**

**Tyler: It was okay. Thank you for the flowers, by the way. They're beautiful. How was your day?**

**Andrew: Busy. Better now that I'm talking to you.**

**Tyler: Good.**

**Andrew: Tyler, I really am sorry for freaking out and disappearing the way I did. I have kicked myself every day since then because I knew I had run away from the first good thing I've had in a long time. I just didn't know how to fix it once I was gone, or if you would even want me to.**

**Andrew: I understand if you're not ready to trust me yet with your heart, but I am prepared to spend every day for as long as it takes to show you how much you mean to me.**

**Tyler: I'm willing to try this again... cautiously. But, we have to set some ground rules. And the very first rule is that we have to communicate. If either of us has a problem, we have to talk about it. Not run from it. I can't handle getting**

hurt again.

    **Andrew: Never again. I promise.**

    **Andrew: Any chance I can take you out for lunch tomorrow?**

    **Tyler: Sure! I didn't realize you were still here.**

    **Andrew: I was trying not to come on too strong. But, I'd really like to see you. I'll pick you up at 11:00.**

    **Tyler: I'll be ready.**

* * *

I spend the morning going through the motions while I wait for Andrew to arrive. After a quick run and half a pot of coffee, I finally talk myself into sitting down and opening a new book from my TBR pile. Of course, it's a lost cause because, after every paragraph, my eyes drift to the bird clock on the wall.

I smile dearly at the clock that I recently recovered from a box in the guest room. Every hour showcases a different type of bird, and when the clock strikes that hour, the clock chimes mimicking the bird in question. Finally, at eleven, the chirping sound of the White-breasted Nuthatch rings through the room, and Andrew knocks on the door.

I gently pull the door open and look up at him. It's strange because every part of me wants to jump into his arms and kiss him. However, I remind myself that I'm being cautious, both with myself and with my heart, so I refrain. "Hi." I say instead.

Andrew, however, must not feel as awkward as I do in the moment. He moves forward and closes the space between us by pulling me into a hug. As much as I know I should resist, I don't. The feel of his arms around me is comforting and safe.

"I missed you." He whispers into my hair.

I melt into him and breathe in the scent of his body wash. "I missed you, too." I tell him, meaning it with my entire heart.

He steps back and smiles gently at me. "Are you hungry?"

My stomach growls in response, loudly enough for both of us to hear, causing him to chuckle.

He gently takes my hand. "Let's get out of here."

Once we are in the truck, I buckle my seat belt and turn to him. "Well, where are you taking me?"

He smirks. "Somewhere special."

"Oh, Red Maple?" I tease, suggesting the downtown diner.

He snickers and shakes his head. "No, ma'am. I'm saving fancy places like that for our second or third date." He motions his head to the backseat of his extended cab. "I packed us a picnic. I hope that's okay."

I grin and squeeze his hand on the center console to show my approval. "Sounds perfect." I say.

Within minutes, we approach the old metal gate that we visited once before. The property he told me he was buying now has a SOLD sign at the driveway entrance. I marvel at the patches of wildflowers blooming on either side of the gate.

I turn to him with a smile. "So, you made an offer?"

He grins. "Actually, we closed last week. This is officially mine and my brother's land."

"That's amazing. Congratulations." I pause and continue to watch out the window. "Where are you staying?"

"I'll show you." He says, making his way up the driveway as the little white house comes into view. Now, however, there's a camper parked next to it. "There's my humble abode." He boasts proudly, pointing to the recreational camping equipment.

"Oh." I say, looking at the little rundown camper. This is a far cry from the type of place I would picture someone living in full time. The camper itself is quite small, honestly it's smaller than most of the minivan's I see driving around Fawn Creek. The exterior looks almost as though it's been painted with spray paint to bring some sort of cohesive look to the metal panels that have been replaced over the years.

"I know what you're thinking. The camper is just a temporary solution. I'm building a barndominium. It's just going to take some time." He says.

"You're building a barn?" I ask, puzzled.

He laughs. "No, a barndominium is a house and shop combination. The exterior is completely metal, so it will go up rather quickly. I have a group from the Amish community slated to take care of that part for me. The rest I can handle on my own, little by little." He pulls up a picture on his phone and shows me. "It'll be really nice once it's done."

I nod and take in the photos in front of me. The front of the house looks like a typical farmhouse. It has a white metal exterior with a large porch and wooden beams. The back of the house has three garage doors leading to the shop. "That's beautiful." I tell him. "So, does that mean you are going to be living there before winter?" That camper can't possibly be warm enough to sleep in once we hit below freezing temperatures.

"Yes. If nothing else, the structure will be up, and I'll be able to park the camper inside the shop to keep myself out of the elements." He assures me with a smile.

I guess at least he has it all figured out.

He pulls the truck to a stop and puts the gearshift in park before turning to face me. His face softens and a wave of seriousness washes over him. "Tyler. I need you to understand something. I'm in this for the long haul and by that I mean I'm here and I'm not going anywhere. I'm sorry that I hurt you and I'm so sorry I disappeared." He pauses. "I got into my head about things that happened to me in my past, and about people that have hurt me before. I realize now that you are not those people. You do not deserve to pay for the crap that other people put me through. And I swear I am going to spend as long as it takes proving to you how sorry I am and how much you mean to me."

A tear escapes down my face and before I can wipe it away, he brushes his thumb against my cheek and does it for me before he continues. "You are everything that I have been waiting for, for my entire life. Everything in my life that has gone wrong until now finally makes sense. I can see now that nothing ever worked out because it wasn't with you. You are my missing piece and I can't wait to show you how much you mean to me."

He leans forward and gently kisses me.

He is going to make being cautious a lot more difficult than I imagined.

# Chapter 24

Andrew lowers the tailgate of his truck before he turns to look at me. "Are you sure you're ready to say goodbye?" He asks.

I shrug. "I don't think there is any other way around it. It just has to happen."

He nods. "Welp, let's get this show on the road, then." I follow Andrew around to the back of my house, where we find Fernandez standing in the live trap we left out for him, eating leftover garlic bread.

"I can't believe no one claimed this guy," Andrew says, shaking his head as he moves to lift the cage. "I mean, look at him. Who wouldn't want him as a pet?"

"Literally every person in this neighborhood." I laugh. Over the last few weeks, I've asked everyone I've seen if they knew where Fernandez the rooster had come from. I got the same response from every Fawn Creek resident. He just randomly appeared one day, but no one knows from where. The general assumption is that he was probably dumped off. "I might actually be given a medal of honor for getting him out of here. I guess standing outside my window waking me up early isn't the worst that he's done. He apparently also loves to destroy people's gardens."

"Well, Rob and Megan are more than happy to let him live on

their farm. Megan said she has something like 50 chickens now and she won't even notice another rooster walking around." He says, as we climb into the truck.

"Good." I say with a nod. "That makes me happy to know that he will have a happily ever after of his own."

He chuckles and squeezes my hand. "You never cease to amaze me, you know that? I can't believe how kind you have been to that mean old rooster."

"He's not that mean." I say. "He's only chased me like three times, and I really think that he thought I was going to steal his food. The guy has just had a rough life. He's been fighting for survival for who knows how long."

"I just hope he will be happy." I say, gazing out the window. Andrew just laughs and shakes his head.

"What? No one is meant to do life alone." I say, turning towards him. "Everyone in this world needs some sort of village to turn to, whether it's a couple of friends, or a whole yard full of hens. Sometimes, you just don't realize it until you get thrown in the middle of it. No one should live in isolation, not even a mean old rooster named Fernandez."

He smiles. "I sure am glad I get to be a part of your village."

"I'm glad you do, too." I say with a smile.

Just then, we pull into Rob and Megan's driveway. An enormous flock of chickens immediately surrounds the truck to meet us. A lady who must be around my mothers age, steps out of the swinging screen door to meet us with a wave and a smile.

Andrew and I climb out of the truck, and Andrew introduces me to Megan. Then he introduces Megan to Fernandez.

"He's beautiful." Megan says, admiring his red and teal tail feathers.

"He is." I agree. "Thank you so much for taking him in. I hope he isn't too much of a handful."

I watch as Andrew pulls the trap from the back of his truck and opens the door. Fernandez comes trotting out with his head held high, like he owns the place. Typical. Within seconds, he joins the crowd of hens, almost as though he's been here all along.

"I think he's going to be just fine." Megan says with a smile. "Feel free to come back and visit him anytime."

* * *

"I have to admit, it really is quite quiet around here." I say, before commanding Alexa to play my red dirt playlist.

"You're missing Fernandez, aren't you?" Andrew teases. "Are you going to go steal him back from Rob and Megan?"

"No." I say with a chuckle. "He's right where he belongs."

It's been two weeks since Fernandez went to his home and one month since Andrew moved back to Fawn Creek. The days have been busy. He hit the ground running with his contracting business and has stayed consistently busy all throughout the week. His brother, Cody, has even started to work with him part-time on his days off from the local oil refinery. I'm so proud of him for all of his success, even though it means that the two of us haven't had much time together. We are simply just trying to enjoy the time that we have together.

Andrew sits across from me with his plate of enchiladas. "This looks amazing." He says, eyeballing his food.

"I hope it tastes as good as it smells." I say with a groan. "That's the good and bad side of working from home. I'm able to cook in between helping customers, which is great, because dinner is already done when I clock out. However, on the flip side, I spend all day today smelling the chicken while it cooked in the crock-pot before I put the enchiladas together. It's a strange kind of torture."

Andrew shakes his head. "Sign me up for that kind of torture, any day. Speaking of, how's work going?"

"Eh. Same old same." I say with a shrug.

He pauses thoughtfully. "Do you like what you do?" He asks, cutting into his food.

I shrug. "I don't know. I don't hate it. It's not my dream job, but it pays the bills."

"What is your dream job?" He pries, but when I don't answer, he continues. "Your bookstore?"

I grimace and stare down at my plate for a second before moving my eyes to his. "That's not an actual job. It's a silly little dream of a ten year old girl."

He scoffs. "Being a business owner is a real job. I should know." He says, before shoving a forkful of food in his mouth.

I roll my eyes. "Sure, what you do definitely qualifies as a real job. You're providing a service that there was an obvious need for in Fawn Creek, otherwise you wouldn't be as busy as you are now."

"So what's the difference? Fawn Creek doesn't have a bookstore."

"No, but Fawn Creek has access to the internet. People don't buy from bookstores anymore, they buy from Amazon and take advantage of two-day shipping."

He shakes his head. "I don't know if you've noticed, but Fawn Creek has a thriving downtown business district. If you open a store, people are going to support it."

I take a bite of my food and ponder what he says. "There's a difference between people buying things here and there, and it being a sustainable business that will support me. I'll still need an income coming in to pay my bills."

"You don't need much." He argues. "Your mortgage is paid off, you don't have a car payment. It's doable."

I frown. "Maybe.... I don't know Andrew. I've thought about it on and off for my entire life, but it's just feels irresponsible to dump money into a business that may or may not work out. Doesn't it make more sense to save it, and just work somewhere where I can bring in a reliable income?"

"At the end of your life, are you going to look back and think, 'Man, I am so glad I worked in customer service for forty years to bring in a steady paycheck?' Or are you going to wish you had followed your dreams?"

I wordlessly continue to pick at my food.

"You never know if you don't try." He says with a wink. "Hurry up and finish your food. I want to go for a walk."

I raise a brow. "Exercise? Who are you and what have you done with my boyfriend?"

* * *

After dinner, Andrew and I make our way downtown, hand in hand, towards Drip. Suddenly, we find ourselves stopped in the middle of the sidewalk, right in front of my little brick building. I look up and see a new sign displayed in the window proclaiming that the building has been SOLD.

I stare at the sign and can't fight the slight frown on my face.

Andrew turns towards me.

"What's wrong?" He asks, taking my other hand and trying to read my expression.

I shake my head. "Nothing. It's stupid." I release one hand and turn to continue down the sidewalk, but Andrew pulls me back towards him, gently.

He digs his hand into his pocket and pulls out a set of keys, jingling them in front of me. "Want to go inside?"

I raise a brow. "But... how do you have those?" I ask, following him towards the building. In one swift movement, he unlocks the door and holds it open, motioning for me to walk inside. "I don't understand. You bought this place?" I ask, making my way through the doorway.

"I did." He answers nonchalantly.

"But, why? Aren't you busy enough building a house and running a business? What are you even going to do with it?" I pull out my phone flashlight and use it to look into the dark, musty building.

"Well, I have some ideas." He turns on his own phone flashlight and leads me further inside. "I could really use a space to meet clients and do paperwork. That could be done in a small room in the back corner, of course." He continues. "I think the rest of it could easily be retail space." He shoots me a sideways glance. "I think this would be a great place for a bookstore, to be honest."

"Uh...." I try to interrupt, but he goes on. "Of course, the upstairs could easily be converted into a couple of apartments, or more office space. The possibilities are endless." He shrugs. "What do you think?"

For a second, I'm lost in thought, surveying the room before I snap back to reality. "Avery told you, didn't she?"

He shakes his head, obviously confused. "Told me what?"

I throw my hands in the air and motion around me. "About me and this stupid building."

"What about it?"

"That I love this place. I've always loved it. She had to have told you I've dreamed of opening my bookstore in this building ever since I was a little kid."

He shakes his head. "No, I promise she didn't say a word about it." He shrugs. "They just kept dropping the price lower and lower, and it had been on the market for months. I made them a low-ball offer and crossed my fingers. They accepted it with no haggling." He shrugs again. "The rest is history. I figure if nothing else, I'll get it fixed up and use it for rental income for office space." He closes the space between us and pulls me closer. "But I would be lying if I said I didn't think of you and your store when I walked in here."

I sigh and release myself from his grip before investigating the space. I creep through the building, taking in the overwhelming amount of work that Andrew has gotten himself into. Most of the drywall is missing, and the exposed studs are all that can be seen throughout the downstairs. Well, aside from the piles of dust, dirt, and broken sheetrock.

"This is going to be a lot of work." I tell him, biting my bottom lip.

"Luckily, I'm pretty good at this kind of thing." He teases, elbowing me lightly.

"So, I'd rent the storefront from you?" I ask, contemplating the crazy idea.

"Yep. I'd get everything fixed down here and then it'll be yours to decorate and fill with books."

"And what happens if I fail? What if I'm right and Fawn Creek isn't big enough to support a bookstore?" I counter.

"What happens if it doesn't fail? What if it takes off and you get to live your dream?" Andrew turns towards me and rests his hands on my shoulders, attempting to calm my nerves. "Tyler. You will never know if something is going to work out until you try. Either you can go all in and see what happens, or you sit on the sidelines and wonder what could have been."

I think back to Hazel's note and my drawings. I think of the money she left me that I've been saving. My eyes move to meet Andrews. "I'm scared." I tell him softly.

He grins. "Good. If your dreams don't scare you, they aren't big enough." He sticks a hand out for me to shake. "What do you say? Are we doing this?"

I let out a deep breath and place my hand in his. "I guess so."

He pulls me in for a hug against his chest before kissing the top of my head. "It's going to be great, Tyler. You just wait and see."

*I hope you're right.*

# Chapter 25

"Hold on, what? He bought you a building?" Avery sits down on my couch with a cup of coffee in her hands.

"Well, no, technically he did not. He bought himself a building. He just.. he wants me to use part of it to open my bookstore." I stare down into my cup of coffee. "This is crazy, right?"

"Crazy romantic." Avery says with a smirk. "You're doing it, right? You have to."

"Well." I pause. "I can't exactly say no, can I?"

She shakes her head. "No, and I won't let you. This is what you've always wanted! And this is even better because you didn't have to drop the money to buy the building and you didn't have to pay someone to renovate it." She takes a sip of her coffee. "Literally all you have to do is set up shop. This is an actual dream come true."

"I guess so." Quickly, I move from my seat on the couch to collect a notebook. "I need to figure out what needs to be done. And what all I'm going to sell because books won't be enough."

Avery's eyes open wide and she claps with excitement. "I have an idea! A book-ish boutique! You can get a wholesale license and have boutique clothing, gifts, and books. It'll be perfect!"

I shake my head. "Avery, I know nothing about fashion, unless it's all leggings and t-shirts."

"That's why you have me. I'll help you pick things out." She says with a shrug. "Oh, we are celebrating tonight. This is so exciting. Call Andrew and tell him we are going out tonight and to pick us up at nine."

"Nine?" I grimace. "At night? Where in the hell are we going?"

Avery grins. "What else is there to do around here? We're going line dancing."

* * *

"I can not believe I let you talk me into this." I grumble to Avery as we pull into the parking lot of Short Creek Saloon, the local dance hall. Short Creek is situated right at the edge of Fawn Creek city limits. It's known for its rustic western decor, cheap beer and huge sawdust dance floor. Basically, it's as close as you'll get to a clubbing experience in Southeast Kansas and it is the place to be on Friday and Saturday nights in Fawn Creek. That is, if you're young and enjoy standing elbow to elbow with a bunch of drunk people. For me, however, this is what I imagine hell to feel like for any introvert.

Sometimes there are so many 18 to 30-year-olds inside this place, you can hardly push your way through the crowd to get to the bar or the bathroom. Obviously, it's not just Fawn Creek citizens that pack the place. People drive from all around to line dance, drink and socialize. I personally have only been here one time. I was home visiting for Avery's 21st birthday and she drug me here, kicking and screaming. Even seven years later, it feels like I'm returning too soon.

"It'll be fun," Andrew says, putting the truck in park and killing the engine. "We just need to get a couple of drinks in you and you'll be out there line dancing in no time." He winks.

\* \* \*

We walk into the bar and wait to have our IDs checked. This is the first chance I've had to really examine Avery's outfit. Like the true fashionista she is, she's wearing hot pink bell bottom jeans with a black crop top and booties. Tonight her hair is wavy and teased high, and she looks like she came straight from Texas. I swear she knows how to fit in everywhere she goes and has an outfit for every occasion. She is definitely going to be an asset for this whole bookish boutique plan. We spent most of the day toying with this plan. By the time she went home to get ready, we had filed for my wholesale license, my logo was designed and we made a plan to shop for used books.

Andrew loves the idea, too. He agrees that anything we can add to the shop to bring people in will be a great idea. He spent a good chunk of the day working on the building and is a good sport for being up to bringing us out tonight. I know he has to be tired, and hopefully we won't be out too late tonight.

Just then, Andrew comes back with shots for the three of us and I know immediately that it's going to be a long night.

"Cheers," says Avery with a wink as we throw them back.

\* \* \*

"Ladies and Gentleman, it is now 1:40 AM, and it is officially last call for alcohol. If you want a drink, you need to get one now. Otherwise, you're out of luck." the DJ's voice booms through the speakers.

Avery and I make our way back to our bar stools from the dance floor and take a seat.

"How did it get so late?" I ask, pulling my sweaty hair away from my face, really wishing I had a ponytail holder on my wrist right about now.

"Um, three glasses of sex on the beach and two shots can sure make time fly." Andrew laughs, sitting next to us.

I nod, realizing that we have all drank more than I thought we would. "We better get an Uber." I say, pulling my phone out of my pocket and opening the app.

Avery and Andrew exchange a look.

"Are you going to tell her or should I?" Avery asks.

"I'm actually wondering how far she will get." He says in response.

I look between the two of them. "What are you guys talking about?"

"How's that Uber coming along?" Andrew teases.

"No rides available." I read from my screen and then hold up my phone to show them. "Seriously? Fawn Creek doesn't have Uber? Are we that far into the dark age?"

Andrew just shrugs. "I guess so."

"So, how do we get home? That's a long walk and none of us are fit to drive."

"No worries. I prearranged our ride home." Andrew says, pulling out his phone. "Give me just a second."

Less than five minutes later, Andrew checks his phone again and says, "Alright ladies, our ride has arrived. Let's get going."

He leads us out of the smoky bar and into the gravel parking lot, right towards a Fawn Creek Police cruiser.

The officer unlocks his doors with a smile. Avery makes her way around to the passenger seat while Andrew motions for me to climb into the backseat. As soon as I'm settled into my seat, I recognize Derek, the officer from the night of the concert.

Quickly, I turn to give Andrew a puzzled expression, but he ignores me and addresses Derek. "Thanks for coming." Andrew says, as Derek puts the car in drive.

"Anytime." Derek replies, pulling onto the main road to take us back towards town.

"Is this really a thing? Like do people do this often?" I ask from the back of the police car.

Avery shrugs. "People with the right friends, I guess."

Derek laughs. "Listen, I'd rather give someone a ride home from the bar than have to tell their family that they were drinking and driving and didn't make it home. I figure I'm driving around town, anyway. I might as well make myself useful."

I nod in the silence. These are the things that make Fawn Creek what it is, and maybe that's just the way it is in small towns. While we may not have department stores and cabs and food delivery services, we have what matters. We have regular folks who love their community and will do whatever it takes to help others. There really is no place like a small town.

# Chapter 26

My screaming phone breaks through the silence at ten o'clock on Sunday morning. I leap to grab it from the nightstand, hoping to avoid waking Andrew, but as soon as I hit the silence button, I see his eyes slowly open and peer at me. The word Mom flashes across the screen and I feel a panic rising in my chest. Immediately, I assume the worst. What if it's about Dad? He's been doing okay for a while now, but the fear is still there in the back of my mind. "Sorry." I mouth to him as I hit the answer button.

"Hello?" I answer quickly, bringing the phone to my ear.

"Tyler? Are you okay?" My mom asks, like she didn't just give me a heart attack.

"I'm fine. I just slept in today." I say, laying back down on my pillow. My head is pounding from those stupid shots last night. "What's up?"

"Well, I'm glad you're okay." She huffs. "Mary Sue cornered me at Bible Study this morning and said something strange. She said that she saw you riding in the back of a Police Car last night."

*Dammit, Mary Sue.*

"Tyler, are you there?"

"Yes Mom. I'm here." I sigh. "It's not what you're thinking.

I wasn't in trouble."

"Well, it certainly sounds like you were." She huffs again into the phone. "Why else would you have been in a police car at two in the morning?"

"I went to Short Creek last night with some friends and we had a few drinks. We decided we were better off not driving, so Andrew called a friend to give us a ride. His friend just happened to be an on-duty police officer."

Mom pauses. "And I'm supposed to believe that?"

Andrew covers his face with a pillow, attempting to stifle a laugh before climbing out of bed and moving towards the bathroom.

"Well, that choice is yours, I guess. I'm not sure what else to tell you." I say. "It's the truth. If I was in jail, I wouldn't be able to answer my phone. I'd be sitting in a cell until Monday morning when the judge gets to work."

"Why didn't you think about how it would look if other people were to see you?" She mutters.

"You're kidding right?" I say, rubbing my temples. It's too early for this shit. "Don't you think it would have looked worse if I had gotten arrested for drunk driving? Or if I had gotten into a wreck and hurt someone?"

"Maybe you shouldn't be drinking." She argues.

"Maybe you're right." I say, rubbing my temples. Mom has definitely gotten back to her old self since Dad's heart attack.

She sighs. "Well, I'm glad to hear that you're okay. I have to get to service. How about you come over for dinner tonight?"

I grimace and play with the fringe on my blanket. "Okay, I can do that." As much as I'd rather not, I haven't spent much time with them lately and that was the entire reason I stayed here. I need to do a better job of that.

"Good. We will see you at six. Bring that boyfriend of yours too. I'd like to meet him."

"I don't have a boyfriend." I lie and turn to face Andrew, who has materialized in the doorway. He raises an eyebrow.

"Nice try." She scoffs. "I've heard all about that Hayes boy. I'll see you both tonight."

Before I can answer, the call disconnects. I guess it's now or never.

\* \* \*

I lean over and take a sip of my tea while I wait for my lunch. Andrew and I are grabbing a bite to eat before going to work on cleaning up his new building.

"So we were the talk of the Baptist Church this morning." Andrew recalls with a laugh, leaning back in his chair. "It's been a while since I've had that kind of problem."

"I don't know about 'we', but I apparently was." I say, stirring my drink with my straw. "I mean, it's fine. It's not like it was the first time I've been the talk of the town. Not even since I've been back. You wouldn't believe the rumors about my breakup."

"Oh, I've heard them." He laughs. "I can't believe your ex is in prison for extortion. I thought this town taught you better than that."

I laugh at his joke, but the look on his face tells me he isn't joking. "Seriously?" I say with a groan.

"That's only the most recent story." He laughs. "There have been a few."

"Man, that's the downside to a small town, I guess. Everyone thinks everyone's business is their business. And most of the time, there is no truth to any of it."

"BINGO." He points to me as our food is placed in front of us. "Luckily, I've never been seen as anything but an angel."

I furrow my brows back at him. "What about that time you released a pig into the hallway of the High School for your Senior Prank?" I ask.

"How did you even know about that? I mean.. they never proved that was me." He says, looking around the diner as though he's making sure no one is eavesdropping.

"Or what about..." I start.

"Okay, that's enough. Eat your food." He laughs.

"Anyway, not only does my mom think I was in jail last night, we have now been summoned for dinner tonight. You can totally skip out on it if you want to. I'll cover for you." I say, stealing a fry from his plate.

"If you wanted fries, why did you order a salad?" he reaches for my hand as I grab another fry from his plate, dipping it into my ranch dressing.

"Because there is no salad in the world, or at least in South-east Kansas, that is as good as a Grilled Chicken Salad at Red Maple. I just want a couple of fries." I say, sticking out my bottom lip for effect.

He rolls my eyes. "Fine. I'll share." And he rotates his plate so I can reach them more easily.

"Want a bite of my salad?" I ask, holding up a forkful of lettuce.

"Gross." He takes a huge bite of his burger. "You are eating my lunches lunch. Anyway, dinner tonight at your moms. I'll be there."

"You don't have to do this, you know." I say. "My parents

219

are... a lot."

"Listen, I told you. I'm in this for the long haul. I might as well meet them now and get it out of the way." He says, reaching one arm across the table to squeeze my hand.

"You don't know what you are in for, though."

"We'll see," he winks, throwing a fry into his mouth.

* * *

We pull up to the curb in front of my parents' house, and Andrew puts the truck in park. Anxiety is coursing through my veins for whatever reason. I'm almost thirty years old. How do my parents hold this much power over my relationship? It's not like I'm going to end things if they don't like him. But it would honestly make life so much better if they all could just get along. Especially since the two of us are already very intertwined.

"You ready for this?" I ask, turning towards him.

He leans forward and lightly kisses my lips, just softly enough that he leaves me aching for more. "Let's do it." He says, leaning his forehead against mine.

I sigh and climb out of the truck, waiting for him to join me before we walk up to the door. He grabs my hand and squeezes it gently.

We approach the house and I knock on the wood entry door. It swings open quickly and my dad is standing in the doorway, beaming at us. I smile as I take in the sight of him. The heart attack was the wake up call he didn't know he needed. Thanks to being a bit more selective of what he eats, and taking evening walks with my mom, he already looks healthier. His face is thinning out and even his waistline is hanging over his pants less and less every time I see him.

"Ty!" He says, about three notches too loudly. "Come on in here."

"Hi Dad." I say as I move in to give him a hug. "This is Andrew. Andrew, this is my dad, Jerry."

"Hello, sir," Andrew says, leaning forward to shake his hand. "Nice to meet you."

"Nice to meet you, Andrew. What's your last name?"

"Hayes." He replies.

"Hayes. Who's your dad?"

My stomach flip flops. We haven't even made it into the living room yet and Andrew is already on the spot with questions about his difficult family dynamic.

"He's actually not from around here. You might know my late grandpa, though. His name was Charlie Hayes." Andrew says, changing the subject, following my dad into the front room.

"Ole Charlie Hayes," Dad says with a bit of a sparkle in his eyes. "He was the mail carrier at one time, wasn't he?" He pauses for Andrew to nod yes. "He was a good man. Sorry to hear about his passing." Dad says.

"Thanks. Yes, he really was a good one." Andrew says, taking a seat on the couch, as I follow. As soon as my body touches the sofa, my mother's voice from the kitchen causes me to bolt right back up.

"Tyler! Is that you?" My mom's voice carries through the house.

"I've been summoned." I say with a nervous laugh. "Be right back."

I round the doorway into the kitchen and I am taken aback just a little as I see the kitchen counters covered dish after dish of food. "Wow, Mom. Happy Thanksgiving." I say. Food has always been her love language, and she is expressing her love loudly today.

"Oh, don't be silly," she says, waving her potholder in my direction.

"Mom. This is a lot of food. How many people did you invite over?" I ask, moving closer to inspect what she had made. The counter is covered in matching dishes full of pulled pork, coleslaw, mac and cheese, roasted potatoes, rolls, and peach cobbler.

"Just the four of us. I just felt like cooking today." She says, pulling her towel off of her shoulder and then wiping her hands as she examines the buffet in front of her. "I... might have gone a little overboard. I suppose."

I put my arm around her shoulder and hug her from the side. "Just a little. It looks and smells amazing, though."

"Did you bring Andrew?" She asks, wringing her hands as though she just needs something to do.

"I did." I nod. "He's in the living room with Dad if you want to meet him."

"I've been asking around about him. No one seems to have anything bad to say about him."

"Well, that's promising." I say, stealing a roasted potato from the pan and popping it into my mouth. "They must not have seen him in the cop car with me last night."

Mom rolls her eyes and lets out an exasperated sigh. "Let's eat, you felon."

I shake my head and follow her towards the living room to retrieve the boys. However, when we enter the living room, there's no one to be found.

"Jerry! Where'd you go?" Mom yells down the empty hallway.

Mom and I exchange a look, both fully aware of where they've disappeared to.

I move towards the den and pull open the door to find both men leaning over a folding card table, with a gun laying in front of them. My dad turns at the sound of us entering the space and smiles brightly.

"It's dinnertime." Mom says with a smirk.

"I was just showing Andrew Great Grandpa's old World War 2 Rifle." He tells us proudly.

"It's actually pretty cool," Andrew says, without moving his eyes from the piece. "It's in amazing shape for how old it is."

"Well, I'm glad you guys had this moment together." I say with a laugh as Andrew moves towards me. We follow my parents towards the kitchen. "Wait until you see this spread." I whisper to him.

We enter the kitchen, and his eyes widen. "How many more people are coming?" He mutters to me.

"I hope you brought your appetite!" Mom sings as she circles into the room.

"And an additional army to feed, too." I say.

\* \* \*

"So," says Mom, passing a bowl of barbecue sauce across the table. "How was jail last night?"

I shoot her an empty stare while Andrew throws his head

back into a laugh. I want to be annoyed, but I'm glad she has a sense of humor about it now. She sure didn't this morning.

"Mom, I'm telling you, we just got a ride home from Derek."

"So now you're on a first name basis with the police?" She asks, using her fork to move food around on her plate.

"Well, it's Fawn Creek. It's kind of hard not to know everyone in town." I say, taking another bite of potato.

"I'm sorry," Andrew says, wiping his face and putting his napkin into his lap. "That was my fault. I didn't want to chance either of us driving, so I called my friend Derek to give us a ride. He was on duty. I didn't know anyone would see us. It was pretty late."

"Well, that was so nice of you to protect my daughter." She says with a smile.

I shoot Mom a look. She gave me a whole lecture this morning about drinking. But, now that it was Andrew's fault, we are off the hook. Whatever, as long as she isn't harping on him about it, I should be thankful.

"What do you do, Andrew?" Dad interrupts the jail conversation.

"I own a contracting company." He says between bites of food.

"How long have you been doing that?" Mom asks.

He thinks for a second. "About five years now. I live near Fort Hood, and I started it as a side gig to help people with odd jobs. Mostly, I helped wives when their husbands were deployed with things around the house. I also did some jobs to help people get their houses listed before they moved duty stations." He takes a drink of his tea. "Eventually, I took on enough work that I could quit my full-time job and work for myself full time. I wanted to set my own schedule because Grandpa wasn't doing well. Because of that, I could run home every other weekend to spend time with him." He pauses. "Grandpa didn't make it long, but I'm glad I got to spend time with him while I could. He raised my brother and I, so I just felt like I owed him."

"That's really sweet, and I'm glad you got that time with him, too." Mom says with a soft smile. "So, do you still live in Texas?"

"Actually, my brother and I just bought some land right outside of town." He turns to smile at me. "We are each planning to build our houses on the land and then use the rest of the acreage to raise cattle. I also bought a building downtown that I'll be renovating and renting out commercially."

I brace myself for him to drop the bomb about my bookstore, but he doesn't. I smile to myself, grateful that he will let me tell them when the time is right.

Mom nods approvingly and shoots me a smile before she goes back to eating her dinner. I can't remember there ever being a boyfriend or even a potential boyfriend that she approved of. This is fresh territory and I have to admit, I'm enjoying it.

After dinner, back in the kitchen, Mom and I work on cleaning up. She busily fills up plastic containers full of leftovers for me while I rinse dishes and load the dishwasher.

"Thanks for taking some of this home. We can't possibly eat all of this." She says, stacking them in a paper grocery sack.

Of course you couldn't, Mom, no one could. I think to myself.

"I appreciate it. Thanks to you, I won't need to cook for a week." I pause thoughtfully. "Well, what do you think of Andrew?" I ask, bracing myself for whatever will come out of her mouth.

"I love him." Mom whispers into my hair as she pulls me into a hug.

"Really?" I ask, half shocked. I can't recall a time that my parents have ever approved of one of my boyfriends.

"Yes! He's so polite and kind. He's obviously a hard worker, and he is handy, which will make your whole life so much easier. Plus, he lives here. That means that you'll stay here too." She beams at me.

Just then, my dad quietly sneaks into the kitchen and grabs two beers from the fridge before moving to stand next to me. He drags me into a side hug. "You found a good one this time, kiddo. Don't let this one get away."

"Thanks dad." I say, taking his acceptance to heart fully. I've never seen this happen before. "I'm really glad you guys like him."

For once in my life, I think I may actually be on the right track. The people I love actually like each other. Is my life finally falling into place?

# Chapter 27

*Six weeks later.*

I place the paint roller into the tray before standing back, hands on my hips, to evaluate my work. Just a week ago, Andrew brought me into the building to show me he had finished the drywall and the downstairs portion reserved for my shop was ready for paint. He wasn't expecting me to practically beg him to let me do the painting.

One thing I learned while working on my house is how therapeutic painting can actually be. Not only is it a workout, but it's also a great opportunity to spend time alone with your thoughts. Not to mention that it's an incredible way to transform a space right before your eyes. I immediately ran to the hardware store for paint and got started the next day. Slowly, I've covered the sheet rock in a creamy off-white satin sheen that created a brightness that this building hasn't seen in decades. I can't wait to fill it with bookshelves and decorate with plants, further bringing this place to life.

I'll admit, I'm also ready to bring in all the inventory that's taken over my guest room. Almost every day I get a shipment of merchandise, clothing and fixtures. Not to mention all the books I've been buying and hoarding from every thrift store and garage sale in the county. Let's just say I probably have more than enough stock in order to get started.

It's still hard for me to believe that this is really happening. All of my life, I have been a bookworm. As a kid, my mom would take me to the library every week and I would check out as many books as they would allow. Within a few days, I was begging to go back to return them and check out more. Hazel always encouraged my love of literature by buying me new books for my collection any chance she had. We never drove past a yard sale without checking out the books, and we certainly couldn't leave the grocery store without a new book for each of us in our basket.

Most people didn't understand my love for reading the way Hazel did. I think what I loved the most was that no matter where I was, I could pick up my book and be teleported to a whole new place. My family didn't travel when I was young, but I knew all about the beach and the mountains and, of course, plenty of imaginary worlds. No matter how sad or mundane or lonely life was, there were so many adventures waiting for me in the pages of a million different stories.

The memories of my relationship with Hazel flood back to me and I'm overcome with how truly lucky I was to have someone who loved and understood me like she did. Someone that not only believed in my dreams, but who made a way to actively support them long after she was gone. There's no better example of love or family. That is everything that I want to be in this life. Hazel was the best role model I could have ever known. I just wish she could be here to see this all pan out. It breaks my heart to know that she can't be my first customer because I waited too long to try this. I can only hope I'm still making her proud.

"Wow, it looks great in here." Andrew's voice breaks through the silence and causes me to jump just a little. He must have snuck in through the back door.

"Hey, this is all you, buddy." I close the space between us and stand on my tiptoes to kiss his lips. "Without you, none of this would have happened. I just painted." I smirk.

"No, ma'am." He hugs me and nuzzles into the messy bun on top of my head. "You are just as much a part of this as I am. I can't wait to see you running your business in here."

"Me neither." I agree, letting out a slow breath. It feels good to finally have my walls down and to let myself be excited about my future.

I gaze around the room while he holds me close. Our plan is to open during the fall festival in mid October. We only have a couple of weeks left, and it's going to be close, but I can finally see the possibility of it being done in time.

I step back to look at him. "Where have you been all day?"

He shrugs. "With your dad."

I laugh. "My dad?"

"He called and asked if I could come help raise a transmission into his old Chevy. Of course, I couldn't say no. It's nice to have someone to work on an old truck with." He says, with his eyes shining. "I miss the days when I used to do those things with my grandpa."

I stand on my tiptoes and run my thumb along his jawline. Something about the thought of him spending quality time with my dad makes me fall in love with him a little bit more. If that's even possible. "I bet he enjoyed having you there to help him. That was really nice of you."

He leans down to kiss my forehead. "I enjoyed it just as much." He says with a smile. "I like hanging out with your dad. He's a great guy and I can learn a lot from him." He pauses for a beat before changing the subject. "Hey, want to run out to the land with me and get some fresh air? You could probably stand to get away from all these fumes for a little while."

Fifteen minutes later, after a quick cleanup, we are riding side by side in his pickup, towards the city limit sign. I rest my arm on the center console and hold his hand as I watch the town move past my window. As we turn onto the dirt road, I look over at him and can't help but smile. Sitting next to him in the truck, holding hands while the radio plays quietly, has become one of my favorite places to be in the last couple of months. Everything I do with him just feels right. He catches me watching him and he slowly lifts my hand to his lips, lightly kissing my knuckles. "I love you." He tells me.

"I love you, too." I say, grinning back at him. I don't think I'll ever be happier than I am right now.

Andrew turns down the long gravel driveway and I watch as we approach the site of his future home. "Check it out!" He says proudly, already unbuckling his seat belt before the gravel around the truck settles. I follow suit and climb out of the truck, as he leads me toward the freshly dried concrete pad where his house will stand.

"Andrew, this is amazing!" I step on to the pad and look around. "It's huge! I'm so excited for you." I say as I turn back towards him.

He grins and takes my hand. "Well, let me give you a tour." He says, as we make our way into the center of the fresh concrete. "The master bedroom will be there." He points to our right. "And then over here will be the living room and a dining room with a table big enough to seat all our friends and family. Back there will be the kitchen with an enormous window overlooking the backyard, where our kids can run and play."

The thought of us having babies causes a rush of butterflies in my stomach. I can't count the number of times I've thought about it just since we started dating, but to hear him say the words out loud sets my soul on fire.

"Over here is plenty of room for a nursery, and a couple more bedrooms, for us to fill with as many kids as you want." His eyes are growing misty. "Back there will be the shop, where I'm going to teach all of those kids how to build and fix things and work on cars."

"And then here..." He pulls me close to him at the front of the layout. "Will be a big front porch where we will put two rocking chairs. Then you and I can sit here in the evenings for the next sixty years, hand in hand, and enjoy our life together."

Before I can respond, he lowers himself down to one knee and grips my hand while pulling a ring from his pocket.

"Tyler." He says. "I know it hasn't been very long and you might think I'm crazy, but I have never been as happy as I have been these last few months with you. You are smart and funny, you're kind and gentle. You are everything I have ever wanted in a partner. Being with you is so easy. You feel like home to me. There is nothing else in this world that I want more than to wake up next to you every day and fall asleep next to you every night in this house. I love you so much. Tyler, will you please marry me?"

The tears well in my eyes and hit the concrete at his feet. I quickly wipe them away and stare into his eyes before realizing that I had been too stunned to even answer him and nod quickly, "Yes, Andrew, of course." I say, as he slides the simple diamond ring on my finger and I pull his hand towards me, bringing him to his feet.

"I can't wait for you to be my wife." He grins before kissing me again. "We are going to have an incredible life together."

I take back everything I thought earlier. Now, is the happiest I'll ever be.

\* \* \*

Andrew rolls himself over and lands on the mattress beside me with a thud. "Well, that was one way to celebrate." I say with a giggle, before climbing out of the bed and moving towards the tight camper bathroom. Upon my return, he is already sitting on the bed, dressed and waiting for me. Carefully, I step around him from where he sits and retrieve my clothes. "I don't know how you live in this tiny space." I say.

He laughs. "Eh, it's a place to shower and sleep. I don't really spend much time here, anyway." He says with a shrug.

It's true. When he isn't working on jobs for customers, he's working on the building, or he's spending time with me.

"You know," I say, "It's going to be getting cold soon. And since we are engaged, maybe you should think about coming to stay with me instead." I pause. "I mean, unless you just really want your own space."

He grins. "No, I want to be in your space as much as I can."

I blush and let out a small giggle. "Well, I guess that means we need to tell my parents we're getting married." I say as I finish buttoning my jeans.

He clenches his teeth. "They kind of already know." When I only answer with a look of confusion, he continues. "I had to ask your dad's permission first. Luckily, he said yes. That would have been super awkward."

I scoff. "I didn't realize you were so old-fashioned."

"Only when it really counts." He laughs. "And for something like that? It counts. I want them to like me. I want to do anything I can to make your life easier."

I grin. "I love you for that, and you already have made my life so much better than I ever dreamed."

"Just you wait," He says with a smile. "We have a lifetime ahead of us."

\* \* \*

"Are you pregnant?" Mom whispers as she leads me into the kitchen. Andrew and Dad are already in the garage, tinkering with the truck. I have to hand it to them. They stayed tuned in for approximately three minutes while I told my parents that we want to get married sooner rather than later before they turned their attention to working on the Chevy.

I roll my eyes and shake my head. "No, I am not pregnant." Not that I would mind so much. "Andrew and I have just had some time to talk about it and we don't want to wait. We don't see the point in spending thousands of dollars for a wedding that will take a year or more to plan, when we could get it done in a few weeks and start our life together. Not to mention that we have basically no spare time between running two businesses and building a house." I say with a sigh. Just thinking about all we have going on right now exhausts me.

She frowns, just slightly. "You know how this town is. People are going to think you're pregnant if you get married so quickly."

I shrug and take a seat at the table. "Then, let them. Who

cares? The worst that will happen is in nine months I won't have a baby on my hip and by then, no one will even remember because I'll be married and they will move on to discussing someone else's reproductive organs."

She pauses for a moment, as though to consider what I said. "You're right." She nods and takes a seat across from me. "When it's right, you just know, and it doesn't matter what anyone else thinks about it." She reaches across the table to squeeze my hand. "You deserve to be happy and if this is what will make you happy, then we will make sure it happens." She pauses for a second and looks at me with soft eyes. "I know I need to get better at not caring what other people think."

"It's a hard habit to break." I say.

"It is." She nods. "But that's no excuse for me to make everyone in my life miserable because I'm so worried about what people on the outside are thinking. I wasn't going to tell you this, but I've been seeing a therapist."

I raise a brow. This is so unlike the mother I was raised by. That woman never would have been capable of talking to a stranger about her problems. And she certainly would have never admitted to me, or anyone else, that she was incapable of handling things on her own.

"Since when?" I ask.

"Since a couple weeks after Dad's heart attack. I figure, if he is going to put in the work to get healthier, I better put in the work to be easier for all of you to deal with." She chuckles before turning somber again. "I know that because of my insecurities, I have really hindered our relationship for so many years. I hate to think of how much time we have lost because of that. Life is so short, and I don't want to miss out on the time I have left here with you because I'm being difficult and causing you to distance yourself."

I wipe a tear from my face and then move to the other side of the table before pulling my mom into a tight embrace. "Thank you." I whisper. "I love you."

"I love you, too." She says, before pulling back to look at me. "We've got a wedding to plan. We better start making calls."

# Chapter 28

*Two weeks later*

I've spent every evening here for the last week arranging inventory, decorating and making sure that everything is perfect for the grand opening. In just half an hour, The Bookish Boutique will officially be open for business. Nervously, I rearrange the bookmark and sticker stands on the checkout counter when a light knock on the glass door breaks my concentration. I peer over the counter to see Avery waving at me from outside while holding Juliet on her hip. Quickly, I move to the door to let them in.

"Hey!" I say, pushing the door open and locking it back up behind them.

Immediately, Juliet reaches for me with a gleeful "Ty!".

With no hesitation, I take her from Avery's arms, giving her a break and allowing her to move through the space.

Our official ribbon cutting ceremony is happening at 10:00 when we open, and I invited all of my friends and family to be here. By then, the Fawn Creek Fall Festival will be in full swing and hopefully that will help bring in plenty of foot traffic for our first day.

"Holy crap," Avery says, as she moves through the space. "It looks so good in here. Better than I ever imagined." For the last week, not only did I ban everyone but Andrew from coming in here but also, I covered the windows with newspaper so no one could even so much as peek at my progress until I was done.

Avery turns to face me. "You did it, friend." She says with a hug. "I'm so proud of you and I know Hazel is, too." She pauses for a beat. "You did, Tyler. And it's beautiful."

I take in a deep breath and choke back the tears that I know will fall at some point today. "Thank you" is all I can say in return.

I move through the building, making last-minute adjustments as I take in the fruits of my labor. Every inch of this space is decorated exactly how I dreamed of.

The main room is filled with shelves full of books separated by genre, with book related gifts, decor and comfy clothes spread throughout the space, breaking up the sections. I never imagined that I would have been able to fill so much space with used books, but once the community learned that I was opening a bookstore, I received countless donations of books that people just didn't know what to do with otherwise. Every wall is full of shelves, with books organized by genre.

In the center of the main room, I will have new arrivals as well as book recommendations for the month. Since it's October, the table is filled with thrillers, ghost stories and books with autumn vibes.

The children's area is in its own separate room, down the hall from the entrance. I had Andrew remove part of the wall, so I can monitor the little people while they are in there, but mostly it's a children's literary fun zone. The shelves are filled with new and used children's books, toys, and some cute clothes that I just couldn't resist. However, my favorite part of the space is all the reading nooks we put in. Besides a child sized egg chair, and a beanbag chair, there's a wooden swing hanging from the ceiling to use for reading and photo ops. The fake greenery on the wall behind the swing with a sign that says "Adventure is just a page away..." completes the space. I can't wait to host story time back there every Thursday after school and I already have books chosen for the first few weeks. It's the exact space that I would have loved to have as a kid, and I can't wait to share it with the children of Fawn Creek.

As Avery and I finish a quick walk through, Andrew comes in through the back door, arms full of iced coffee and breakfast burritos from Drip. He greets us and then sets everything down on the counter before turning to look at me. "You ready for today?" He asks, kissing my forehead.

"I'm probably going to vomit." I admit, my nerves are shot. "What if no one comes in? Or what if no one shows up for the ribbon cutting?"

He laughs and shakes his head. "They will. It's going to be a great day." He promises.

I nod, only half believing what he says.

"Is the website live yet?" Avery asks, interrupting us.

"Not yet." I say. "I'm going to get through today first and then I'll work on opening it up on Monday. Surely, we will be a little less busy that day and I can give it my full attention in case something goes sideways." I'm hoping that will help us with sales, even on days that are slower around here, by posting and sharing links on our social media pages.

"That's a good call." She agrees. "I think today is going to be crazy. The free parking lots are already filling up for the Fall Festival. Being right next to the pocket park will be a huge plus for you, too. There is a lot going on over there today for the kids."

I hope she's right. I need this to work out.

By 9:55, the store is filled with all of our family and friends. Avery, Juliet, Andrew, Derek, Cody, Sierra and my parents have all come to be a part of this moment with us. I take a moment to look around at my community and I can't help but feel so blessed. It's crazy to think that I lived in a city with thousands of people for years and never felt as connected as I do now in my small town.

At ten o'clock on the dot, we move outside and stand on the sidewalk in front of the door with the members of the city chamber. The street in front of my building is full of Fawn Creek residents cheering us on as we start our new adventure.

After a small speech from the Mayor and an awkward attempt to cut a thick ribbon with oversized scissors, the store is officially open to the public. The crowd funnels into the store and I take my place behind the counter.

My first customer is Piper, the little girl I met at Juliet's daycare. Piper steps up to the counter and beams, before placing a book about female role models down and pushing it towards me.

"Hey Piper, remember me? This looks like a good choice." I say with a smile.

She quickly nods, causing her pigtails to fly wildly around her head. "Good job brushing your hair today." She says with a grin.

"Piper!" a shocked voice calls out from across the store. Ava, the real estate agent, comes around the corner. "I am so sorry." She says to me, with a red face. "Piper... she has no filter." She says as she hands me her debit card.

I chuckle to Ava and ring up Piper's purchase. "It's okay." I say with a genuine smile. "She's spunky. I like her." I add.

"She's one of a kind, that's for sure." Ava says with a smile.

I nod, realizing in the moment how much that spicy little kid reminds me of Grandma Hazel. She's fierce, filterless and marches to the beat of her own drum. Of course, it only makes sense that Piper would be my first customer. She's Hazel in little kid form, and I almost feel as though I get to experience Hazel as a child.

The rest of the day flies by in a blur. We stay consistently busy for a majority of the day. A lot of familiar faces come in to just look around, but overall we sell much more than I had ever imagined.

Around one o'clock, Andrew brings me a burger for lunch and as soon as it slows down a little, I eat and check out the sales report for the day.

"How's it looking?" Andrew asks, peering over my shoulder.

Shocked, I stare at the screen. "I think we are going to break a thousand dollars in sales today." I tell him. "This is crazy."

"Good job." He says, high-fiving me. "I told you that you'd rock this. I'm so proud of you."

"Well, don't get too excited. It's only the first day. I have to somehow keep up the momentum." I tell him.

Andrew stops to glance around the room. "Honestly, I don't think it's going to be a problem."

I sit down on my stool and for the first time all day, I really look around at what I've created. Suddenly, I see so much more than a space full of books and merchandise. I see a mom with her little girl, sitting on the floor reading a story together. I see a teenage boy, studying the back of a book about wizards, and an older woman clutching a pile of worn romance novels. Then, my eyes wander to a stack of coloring pages that the children of Fawn Creek have been coloring and returning for my monthly coloring contest.

I can finally see it's not just a store. This is what my heart needed so badly, and what Fawn Creek needed, too. Silently, I thank Hazel for the push to get me here.

# Chapter 29

*One month later.*

"Knock, knock." Avery calls out as she walks in through the front door of my house. Sierra is putting the finishing touches on my hair when Avery steps into the room. She quickly lays her dress bag onto my bed and then walks over to talk to my reflection in the mirror. "You look beautiful." She says with a grin, her own long dark hair is in loose curls framing her face.

"Sierra is a magician." I say, admiring the half up do she had given me, with curls trailing down my back. I turn to Sierra and smile. "Thank you so much for your help. I am terrible at being a girl and couldn't have pulled anything like this off without you."

"You are not terrible at being a girl." She laughs. "We all need a little help sometimes, and I'm honored to do it."

It's insane to think of how quickly, yet easily, this day came together. Our wedding, while small, could not have been made possible without so many community members helping.

Mom's church let us borrow tables and chairs. Sierra did my makeup and hair, and Avery's mom altered my dress. Much to my surprise, Cassidy is ordained to perform weddings, and I couldn't think of anyone else that I would want to marry us. The local bakery made us an adorable cake, McDaniel's made the bouquets, one of Derek's friends apparently moonlights as a DJ and Avery hooked us up with an amazing photographer. Just like always, our community came together to make everything work out. And they did it, expecting nothing in return.

I watch my two friends in the mirror's reflection for a second and realize how thankful I truly am. It's baffling to think that just over half a year ago; I was living a completely different life. My job was a dead end. My relationship was hanging on by a string. I lived in a giant city surrounded by people, but I was alone. It was what I thought I wanted, but in reality, it couldn't have been further from what I needed.

Now here we are. I'm back home and marrying a man that is head over heels in love with me. I have the group of girlfriends that I've always needed. Mine and Andrew's businesses are thriving. My parents and I are closer than ever and I have a whole community rooting for me.

"Okay, no tears." Sierra interrupts my daydreaming after recognizing the look on my face.

I blush. "Sorry. It's been a whirlwind few months. It's wild that I've always thought of you as my little sister, but after today we will actually get to be sisters." I squeeze her hand and then look at Avery. "And you, Avery. You've always been my sister from another mister." I laugh. We always used to joke that our mothers couldn't have handled us as actual sisters, so we had to be best friends instead. "I love you girls so much. And I'm so thankful to have you both with me today."

"Now you're going to make me cry." Avery groans and waves at her face. "There's nowhere else we would rather be. How are you feeling? Are you nervous?"

"Not really." I pause, "Well, okay, I'm a little nervous about tripping or forgetting what I'm supposed to say in front of everyone. The actual getting married part isn't worrying me so much, though." I laugh. "I think I'm just ready."

Sierra makes some last-minute touch ups to my makeup and spins my chair so I can look in the mirror one last time.

I stare at myself in awe. My hair and makeup have never looked better. "Can you come over every day to fix my hair and makeup for the rest of my life?" I ask. "You know one day soon we are going to be neighbors, after all."

"I could teach you to do it yourself?" She offers with a shrug.

"I'll never be able to work this kind of magic." I laugh and shake my head at her, still shocked to see the person staring back at me in my reflection.

"You need to get dressed and we need to get going." Avery interrupts. "Your groom is waiting."

\* \* \*

The girls and I park in the gravel driveway, ensuring that I'm hidden from the guests and while we wait for my dad to come retrieve us to walk down the aisle.

The exterior of the house has gone up, and we opted to have the wedding in what will be our backyard, under an oak tree. In Kansas, the weather is unpredictable at any time of year, but in the fall you just never know. It could be anywhere from seventy degrees and sunny, to thunderstorms, to a snowstorm. We regularly experience every season over the course of a weekend, so it was a bit of a gamble. However, I had my heart set on getting married in our backyard, where we got engaged and where we plan to make so many more precious memories. Thankfully, it's a beautiful day and everything is going according to plan. It's crazy to think how easily things fall into place, when it's meant to be.

The trees surrounding the house have turned colors and we have a backdrop of yellows, oranges and reds behind the wooden arbor Andrew and Dad built together last weekend. The arbor is perfect for us to be married under, and then Andrew plans to hang a porch swing from it later so we can enjoy it for years to come.

A knock on the window interrupts my daydreaming. I turn and smile at my dad in his white button-down shirt with his blue jeans as he beams back at me. Carefully, I climb out of the car and Avery fixes the jumbled mess that my skirt has come. I glance at my silhouette in the reflection of Avery's car. I just can't believe it's finally happening.

The girls give us a little bit of space, and I look up at my father. I see tears in his eyes as he looks down at me proudly. "You look beautiful." He tells me before moving in for a hug. "I'm so glad my heart didn't take me out and make me miss this."

Sierra quickly rushes to my side and holds up a finger. "Mr. Burris, I love you, but please don't make her cry. I don't have time to redo her makeup and she's been right on the edge of it all day." She teases.

"Fine." He laughs in response, shaking his head. He turns to me and says, "Well, kiddo. We better get going then."

And just like that, I start down the path to my very own happily ever after.

# Epilogue

I bend down over the playpen to lay a blanket on top of our sleeping three-month-old, Molly Anne. She has a faint smile on her face while she is smacking her lips and dreaming about whatever babies dream of. My stomach flutters every time I see her sweet face, and I could look at her all day long. To be honest, staring at her is just about all I've done for the past several weeks. She's the perfect mixture of her father and I, with my green eyes and her daddy's nose, and dark hair that matches up both. I can't wait to watch her grow up and see what her personality is going to end up like.

The last six weeks have gone by in a blur. Honestly, that could be said for the entire last year. Just a couple of weeks after we got home from our honeymoon, I opened a box of Christmas scented candles for the store and it about took me out. I immediately had to run behind the counter to throw up in the trash can because of the overwhelming scent. A pregnancy test from the drugstore across the street confirmed we were, in fact, expecting. We had apparently brought home more than just a shot glass and some sand from Mexico. We weren't really ready to try, but once we were married, we weren't really doing much to prevent it from happening, either. It was just another clear indication of what was meant to be.

The pregnancy went smoothly and after a 22 hour labor, Molly Anne was born at the beginning of August. Thanks to my mom and a couple of high school girls, the store kept running smoothly while I stayed at home with her for a few weeks. After that, I peeked in and helped a little, all while baby wearing Molly, of course.

I just started working full time again this week. Just in time to gear up for the store's One-Year Anniversary Celebration next month. The growth of the store over the last year has been beyond my expectations and even my wildest dreams. While the physical store is still doing great, our online presence is even bringing in a substantial income. I owe that all to my high school employees, who started using TikTok to showcase our products while I was on maternity leave. I never imagined that the store would be this profitable, or that I could support two part-time employees.

The office spaces upstairs are rented out and bringing in additional income. One is being used by Sierra. She opened her own salon space, allowing her to work for herself. She's already busy enough that she's had to bring in a second stylist to cover her expanding client list. The other office is being rented by Ava. Her real estate business is booming, and she is in the works of starting her very own brokerage firm, at the age of twenty-three.

Cody and Sierra are almost done building their house and we are all so excited to be neighbors while we raise food, babies, and animals alongside each other.

The bell on the door lets out a loud jingle, alerting me of a customer and bringing me out of my daydream. I make my way out of the break room to find Andrew waiting for me at the counter.

"How are my girls?" He asks, as I close the space between us and he pulls me into a hug, kissing my forehead gently.

"It was a good day." I say, checking my watch and walking over to lock up for the day. "We are just about ready for the Fall Festival and our one-year anniversary." I tell him, hands on my hips, feeling accomplished.

"You are Superwoman, I swear." He tells me, just as he leans down to kiss me again, until the door interrupts us by swinging open.

In walks Avery with Juliet on her hip and Derek following behind her.

"Ready for our double date?" She asks with a grin, as she squeezes Derek's hand.

"Yep. Let me grab Molly and lock up and then we can go." I say.

I turn around one last time to look at my group of people standing in the middle of my store, and my heart wants to just explode. All my life I was searching for my place in the world and it was here in Fawn Creek all along. There really is no place like home.

# Tyler's Margarita Recipe

**Here's Tyler's favorite margarita recipe!**
It's super easy and delicious.
*Proceed with caution if sharing with your hot neighbor next to a fire pit.*

### Ingredients

- 1 can frozen limeade, thawed
- 12 oz tequila
- 1 (2-liter) bottle of Sprite

### Instructions

1. Pour the thawed limeade into a large pitcher.
2. Fill the empty limeade can with tequila and pour it in.
3. Slowly add the Sprite — start with half, taste, and add more to your liking.

Serve over ice with a salted rim (if you're feeling fancy).

# About the Author

Michelle Lynn Ross is the author of humorous and heart-warming small-town romances set in Kansas, in the fictional town of Fawn Creek. When she's not writing, she enjoys traveling, reading, and spending time with her husband and three daughters.

**You can connect with me on:**

🌐 https://michellelynnross.com
📘 https://www.facebook.com/ThatsWhatShellSaid
🔗 https://www.instagram.com/michellelynnrossauthor
🔗 https://www.tiktok.com/@thatswhatshellsaid

# Also by Michelle Lynn Ross

**Small Town Famous**

After escaping a toxic relationship, Avery Thompson is focused on rebuilding her life and raising her daughter—solo. But when a new side hustle as a content creator brings unexpected attention (and chaos), she starts to find her spark again. Add in a swoony local cop who sees past her scars, and Avery must decide if she's ready to risk her heart... or let fear hold her back.

**Single In A Small Town**

After a messy divorce, Madison King is determined to start fresh—new hair, new walls, new life. The only rule? Absolutely no more Bryan Thompson. But in Fawn Creek, where dating options are scarce and secrets don't stay hidden, resisting temptation might be the hardest rule she's ever tried to keep.

**Signed, Sealed, Delivered**

When love shows up at Ava's doorstep—along with a charming UPS driver—life in Fawn Creek gets delightfully unpredictable. Between spilled ranch, second chances, and small-town surprises, Ava learns that the best deliveries aren't packages, but the people who make a place feel like home.

**Back To You**

After a messy divorce, Reagan Miller returns home to Fawn Creek hoping for peace—not romance. But when she runs into her high school sweetheart in the pickle aisle, old sparks reignite and the past comes rushing back. Cozy, heartfelt, and full of holiday charm, *Back to You* is a story about first loves, fresh starts, and finding your way home again.